BRAIN TRANSPLANT

8:45 AM. Both teams are clustered around the orange heads bulging through the green drapes. I can smell the tension. My own palms are wet with sweat. . . .

8:50 AM. Gonzaga and Steinke begin their incisions at the same moment. The cut starts on the side of the head, above and behind the ear, sweeps forward over the front of the scalp just behind the hairline, then backward across the temple on the other side. A huge flap of scalp and bone is turned to expose the entire brain. . . .

Also by Birney Dibble, M.D.

*PAN
IN THIS LAND OF EVE
THE PLAINS BROOD ALONE*

BIRNEY DIBBLE, M.D.
BRAIN CHILD

LEISURE BOOKS   NEW YORK CITY

For Edna

Also, thanks to Dr. Leonard Larsen, professor of computer science at the University of Wisconsin, Eau Claire. He aided me immeasurably in devising the hardware and in writing the computer programs for the post-operative control of brain transplant patients.

A LEISURE BOOK

Published by

Dorchester Publishing Co., Inc.
6 East 39th Street
New York, NY 10016

Copyright ©1987 by Birney Dibble

All rights reserved. No part of this book may be reproduced or transmitted in any form or by any electronic or mechanical means, including photocopying, recording, or by any information storage and retrieval system, without the written permission of the Publisher, except where permitted by law.

Printed in the United States of America

BRAIN CHILD

PART ONE

> *Do not go gentle into that dark night,*
> *Old age should burn and rave at close of day;*
> *Rage, rage against the dying of the light.*
>
> Dylan Thomas

1

They challenged death to a race. The sense of urgency deepened now that they knew the two actors in their drama. No longer could they sit in the ivory tower and contemplate their navels, nor thoughtfully discuss the theory of brain transplants, nor even ponder the alternate routes to their goals. They had made the decision to go forward. They could not borrow from the future, but must use the technology of the present.

They were mountaineers striking base camp, astronauts entering the LEM. They came now to that last stage of assault where action proves—or disproves—

theory. In three days two lives would be altered in the most radical way man had yet devised. One of them, Gerard Houston, already legally dead of a brain hemorrhage, would be allowed to die. The other, James Abernathy, would be resurrected from the dead like Lazarus from his tomb, for although not legally dead, his link to life was tenuous indeed.

Theologians were arguing wildly in pulpits, anthropologists and sociologists in the press. Pseudo-scientists and philosophers of all stripes were bickering on the bus and in the *Voice of the People*. There were as many opinions as there were people. The minds of the scientists at Hektoen were untroubled by such things, and they would have been the first to claim that they brought only solid, amoral, common sense from the laboratory to the operating room, unfettered by armchair philosophies.

Or so Mercury Reynolds thought up until a few days before T-day. A central fact stood out clearly, one so awesome that none of them could fully take it in. They were creating a new life. Musing on this one night, Reynolds remembered something Pearl Buck once said, and looked it up. She described the creative mind as one which had the "overpowering necessity to create, create, create—so without the creating of music or poetry or books or buildings or something of meaning, his very breath is cut off from him. He must create, must pour out creation. By some strange, unknown inward urgency he is not really alive unless he is creating."

Humbly he acknowledged that the description fit him. He really was creating something of meaning. Not a book or a symphony, but perhaps a man who could write a book or a symphony.

They were all affected, of course, but in different ways. Two days before T-day, Reynolds sat with Gonzaga in the stuffy little room off the main neurosurgery ward. The contrast between the two men was striking. Reynolds, twenty-four years old, tall, lean, blue-eyed, van Dyke-bearded, was a doctor of biomedicine, originally from Virginia. Gonzaga, twenty-seven years old, short, stocky, muscular, brown-eyed and dark-skinned, was a doctor of medicine, a fourth-year neurosurgery resident, originally from the Philippines. The two young men had only one thing in common: a goal.

On Gonzaga's desk were the tools of his trade: books helter-skelter, several lying open; papers; reflex hammer; stethoscope; a skull with the top sawed off to expose the cavities into which a brain fits; a plastic model of the base of the brain showing all twelve cranial nerves in yellow, the arteries in red, the veins in blue. Behind him, just above a human brain in a jar of formaldehyde, was a picture of a shapely, bikini-clad rump with a three-year-old-calendar stencilled on it. Reynolds liked the juxtaposition of dead brain and sex symbol. He wondered if Gonzaga had done it on purpose.

"It's odd," Gonzaga said, tipping his head back and looking at the ceiling.

"What's odd?" Reynolds asked, a little surprised that all of a sudden Gonzaga felt like talking about the project. So far he hadn't really opened up, hadn't shown what cultural conditioning a Catholic Filipino brought to this surgical investigation.

Gonzaga pushed his chair back on two legs, dropped his gaze to a neurosurgery text which he held almost idly in his fingers. His usual bravado was muted. There was a hunted, vaguely frightened look in the dark eyes he raised to Reynolds. Faint shadows seemed to pass behind his pupils as he said, "That body in there, the carpenter, doesn't know any of this is going on. He doesn't know that his brain is dead. Bloody mush. He hasn't the slightest idea what's going on."

Reynolds nodded. He had thought of that.

"We're going to take his body," Gonzaga went on, "and put another force into it . . ." His voice trailed off.

"An interesting way to put it," Reynolds said. "Another force . . . power . . . guiding mechanism. Yeah, I like that."

He could readily read Gonzaga's thoughts, understood better what his brain was doing than Gonzaga himself. Gonzaga was dehumanizing the project by dissociating the people from it, taking away their names and personalities. If he could think of Abernathy's brain as a new source of power for Houston's body, then he could rationalize the whole procedure.

"You having trouble," Reynolds asked, "accepting this transplant because of your religious training?" He sat forward in his chair. "Because if you do, you should get out now."

Gonzaga raised his hand, palm outward, then waved it back and forth. "Don't worry, Merc, I've got it all worked out, and I'm going all the way. But I do wonder . . ." His voice trailed off again, and his eyes seemed to sink back into their sockets.

"Alright, so do I," Reynolds said. "Do you want to talk it out some more?"

His eyes glowed, blinked, lost their indecision. "No." Back in control, all business again, his eyes quickly regained their sparkle. He reached for a clipboard and started to tick off the items. "First, Gerard Houston. He's had a final EEG, which I'll have Matt read this afternoon. It's been flat for a week and I don't see it changing now. After all, we'd have pulled the plug long ago if Steinke'd let us."

"Good thought, from a medico-legal standpoint if no other." They were plowing a virgin prairie where no man had ever sown before.

"I did a carotid angiogram this morning. Looks good. I don't see any problem with the main arteries to the brain—no significant arteriosclerosis, no placques. Dr. Czrza and his boys should be happy."

"What about Abernathy's blood vessels?"

"I'll do that with Kettering tomorrow morning. Let's stick with Houston for a minute. I've got signed releases from his brother. His wife's in a nursing home, *non compis*. His brother seems to understand what's going on, though he's not any too bright. All legal, though. I've done a complete blood count, run an SMA-12—"

"Run those by me again, Fred."

"Total protein, cholesterol, blood urea nitrogen, blood sugar, bilirubin, alkaline phosphatase, LDH, albumin, calcium, phosphorus, uric acid."

"OK, they're alright?"

"The BUN is up a little, but no more than we'd expect from mild dehydration alone. We're loading him with fluids to make sure it comes down. We've done another chest X ray to rule out CA and pneumonia—he was a heavy smoker—and an EKG. That's about it."

Reynolds left him then, satisfied that Gonzaga would be OK. If he wasn't, he'd had his chance, and he'd have to go. That would be Steinke's decision, and he'd be ruthless.

Reynolds met with Kettering that same

afternoon in his own office. Kettering was getting Abernathy ready for the most important surgery he'd ever have.

"He's ready to go," Kettering said, then added, "Ready as he'll ever be."

He paused a second, seemed about to say something, thought better of it and plunged into a recitation of his work-up on Abernathy. He'd done an EEG, EKG, SMA-12. "No need for a chest X ray," he said with a sad smile. "But we've got ten units of packed red cells ready to go if we need them."

"Ten units?"

"J'ever see a bulldog slip off a carotid?"

Reynolds smiled. "No."

"Well, I have. Bloody, man, bloody."

"How's he holding up, in general?"

"Not bad. We're having to give him about three pints of blood a day just to keep even. But if he doesn't bust loose before Friday, he's going to be OK."

"See that he doesn't," Reynolds said, the preemptive tone in his voice startling him. Kettering ignored it. He, more than anyone else, seemed to empathize with Reynolds, to sense the strain under which he was working. He said, "We'll put down a Sengstaken if he does. That'll keep him quiet. Uncomfortable as hell, though, that's why we don't have it down now. And it sometimes causes necrosis of the nose . . ." He stopped, grinned a little foolishly, and added, "but then we aren't too concerned with that, are we?"

Reynolds shook his head and said, "That it, Jon?"

Kettering nodded and stood up. He moved slowly to the door, then turned and said, "Merc, d'ya'ever have second thoughts about all this?"

My God, Reynolds thought, this is getting to everybody. First Gonzaga, and now Kettering. He had not expected either to have problems, Gonzaga because he was a neurosurgeon, Kettering because he was one of the new breed of internists, less interested in the art of medicine than the science.

"Not any more," he answered. "I've sweated it, though, and I know exactly where you're coming from. I will say this, Jon, if you're having trouble, get out now, before we start. Don't wait till we're in the middle of it, or till we lose our first brain by rejection, or some other god-awful thing. That might happen some day, you know, maybe even this first one. We know that none of our lower primates' brains have been rejected. But we've got no data on humans yet. It's going to be one hell of a mess if it ever does happen."

Kettering shook his head vigorously. "No, Merc, don't count me out. Just thinking out loud, wondered how you felt. Guess what bothers me most is this: what if Jim's brain stays alive and yet the spinal cord and the cranial nerves never grow out of it to make Houston's body work?"

He leaned forward, eyes wide, mouth slack. He shook his head slowly from side to side. "He'll be alive inside that cranium, knowing he's alive, unable to tell us. What do we do *then*?"

"I don't know, Jon, I don't know. But I do know that the difference between what *is* and what *might be* is what drives us all. It's the only real source of power in the world."

"A philosopher yet," he said with his quiet laugh, but there was a confidence in his stride as he left.

Reynolds crossed the hall to Victor Steinke's office. Steinke was Chief of the transplant service and the senior neurosurgeon involved in the brain transplant experiments. He was fifty-nine, a German Jew who had survived the war in a concentration camp because he was young and strong and useful to the Germans. His right forearm bore now-fading numbers tattooed in 1940, fifty-two years before.

He had the charts of Abernathy and Houston on his desk, but he wasn't looking at them. He leaned back in his chair, scratched idly at his tattoo and smiled broadly.

"Dr. Reynolds, come in, come in. I just sent for you. We need to talk."

He was so euphoric Reynolds hardly knew how to deal with him. Finally he decided on just plain business.

"I see you're looking over the charts. Any last minute ideas?"

"No, none. But once more now the mechanics we go over."

As he talked, Reynolds watched his eyes and body movements and listened to his brain working. There was no mistaking what he was doing. This brain transplant project was to be his vindication, his *raison d'etre*. He would no longer need justification for *being*. Very strange, Reynolds mused, that he hadn't seen this side of Steinke before. Deep inside Steinke was the niggling question: *was* I inferior to those Germans who killed my family and tried to take my life? Didn't the fact that they so easily led us to their gas chambers indicate that they were superior? Why didn't we fight back? Why did we go so docilely into the cattle cars?

All this Reynolds read in him that hour, knowing that Steinke never knew how plainly he came through. Perhaps, Reynolds thought, clairaudience wasn't even necessary; maybe anyone could have read Steinke's thoughts that day, just by listening to his incisive words. At first Reynolds had a vague feeling of pity, but he suddenly recognized that his own mind was following the same tracks, justifying his existence. When this insight came it struck him dumb. He sat straight in his chair and listened even more intently to what Steinke was saying. He was summarizing the logistics of the operations, synchronizing in detail the conduct of the two independent surgeries, then the hours of tedious anastamoses: first the dissection and cutting of cranial nerves and spinal cord, then the arterial supply and venous drainage, then the passage of enlon strands into the spinal canal, then the anastamoses of cranial nerves and the brain stem itself, and finally the complicated introduction of the enlon-borne depolarizers into each cranial nerve. He could see it so clearly in his mind. It was as if he had already done the procedure a dozen times.

"You know, Dr. Reynolds," he was saying now, "we do nothing here new. Hundreds of neural anastamoses I have done on people—none so extensive, but same thing. And I have now done fourteen spinal cord anastamoses in dogs and five in apes. The artery surgeons have done these anastamoses for decades. Just under such pressure before we have never done it. Do you see?"

"I do, sir. It's like when Christiaan Barnard did the first heart transplant. It was easier than a lot of operations he'd done for years. It was the psychological hurdle he had to jump. Like the four minute mile."

"Four minute mile?"

Amused for a moment at his ignorance, Reynolds could hardly blame him for not knowing. "Thirty years ago many runners had come within seconds of running a mile under four minutes. They couldn't quite crack the barrier. It was psychological, no doubt about it. For when Roger Bannister finally crossed that artificial barrier, everyone started running the mile under four minutes."

"I see what you mean."

A drizzly rain, typical of January weather in Chicago, had started outside and gusts of wind blew showers against the window pane. A pigeon sat on the sill, its feathers ruffling in the breeze. Steinke spun in his chair and gazed out on the dreary scene. He baited Reynolds. "Miserable day out there, doctor."

"Only day we got, sir?"

"The only day. You're right. You were right all the time."

Reynolds smiled. "Thank you, sir."

2

T-day came. The transplant team from Hektoen Institute for Advanced Research did the first human brain transplant. The news was printed on the front page of every newspaper in the world, from *The Times* of New York to *The Times* of London, from the *Daily News* of Chicago to the *Pacific Daily News* of Guam, from *Pravda* to Patagonia. All the stories relied on scanty information scratched from nooks and crannies because the operating-room team wasn't talking to anyone, not even to their own PR people.

So it seemed proper—a day later—to make public just what had happened to

Jim Abernathy and Gerard Houston. At first Reynolds was dead set against a minute by minute recitation of the events of that historic day. It was gauche, he said, in bad taste, and not all that interesting.

"Borscht!" exclaimed Phil Adler, Cook County Hospital's top PR man. "Don't you remember the *moon* landing? 'Course you don't, you weren't *old* enough. But people couldn't get *enough* of the technical stuff. And they just abso*lute*ly ate up the *personal* comments of the astronauts. Made them seem *human*."

"This's different," Reynolds persisted.

"I'll say it is. This's *more* important. And *more* interesting. Every guy *out* there is asking himself how the *hell* you can take a man's *brain* out, keep it *alive,* and put it *back* in another head. *Please,* doctor, *trust* me."

Reynolds laughed for the first time since surgery. "I never trust anyone who says 'trust me.'" But he helped Adler edit the journal he had kept during the first half of the operation, when he was at his computer console in Hektoen. To cover the second half, when he was in the OR watching, Reynolds dictated an account which Adler used almost verbatim. Reynolds sent the manuscript to his mother with comments scribbled in the margin. He thought she might be interested. She was. Especially in those scribblings. She sent it back with a few marginal comments of her own.

BRAIN CHILD

A PERSONAL ACCOUNT OF THE WORLD'S FIRST BRAIN TRANSPLANT
by Mercury Reynolds, M.S., Ph.D.

FRIDAY, Jan. 13, 1993

6:30 AM. At my computer console in the lab at Hektoen. (Editor: *Cook County Hospital's Hektoen Institute for Advanced Research.*) Closed circuit TV from Operating Room E, at my left elbow, checks out well, scans 180 degrees, slowly picks up operating table, lights, bank of vital sign monitors, gas lines, etc. TV cameramen hear me alone, obey commands instantly. Gerard Houston's room, Dr. Alfredo Gonzaga in charge of recipient body.

Roving TV from Operating Room F OK, screen at my right elbow. James Abernathy's room, Dr. Victor Steinke in charge of donor brain.

Permanent-film cameras, one in each OR, and crews, standing by, functioning.

6:50 AM. Steinke and Gonzaga come into their rooms.
Steinke: "Ready to go, Dr. Reynolds?"
I answer in the affirmative. Gonzaga the same.
I can hear both of them. Neither of them can hear the other.

(It was eerie, Mother, watching the start of that operation, an operation never before done on earth. I thought I could hear a roaring in my ears, like a soughing of wind through pine trees, high in the arcane corridors of Arcadia.)
(Phoebe: *I hear it, too, but why do you?*)

7:00 AM. Houston—recipient body—is rolled into OR E, nurses and orderlies dragging respirator and oxygen machine and IV standards. Anesthesiologist straps on B/P cuff, checks IV, starts another one, takes over control of respiration from respirator. Will probably not need anesthesia, just breathing help. Transfer to OR table face down, forehead on special brace. Head shaved by intern. Gonzaga sits in the corner on a steel stool. Looks calm.

7:15 AM. Abernathy—donor brain—rolled into OR F. Color better than ever, has had massive blood transfusions. But jaundice apparent on zoom. Eyes open. Steinke bends over him and asks how he's doing. Abernathy just nods. I wonder just how much he comprehends.
(Be a hell of a note to wake up in another man's body and not remember how the hell you got there.)
(Phoebe: *We all have "another man" within us. Your father did, and it killed him. You do, and it will save*

your life some day.)

7:20 AM. Anesthesiologist connects Abernathy to vital sign monitors. The read-out appears on my console. Anesthesia started, IV pentothal and a muscle relaxant (*succinyl choline chloride*). Intubation. Head shaved. Continuous read-out on pulmonary wedge pressure, arterial blood gases, blood pressure, pulse rate, body temperature, everything OK.
(*Kudos to Jonathan Kettering (the medical resident)*)

7:35 AM. Steinke: "Start cooling."
Room nurse switches on cooling blanket. Thermocouple reading drops slowly. I read off each degree to Steinke.

7:45 AM. Houston in OR E ready to go. Multiple heavy drapes around his head, over entire length of body. Gonzaga gowned, capped, masked along with two assistant junior residents. Paints entire scalp with betadine, wipes off excess. Marks proposed incision with sterile magic marker.

8:10 AM. I tell Steinke that Abernathy's body temp is down to 93 degrees. Rolled off cart onto table, face down, like Houston, with cooling blanket. Abernathy's head painted and draped out just like

Birney Dibble M.D.

Houston's. Incision will be identical.

8:25 AM. Dr. Hiri Czrza, Chief of Vascular Surgery, walks into OR F, stands talking to Steinke. Czrza will be in charge of sewing together the arteries and veins. The last to be severed will be the blood vessels, and the first to be re-united.

Steinke, to Czrza: "I think maybe you scrub right from the start."

Czrza: "That would be a great waste of time."

Steinke: "You got something to do more important?" Czrza thinks this over, shakes his head and backs a step or two away. (*Czrza is from Czechoslovakia and one would think he and Steinke would have a common bond in their hatred for the Soviet Union. Maybe they do, but it does not allow them to be friends.*)

(Phoebe: *They're both prima donnas, jealous of each other's fame.*)

8:30 AM. I watch the monitors and the TV screens carefully now. One of my jobs is to synchronize the two operations so that when Abernathy's brain is ready for the final excision, Houston's braincase will be ready to accept it. The room nurse in OR F reports that Abernathy's body is now cooled to 90 degrees. Steinke has overruled some strenuous objections and the brain will be cooled to 78 degrees. Steinke looks up at the roving TV camera, speaks to me. "Any problems, Merc?" (*The first*

time he's called me by my first name.)
(Phoebe: *He needs you more than you need him.*)
None, I reply. Want a read-out?
Steinke: "No."

8:45 AM. Both teams are clustered around the orange heads bulging through the green drapes. I can smell the tension. My own palms are wet with sweat. I dry them on the seat of my pants. (*I reached down into my subconscious and empathized with the first Dr. Reynolds as he sat alone at his microscope, micro-scalpel controlled by the scored dials at his finger tips, fashioning a new kind of creature never before seen on earth.*)
(Phoebe: *A magnificent creature he turned out to be—a real man.*)

8:50 AM. Gonzaga and Steinke begin their incisions at the same moment. The cut starts on the side of the head, above and behind the ear, sweeps forward over the front of the scalp just behind the hairline, then backward across the temple on the other side. A huge flap of scalp and bone is turned to expose the entire brain. By now Steinke is well ahead of Gonzaga and I tell him.
Steinke: "Naturally. It is alright. I have to slow down later when he can catch up."

9:10 AM. The bone is still closely

adherent to the under-surface of the scalp, will remain alive and capable of healing when replaced. This doesn't make any difference in Abernathy's case, but it is of extreme importance in Houston's. (*Confusing. It does make a difference to Abernathy. It is of no importance to him if his present body fails to heal, because it will be dead in a few hours. But it is important to him that Houston's body heals. It will make no difference to Houston if neither body heals.*)

9:15 AM. The brain is exposed. I automatically watch Steinke now because it is Abernathy's brain that must be saved. Any little mistake . . .

9:25 AM. Steinke tips up the frontal lobe to visualize the structures directly beneath it. The genius of the man is now apparent. One by one he dissects the cranial nerves free and cuts them. His first challenge is Cranial Nerve #1, the olfactory (*smell*) nerve: it has to be cut behind the nucleus for it would be impossible to re-connect all the tiny nerves which leave the nucleus and penetrate the nasal bones. Steinke does a masterful job.

Cranial Nerve #2, the optic (*vision*) nerve, is large and is one of the easiest to re-connect. Steinke cuts the nerve after it reaches the *chiasm*, where the fibers from the inner part

BRAIN CHILD

of the retinas cross the midline and go to the opposite cerebral hemisphere. (*We had argued about that level. Steinke didn't argue when the data from our experiments with the anthropoid apes proved me right.*)
(Phoebe: *It takes a great man to admit he's wrong, especially to a 24-year-old hillbilly!*)

10:25 AM. Steinke has now cut loose all twelve cranial nerves and lifted the pituitary out of its bony cave. The cerebellum, seat of control of balance and coordination, he has teased out of the posterior fossa of the cranium.

Through the zoom lens of my monitor I can see the pulsations of the myriad arteries coursing over the ridges and crevices of the *cerebrum*, the main mass of the brain proper. Care has been taken to avoid injuring even the smallest of blood vessels. This has made for painstaking work, especially around the fifth, sixth, and seventh nerves which exit from the *pons*, another part of the primitive brain.

10:30 AM. Steinke: "Progress report on Gonzaga."
I answer: "He's working on the trochlear now, almost done, about ready to trace the abducens forward."
Steinke: "Gottverdammen! The idiot. Tell him to transect the abdu-

cens first, as far anteriorly as he can, then he has much easier time with the trochlear."

I relay this information and get a pained, pithy answer in Spanish as Gonzaga realizes his mistake. I reassure him, "No harm done."

He answers, "Just time."

Steinke steps back from the table and with his hands clasped closely to his chest, accepts a straw under his mask from a glass of orange juice. The nurse rubs his lips with his mask to dry them. He nods his head in thanks.

He stands there for a moment. I know what he's thinking. The next step is to make another incision on the back of the neck and remove the bony covering over the spinal cord.

Irrevocable transection of the brain from the spinal cord imminent.

Point of no return near.

The psychological barrier about to be breached, the four-minute mile a fact. (*I wondered at that moment when John Reynolds crossed that same barrier. Was it when he conceived the Grand Experiment? When he isolated the egg from Penelope? When he finished that last gene translocation? When?*)

(Phoebe: *He never crossed it. He was already on the other side. His misguided genius was incapable of recognizing a psychological barrier.*)

10:40 AM. Steinke: "Scalpel." He makes the incision, cuts away the bone with rongeurs, opens the dura between two tissue forceps held by his assistants, and gazes at the smooth, glistening surface of the spinal cord.

Never before has any man ever purposely taken a scalpel and cut through the spinal cord at that level.

A moment in history never to be forgotten by anyone in that room.

I can almost feel the intake of breath by everyone watching. I hold my own breath for so long that I gasp for air when I hear Steinke say again, "Scalpel."

11:03 AM. Friday, January 13th, 1993. Dr. Victor Steinke palms the scalpel and deftly, incisively, cuts the spinal cord.

3

11:05 AM. Steinke: "OK, Merc, you may come over here."

I quickly shut down my consoles. There is no need for further synchronization of the operations. Steinke is now free to move back and forth between the two ORs until he is again involved in the anastamoses and placement of the enlon strands.

(Editor: *Dr. Mercury Reynolds' laboratory journal ends here. His narrative continues, as told to Mr. Phillip Adler of the hospital's Public Relations Department.*)

BRAIN CHILD

I crossed the street from Hektoen to the Operating Rooms of Cook County Hospital. In the seventh floor surgeons' dressing room, I got a few curious looks until one of the surgeons recognized me and said, "Oh, Dr. Reynolds, your big day, isn't it?"

"Yes, they're at it now. Just about ready for the blood vessel anastamoses."

"Good luck," he said, as if I were going in to do an appendectomy. I smiled, remembering that a prophet is not without honor except in his own home town.

I ran the stairs to the eighth floor, slipped into shoe covers, pulled a paper hood down over my hair and beard and tied on a mask. The corridor of the main operating rooms extended in front of me for hundreds of feet, running the entire length of the main building which covers a full city block. Scrub-suited interns, residents, nurses, medical students, orderlies, aids, and anesthetists scurried back and forth. It was now 11:30 AM.

I slipped quietly into OR F, where James Abernathy lay. Dr. Czrza was just beginning to dissect out the main right carotid artery just where it enters the skull between the second and third cranial nerves. At this point the artery is intimately associated with the inner wall of the cavernous sinus, the huge venous lake which drains the frontal, temporal and occipital lobes of the brain, as well as the eye and nose. When he was through with the right side he moved over to the left and repeated the intricate dissection.

I could see that Dr. Czrza was slowing down. I thought I knew why. He had the toughest part of the entire transplant ahead of him. The veins.

The veins of the brain all drain into a complicated network of collecting systems called *sinuses*, large, thin-walled, easily torn blood-spaces through which the blood moves sluggishly toward the internal jugular vein. All these would have to be dissected away from the bony cranium millimeter by millimeter.

By now the tension in the operating room had reached its highest peak. The only person seemingly unaffected was Czrza himself. He had slowed down, it's true, but under his breath he was whistling a little folktune which I assumed was Czechoslovakian. Incongruously I wished that he would sing the words, for it was a catchy little ditty.

Czrza stood back from his work for a moment and drank some orange juice through a straw. The nurse gently wiped away drops of perspiration from his neck. Steinke sat slumped on a cross-taped stool in the corner. Lines of fatigue showed at the corners of his eyes. Through the door I could see the other operating team, also motionless with fatigue, their work temporarily suspended, waiting for Czrza to finish.

The arterial dissection had taken about forty-five minutes. The venous dissection took two hours. So far Abernathy had received five units of packed red blood cells, replacing the loss from his esophagus as well as from the surgery.

It was now 2:25 PM.

The brain of James Abernathy lay loosely in its bony cranium, attached only by the carotid arteries and the jugular veins. None of the blood vessels had been transected yet except for the vertebrals, and these Czrza had clipped with heavy stainless steel clips. The cut ends pulsated vigorously.

The body of James Abernathy was almost redundant now. The heart still beat, slowly to be sure for it was no longer under nerve control. The lungs functioned as long as the respirator sucked in pure air and pumped out used air. The intestines still churned. But the body had just about served the purpose for which it had been created a half century before. In an hour or two it would cease to be, would fulfill the biblical adage of ashes to ashes, dust to dust.

> (To Phoebe: *Were we playing God? No, I reason. In a day or two, or a week or two, whenever Kettering decided to stop the blood transfusions, Abernathy's heart would have stopped beating anyway. All the*

functions of that great 57-year-old body would have come to a standstill. We were just speeding up the process, meanwhile saving the brain, re-cycling it, to use an ecological term. I tell myself all of this. And shudder a little. And wonder what thoughts went through the mind of the first Dr. Reynolds as he created a new life out of the Phoenix-like ashes of Penelope's death.)

(Phoebe: John Reynolds did not mourn for Penelope any more than you mourn a dead mouse. He was just glad that he had saved the baby Pan, for Pan was to prove John Reynolds' genius to the world.)

At 2:29 PM, Dr. Czrza peered intently one more time into the brain case of Jim Abernathy, gave a quick nod of his head, and with quick mincing steps dashed from OR F into OR E. He was re-gowned and re-gloved by the scrub nurse. With a rapidity which belied the long hours he had already been operating, he doubly clipped Gerard Houston's anterior and middle cerebral arteries and cut in between.

Houston's brain did not need to be kept alive: it was already legally dead. This allowed Czrza to tip the brain much higher than he could in Abernathy's case, speeding the removal of the sinuses. In less than an hour he clipped the vertebral arteries.

BRAIN CHILD

At 3:25 PM the brain fell loose in his hands.

Sudden bewilderment drew deep lines in Czrza's face. His eyes stared, the pupils dilated. Then slowly the wonderment faded. Tiny crinkles formed at the corners of his eyes. He looked up at Steinke and said, "Forgive me, Dr. Steinke. It is not every day a man's brain comes loose in my hands." Steinke nodded. They understood each other at last.

He cradled Houston's brain in both hands and stood silently for some seconds. I wondered if perhaps he was saying a prayer, or meditating on the enormity of what he had just done. Finally he turned slowly and almost lovingly placed the dead brain in a stainless steel basin held out to him by the scrub nurse. She in turn handed it on to the unscrubbed circulating nurse, who nonchalantly lifted the brain out of the basin and slid it into a large glass jar partly filled with formalin. I could see that the original brain hemorrhage had destroyed the normal architecture of almost half of one hemisphere, discoloring it a dark reddish-purple.

Gerard Houston now was not only legally dead, but actually dead.

I watched the circulating nurse sit at the small stainless steel table in the corner, take a pen from her pocket, pull the OR flow sheet toward her and write, "Patient pronounced dead at 3:25 PM by Dr. Hiri

Czrza."

> (To Phoebe: *Her eyelids fluttered as I watched her. She was totally unmindful, for that moment, of her surroundings. I could feel her thoughts coming through to me as I stared at her. "He didn't really pronounce him dead," she thought. "He killed him . . . in any other circumstances this would be murder . . ." Not for the first time I thought how odd it was that my father Pan had been able to send messages, whereas I could receive them.*)

Dr. Czrza returned then to OR F, Jim Abernathy's room, and quickly transected the carotid arteries. Cupping the brain in both hands, like a mother with a newborn baby, Czrza walked back into OR E, placed Abernathy's brain on the sterile back table, covered it with a large gauze wrapping, and saturated the wrap with cold saline solution.

He emptied the brain of blood and injected cold heparin solution into the carotid arteries. Carefully he removed the gauze, lifted the brain from the table and gently placed it into Gerard Houston's brain cavity. He pulled the operating microscope into place, and began his work.

I was astonished to note that it was already 3:40 PM. And yet, paradoxically, it seemed only moments since the nurse had "pronounced" Gerard Houston dead.

Meticulously Czrza sutured the cerebral arteries and then the jugular vein just above the bulb in the foramen, moving quickly and surely as if he had done this a thousand times. And of course he had, in a thousand other circumstances. But never Jim Abernathy's brain in Gerard Houston's braincase. He watched, mesmerized, as the arteries coursing over the brain began to pulsate strongly and firmly.

Czrza looked up now at Steinke. "May I break scrub now, Dr. Steinke?" The words were formal, but the tone was one of deep affection.

"Get the hell out of here, Dr. Czrza," Steinke said, his voice almost tender.

Steinke was re-scrubbed, gowned and gloved. His eyes shown with strength and confidence. The brain was now revascularized; he could work as slowly or as rapidly as he wished. Gently he pushed the short, cut end of Jim Abernathy's spinal cord down through the base of Gerard Houston's braincase. Then meticulously he sewed the cut ends together. Everyone was more relaxed, the palpable tension gone, the brain receiving blood again. Not that Steinke slowed down any. His fingers fairly flew. But the heavy, heavy load was lifting.

I scarcely noticed the nurses in OR F detaching Abernathy's body from the machines, covering it with a sheet and carrying it away. One of the junior residents, or perhaps it was an intern, had sewn his scalp back down, its brainbox now empty, the body a useless shell. So what looked like Jim Abernathy was being carted away to the incinerator, but the real Abernathy was still here, right in front of me, 1500 grams of white and grey matter that would fit easily—had fit easily—into a man's hand.

Or another man's skull.

It was almost too much.

And then, in the quiet of that almost holy moment, intruded the clear, cold, dreadful word, "Arrest!"

(Editor: *Dr. Reynolds' story ends here. For Jim Abernathy, in Gerard Houston's body, could not be revived and he too was dead.*)

Later that night, in the darkness of their living room, with Britt's arm around his shoulder, he asked himself over and over again, what the hell went wrong? Kettering said that the electrolytes, particularly the potassium, were normal. The EKG tracing showed a steady heart rate, without any electrical conduction defects or even extra systoles. Nothing, in fact, that would account for the sudden arrest. One moment everything was alright, Steinke and Gonzaga working steadily on the spinal cord anastamosis, Reynolds hovering at his elbow, Czrza keeping an eye on his blood vessel anastamoses.

Then, the classic drama which so

thrills the layman and constricts the surgeon's coronaries: cardiac arrest. A deathly silence surrounded them for several seconds while the full significance of the word impressed itself on all their minds. Reynolds looked up at the EKG monitor, as did everyone else in the room. And there it was, an almost straight line, just an occasional little flip which heart doctors label "agonal." A dying heart.

A dying patient.

Gonzaga took charge. He stood in the middle of the room, well away from the table, arms folded on his chest, eyes constantly moving, voice scarcely louder than in normal conversation. Cut the head tapes. Pack the wound. Roll him onto the cart. Cardiac massage, eighty a minute, slow down, Joe. Calcium chloride. Sodium bicarbonate. Let's shock him. Stand back everybody. Hit him. No go. Massage again. Not so fast, Joe.

The CPR team moved smoothly, despite the apparent confusion, everyone doing just exactly what she or he was programmed to do in such a situation. The circulating nurse called out the minutes, which at first seemed like only seconds. The anesthesiologist pumped his bag.

Reynolds stood in awe and in fear. Fear which only now, in the stillness of his living room, began to take a spectral form, belying the confidence with which they had all approached the transplant of a human brain.

Britt finally went to bed, saying softly as she left, "There'll be others, Merc." But Reynolds sat desultorily in the big easy chair, playing with the brown linen cloths which covered the threadbare arms. His adrenalin-fed mind trundled out everything that had led up to that moment of colossal failure. It had started on a warm, rainy day just six months before, when he arrived at Hektoen Institute to begin work with Steinke.

Since then, so many things had happened. He had met Britt and Maia. Hal Forester had come back into his life. His mother, Phoebe, had challenged him to sort things out before he did his first brain transplant. Steinke had pushed him too fast. No, it wasn't Steinke's fault. They had all been eager to get started. Inevitably his thoughts drifted back to that first day, standing in the rain at the bus stop where the taxi from O'Hare Field had dropped him. . . .

4

Mercury Reynolds climbed out of the taxi and stood in the warm, early spring rain on the corner of Harrison and Wood, awed by the thought that he, a twenty-four-year-old Virginian hillbilly, was about to report to the great Victor Steinke. Steinke, the world's most famous neurosurgeon, had asked for him. Reynolds rolled the name around on his tongue and had the urge to shout it to the world.

He moved out of the way of a load of passengers hurrying off a bus, crowding each other in their eagerness to be somewhere else. He had come directly from O'Hare Field after a two-hour flight from

of the Chi-
yet pene-
of his
a dream.
ad all of
ants. He
course,
ificant
ing to
hing.
tively
rmal
able
whose body
his brain. Remove the
both specimens (horrible
word), transplant the good brain into the good body. Incinerate the dying brain and the dying body.

To execute this simple concept would be incredibly complex. Selection of the brain alone would try the wisdom of a Solomon in the Greek caves at Delphi; that was Victor Steinke's problem. Mercury Reynolds' job was to ensure regeneration of the cranial nerves and the spinal cord. At this point in time, 1992, he was the only man in the world who knew how to do that. For two years, surgeons had used Reynolds' invention, enlon, to cause the lower cord to grow; for twenty years surgeons had transplanted animal brains which lived but never joined their new bodies. No one had ever transplanted a brain which linked up with its new body, in animals *or* man.

Steinke's laboratory lay half a block south in the Hektoen Institute for Advanced Research. Reynolds walked down Wood Street to the seven-story Children's Hospital and stood on the sidewalk across from Hektoen for a moment. It was here, in this building, that he hoped to perform a miracle which would surpass even the evil genius of the first Dr. Reynolds.

The building was only twenty years old, a mere child compared to the eighty-year-old monolith of Cook County Hospital across the way. Nine stories of glass and yellow brick rose above him, supported by two-foot-thick concrete pillars twenty feet high. Tucked under the pillars was a glass-enclosed foyer. A young black girl wiped the inside of the windows while an Afro-haired student in a white lab coat chatted with her.

The original Hektoen Institute stood forlornly beside its gilded stepchild, connected to it by only an enclosed skywalk on the fifth floor. But it had had its days of glory, had housed the scientists who had made medical advances every bit as startling in their day as those Reynolds hoped to make in his.

As he stood musing, a dozen white-coated young men pushed through the central doors onto the sidewalk. Some carried stethoscopes and all had pockets crammed with papers and notebooks. Identification cards were clipped conspicuously to lapels or pockets. Reynolds felt old and too well-dressed as the wave of tomorrow's doctors washed around him. They didn't even know he was there. The sophomoric thought crossed his mind that he would show *them!*

He found the office of his new Chief on the ninth floor, a large corner room where light streamed in from four windows. As he strode across the tiled floor to shake hands with Victor Steinke, Reynolds' quick glance around him gave him an idea of the no-nonsense personality of the great man. A massive oak desk jutted at right angles from one wall into the center of the room. The walls were totally bare except for a placque inscribed with the Oath of Hippocrates and a framed certificate of the American Board of Neurosurgery. The desk was almost as bare as the walls: several texts, a green blotter on which lay several journals and typed reports, a white lab coat bulging with instruments.

"Sit down, Dr. Reynolds. Miserable day, no?" Steinke's voice was high-pitched and heavy with a German accent.

Reynolds smiled and answered, "Yes, sir, but the only day we've got."

"A philospher you are already, Dr. Reynolds?" he said with a hint of sarcasm which Reynolds chose to ignore.

"Not really, but yesterday's gone and

we can't do a damn thing about it. Tomorrow's not here, and we can do damn little about *that*. Therefore, it's today that counts."

Steinke's face remained stolid, his little pig eyes emotionless. "Here in the Hektoen I want men who think they can do damn much about tomorrow. Maybe we choose wrong?"

Reynolds tensed, the muscles in his jaw setting hard. He had met Victor Steinke when the whole department interviewed him the month before, but most of the interrogation had been conducted by others. Steinke had just sat back and watched.

Now he continued to hold Reynolds with his little pig eyes. The thought crossed Reynolds' mind that he had never seen a fat Jew before. His Jewish friends were lean or at most slightly overweight. Above the rolls of fat on Steinke's neck, his bald head reflected even the dull light streaming in the huge windows. His skin was pink, his full beard and mustache blond and beginning to grizzle. Except for his dark brown eyes, he looked more Aryan than most Germans.

Reynolds smiled, determined now to fight fire with water. "Oh, I think I'll be your man, Dr. Steinke."

Steinke scratched his tattoo as if a mosquito had just bitten it, his eyes never leaving Reynolds. He leaned back in his chair, folded his arms over his bulging belly, and grunted. "You better be. This study will be pilot project watched around the world." His w's were halfway between w and v, his d's almost t's, and his s's sibilant. So what he actually said was, "Thiss shtudy vill be pilot project vatched around the vorlt." He had tried to eradicate the hated German accent and hadn't done it.

"I'm aware of that, sir," Reynolds said. "I'm prepared to spend the next two years living in this laboratory if that's what it takes."

"You're not married?"

"No."

He waved a pudgy hand. "But that is not my business. What you do here in this building is my business. Even about the smallest details you will consult me."

Reynolds shook his head slowly, his smile wooden. "That's not the way I work, Dr. Steinke. I've got to be allowed some freedom . . ."

"Not in my laboratory, by God!"

Reynolds almost told him he wasn't being reasonable. Two things stopped him. One, he remembered Fred Bucy's law: nothing is ever accomplished by a reasonable man. Secondly, and more importantly, Steinke would throw him out. He felt his jaw tighten again and a drop of sweat trickled down his back. Hang in there, Merc, he said to himself. Steinke can't be everywhere at once, and when the work is well under way, there's no way he can supervise every bit of it.

"Alright, sir," Reynolds said.

The flush faded from Steinke's face. Odd, Reynolds thought, that Steinke could have survived Auschwitz or Bergen-Belsen, or wherever the hell he'd been. He sat behind those rolls of fat just itching for a fight. An attitude like that would have been a free ticket to the showers. Maybe he'd been able to control it when his life was at stake. And maybe he'd been mellower when he was young.

Kill him with kindness, Reynolds thought, or kill him with a song. But bring him around somehow, so he doesn't have to be fought.

Steinke sensed the hostility draining from Reynolds and his manner changed abruptly. "You know about me, doctor, now tell me about you."

Reynolds smiled. There were a great many things about himself that he would not tell. No one, for instance, need know about his grandfather. Or that he suspected his foster father—the first Dr. Reynolds—of murder. There were real, honest-to-goodness skeletons in his closet that should be kept there.

But he would tell Steinke what he wanted to know about his professional life. Steinke would already know his qualifications; he wouldn't have hired him if they hadn't been satisfactory. No, Reynolds thought, he wouldn't have hired him if his qualifications hadn't been *superior*. He had the urge to start out, "I was born of poor but honest parents," and that was certainly true. But it was a little corny and Steinke wouldn't think it at all funny.

"You've seen my CV, Dr. Steinke. Is there anything specific you'd like to know?"

Steinke smiled for the first time, a gentle smile which betrayed a trace of envy in the minute elevation of the left corner of his mouth. "What your CV says, I know, but I like to know about your discovery of enlon."

As Reynolds began talking, Steinke sat back and watched him. What he saw was a tall, lean, young man with a slight hunchback and not too obvious a limp, a clean-lined narrow face, almost ascetic in its boniness, with reddish eyebrows and a neatly trimmed van Dyke beard. In the depths of his pale blue eyes Steinke sensed a timelessness, a feeling that Reynolds could reach as far back into the past as he wanted to go. There was in him a disconcerting ingenuousness for a man so young and famous. Steinke, lacking all physical attributes attractive to women, recognized that Mercury Reynolds was loaded down with an animal magnetism which would escape no member of the opposite sex, no matter how old.

"Well," Reynolds said, "it's a long story or a short one, depending on how it's told. I knew long before I got to college that my field was going to be medicine. In some capacity. For a while I saw myself as a neurosurgeon..."

Steinke's grunt was eloquent, his face stolid.

"... because I could see the incredible advances being made in the surgery of cerebral aneurysms, brain tumors, and cranial nerves. I wanted to be a part of that. But very quickly I recognized I'd be no good at handling the daily crises with the patient and his relatives. I don't mean the medical crises, I mean the interpersonal relationships. I'd have to stay aloof in order not to identify too closely with them, and either route would be bad." He smiled broadly. "And I knew instinctively that I'd never be able to spend the necessary time in the office signing insurance forms, sending bills and trying to collect, attending staff meetings, and all the other chores the practicing physician must do."

He leaned back in the chair and crossed his legs. Steinke relaxed and leaned forward, hands folded on his desk in an almost prayerful pose.

Reynolds continued, his voice low, slightly pedantic. "The laboratory was my milieu. In my senior year in college I saw clearly what my field would be. Medical scientists were on the brink of perfecting a technique to stimulate regeneration of the spinal cord. At first it was just a whisper—

you'll remember that time. And you'll also no doubt remember when that whisper became a roar; it was found that total depolarization of the spinal cord distal to the transection was all that was necessary for the unmyelinated nerve fibers to grow again. I felt like the parson's son in Service's poem: 'Till sudden there came a whisper that maddened us every man; I got in on Bonanza before the big rush began.' "

Reynolds' pale blue eyes flashed across the room to Steinke, burning like dry ice, hot and cold at the same time. He leaned forward, his voice low and vibrant. "I got in on Bonanza all right. I was right there in the thick of it, helping with those first tests . . ."

"There is one major parallel in medical history," Steinke said, "you probably know . . ."

Reynolds smiled, the icy fervor draining slightly, his eyes still bright with repressed excitement. "Yes, I know. Charles Best was an undergraduate assistant in Dr. Banting's lab when they extracted insulin. That was almost seventy years ago." He shrugged his heavily muscled shoulders. "That discovery helped more people than we . . ."

Steinke slammed his hand on the table. "We do not compare successes. *Every* discovery is important."

Reynolds nodded vigorously. "I couldn't agree more. Sorry if I sounded . . . well, to go on with my story. We'd begun

BRAIN CHILD

with tests *in vitro*, then finally went to experiments *in vivo*, and eventually to the human himself.

"I did my master's thesis on methods to depolarize the spinal cord after total transection. I've never worked so hard and long. The months flew by. I lost track of friends, even my old roommate Hal Forester—he's playing for the Philadelphia Eagles now—for long periods of time. The only relaxation I got was when I visited my mother once a month or so for a weekend, or she'd come to my apartment and settle in for a few days. She understood my compulsion as few mothers would, although she occasionally wondered out loud why I hadn't gone into genetics. We talked long hours about my work. She has a brilliant mind and showed it in the astute questions she asked. She has a scientist's mind herself, got a doctorate in botany while raising me."

Reynolds paused for a moment, thinking of his mother still living at Standing Oaks, the place where Dr. John Reynolds and his wife Sylvia had conceived the great experiment to merge the forty-six chromosomes of *Homo sapiens* with the forty-eight chromosomes of *Pan troglodytes*. He would never tell Steinke that. Would probably never tell anyone.

"Our first attempts at depolarizing the spinal cord were hopelessly clumsy. We actually opened the spinal cord through-

53

out the entire length of the cord below the level of the injury or disease, because we knew we had to place the electronic depolarizers every centimeter for them to work. We had to put each depolarizer in place, gather the wires for approximately ten of them, and bring them out to the controls where we could adjust the transmission. No one had thought to control the transmission at the depolarizer, to use the CT scan, or to use body-jacket sensors to monitor the nerve growth." He smiled. "We didn't even use the computer to help us interpret the results. All four of those ideas were mine."

"So I understand. It was a brilliant piece of work."

Reynolds waved a deprecating hand. "It was work, alright. I'll say that much. For my doctoral thesis I worked on placing tiny depolarizers every centimeter with all the electronic circuitry needed to provide the switching and transmission controls at the depolarizer site. And all of this is a strand of plastic only one-half millimeter thick. At the heart of all of this was my luck in finding someone willing to put the correct circuits on a 1K micro-silicon chip. Without that reduction to .4 millimeter size, I could never have swung it.

"I've got a scale model I'll show you when my gear gets here from Charlottesville. And I'll explain it all in much more detail. Other members of the staff will be

BRAIN CHILD

interested, too. Anyway, for two years I filled wastebaskets with notes, computations, and tangled lengths of almost invisible plastic wires. And I filled gunny sacks with experimental models of the skullcap sensors and body sensors before I got them right. When I finally produced a working module, it caught the imagination of even the stuffiest scientists and of course the always-eager public. The scientists, like you, said it was a brilliant piece of work. The public called it serendipity."

"You knew though, as Pasteur did," Steinke said, "that serendipity favors the prepared mind."

Reynolds nodded. "I called my invention 'enlon.' The press called it 'the magic thread of life.' "

Steinke was very quiet. Reynolds sat quietly, too, thinking that, yes, he had gotten his doctorate for his work and there was now another Dr. Reynolds. The first was a micro-biologist whose drive for recognition eclipsed all human ethics and led him to kidnapping, murder, and total immersion in a terror-riven life.

And he, Mercury Reynolds, the second Dr. Reynolds, would spend his life expiating the sins of the first. He could do no other, no matter what pain and frustration might come in his personal life, and what it might cost him in his professional life.

5

A gust of wind threw a splattering of raindrops against the window and the room darkened a bit. Steinke leaned back and rested his hands on his belly. "Thank you, Dr. Reynolds," he said. He was impressed with Reynolds' clarity, recognizing that there was something unique about him, not knowing just what it was. He was to find out.

"Perhaps we now go see . . ." The phone rang and he put out his hand to it. "Your workshop." He lifted the receiver and put it to his ear. "Yes. Yes. No, I come right away." He replaced the receiver on the cradle. "A case I must see. You will come?"

"Of course."

Steinke heaved himself out of his chair and put on the long white lab coat. The breast pocket bulged with pens, pencils, index cards, tongue blades, a penlight. A tuft of cotton was fastened with a straight pin to his lapel. In one side pocket a stethoscope bulged, the earpieces and diaphragm entwined with the flexible grey tubing, reminding Reynolds of a caduceus, his own symbol of healing and power. A reflex hammer and an ophthalmoscope protruded from the other pocket.

Reynolds knew that the diagnostic equipment displayed so openly was Steinke's statement to the world that he was a clinician first and a researcher second. That was alright with Reynolds. Both disciplines were necessary. Reynolds didn't know how to transplant a brain. Steinke didn't know how to use enlon strands.

Because of the rain, they took the tunnel to the main hospital. They made a rather odd pair. Steinke walked like a fat man, legs swinging awkwardly from the hips, toes pointing out, arms swinging widely in an almost effeminate manner, head down but eyes peering straight ahead. Reynolds was six feet tall even with the stoop resulting from his mild kyphosis. He dragged his left foot slightly, giving him a rocking gait much like a sailor on a badly tilted deck. But his upper torso was heavily muscled, the shoulders and arms bulging the fabric of his tailored coat, his lower body tapered and lean. He had been a wrestler in high school and was prevented from being a star only by a weakness in his left leg. Both defects were congenital. When his mother told him the details of his birth, he was surprised that there weren't more problems.

The walls of the tunnel were damp, the odor a disagreeable mixture of cave, sewer, hospital and boiler room. Overhead water pipes and electrical conduits hung from the low ceiling and Reynolds found himself ducking to avoid striking his head. Steinke turned to the right when they reached the main tunnel connecting all the buildings of the huge hospital complex. Here there was a steady stream of whiteclad interns, residents, nurses, students and a few patients straggling along from one clinic to another.

"We combined neurology and neurosurgery on Ward 30," Steinke said as they strode along a broad yellow corridor on the third floor. "Dr. Johnny Howser's old ward. Much time it saves for all of us, especially the residents. But you are not interested in ancient history."

Just outside the ward he thumped his fist on a door marked "Chief Resident." A handsome young Filipino opened it and said, "Oh, Dr. Steinke, I'm glad I caught you. I think we got a subdural."

"Acute?" His eyes were bright with anticipation.

"No, sir. Subacute."

"Let's see him."

"Her."

Reynolds tagged along, liking Dr. Gonzaga from the very first. He was short, muscular, Filipino by birth but trained in the U.S. and now an American citizen. His voice trailed back to Reynolds, eager and persuasive, confident, quickly detailing the clinical history for Steinke.

"She was drunk for a week, tried to get up to her room last night and fell almost a flight of stairs. Lay there for an unknown length of time. Found by another tenant, who surprisingly brought her in and says she talked to him all the way. Now she's unconscious and going fast."

Steinke grunted. "Any other injuries?"

"No, sir."

They had reached the main ward and turned into it. Dr. Gonzaga slipped into the first little room on the left and came out with a test tube. "Her spinal fluid. Clear as a bell, grossly. Few red cells under the mike."

"Pressure?" Steinke asked.

"Out of the manometer."

Steinke grunted again.

The huge ward stretched into the distance for two hundred feet or more. Along both sides of the first hundred feet, small doorless rooms held a bed or two for the desperately ill. In one room, three serious young men in long white lab coats bent over an elderly man who seemed to be unconscious.

With the lumbering alacrity of a sumo wrestler, Dr. Steinke strode into the small nurses' station halfway down the hall. The head nurse jumped to her feet, reminiscent of the days when all nurses stood when a doctor entered. She was tiny, with the figure of an adolescent girl, and wore her hair *en bouffant* to give more height. Her movements were quick, purposeful, and reminded Reynolds of a junco under a birdfeeder. The other two nurses in the room were suddenly quiet, their lively conversation muted by the sudden presence of the great Victor Steinke. They bent their heads quietly over a patient's chart, occasionally glancing out of the corners of their eyes at Steinke.

"Good morning, Miss Rogers," Steinke said and sat heavily on the wooden covering of the steam radiator. "My new associate, Dr. Reynolds. Him you must break in right."

Helen Rogers stood before him like a doll in front of a bear. She wrung her hands with quick little movements, then shook her fingers as if there were water on them. "Don't worry, doctor. I'll make him toe the line."

She smiled at Reynolds then, a smile so frank and candid that he was put on guard immediately. Whatever obsequiousness she reserved for the Chief would not be wasted on his new assistant. "Welcome, Dr. Reynolds, to the cuckoo's nest."

"Helen!" Steinke roared, and the two staff nurses jumped.

"Sorry, doctor." She flushed and wrung her hands again.

"Show him the ward, Miss Rogers," Steinke said, formal again, "while I look at the subdural."

Helen Rogers inclined her head toward the door and Reynolds went out. She followed slowly, readjusting her little round cap securely on the tall blonde hair. Steinke and Gonzaga moved off down the ward and disappeared into one of the private rooms.

"There's not much to see," Miss Rogers said, "that you can't see from here. But come along."

She walked bird-like down the hall. "The big ward used to hold fifty beds, jammed so close you could hardly squeeze between. And another twenty in a double row down the center. That was when County had 3500 beds. We're down to about 1200 now."

"Why?"

"Social progress. The blacks don't all have to come here now, what with insurance on their jobs, medicaid, medicare, what have you. And it's against the law to discriminate. So the private hospitals take them."

They passed the room where the "subdural" lay. Steinke was shining a little penlight into each eye and Reynolds heard him say, "Right pupil's fixed." Gonzaga answered with a smug, "I know."

Steinke heaved his bulk to the foot of the bed and pushed his hands against the soles of the patient's feet. The left foot pumped up and down against his hand.

Reynolds and Miss Rogers returned to the nurses' station. She stopped before she went in. "Your fame has preceded you here, doctor," she said. There was an accusatory note to her voice, as if somehow he were an interloper. In the harsh light, anxiety spread from her eyes into the muscles of her face, made her jaw muscles quiver. Interesting, Reynolds mused as he watched her carefully and tried to catch her thoughts. She was about as old as his mother, though not nearly as pretty or confident, and there were no rings on her fingers. For a moment he wondered if somehow she considered him a threat, then suddenly knew that she was asking his help in some indefinable way. When she spoke he knew what it was.

"He's not nearly as gruff and tough as he sounds, not nearly. You should see him talking to an injured child. Makes you want to cry."

"I understand."

"It's his background. His mother was gassed. He was torn right out of his father's arms. Never saw him again. Doesn't know if he's alive or dead. Victor's never married, unless you call Hektoen and this ward his life."

Reynolds nodded. And didn't miss the "Victor."

"So don't cross him unless you're really sure you're right." She turned toward the nurses' station, then glanced at him over her shoulder. "And he's rarely wrong." He would remember those words when he heard Andrea Hughes die.

"We'll get along," he said.

"I'm on his side if you don't," she said and went into the nurses' station.

He followed her in and sat at the nurses' desk to wait. A few moments later, Steinke barged in, motioned Reynolds out of his chair, and sat heavily in it. Without hesitation he dialed a number and waited impatiently. Behind him, Gonzaga stood almost at attention, eyes fixed on Steinke as one would look at a god.

"Miss G. please," Steinke roared into the phone, then whipped his stethoscope from around his neck and stuffed it into his pocket. He twisted the ends of his drooping mustaches, scratched his shaved pate, then shifted his eyes suddenly to Gonzaga. "Would be quicker if you just run up there."

Gonzaga started for the door but Steinke waved him back and talked briskly into the phone. "Miss G. A subdural we have here on Ward 30. Going fast. No anesthesia. A room, two nurses, the emergency burr-hole tray." He paused, listening. "Bump him. This is more serious. I talk to him, keep him off your neck." Another pause. "Right now. We send her up, OK?"

He hung up.

Less than a half hour later Reynolds sat in the little balcony overlooking the main operating room, thin blue paper hat on his head, soft green paper mask covering his face. Ten feet away, Gonzaga's intern was finishing a quick shave of the patient's scalp. Blood trickling from several nicks attested to the rapidity of the prep.

The base of the patient's head was held firmly on two padded head-pieces by a wide strip of tape across her forehead. An anesthetist sat idly on the other side of the arm board, with nothing to do except monitor the vital signs and keep the intravenous line open. He had placed a plastic airway deep in her throat; she tolerated it without choking or gagging.

Steinke and Gonzaga came in, were gowned and gloved by the scrub nurse. Reynolds watched them carefully. These two men were more important to the success of the brain transplant project than anyone else, including himself. If he didn't like what he saw right then, he could still get out.

From the moment they started the operation, there was no longer any doubt in his mind about the technical skills of the surgeons. Gonzaga did the actual surgery, but they acted so well in concert that it was sometimes difficult to say who was surgeon and who was assistant. Smoothly they covered the entire patient with sterile sheets, except for the top half of the head. Gonzaga used the back of a scalpel to make tiny crosshatches in the four places he planned to explore with the trephine. Then, without a word, he looked first at the anesthetist, then at Steinke. A brief nod from each.

His eyes never wavering from the orange scalp, and without a second's pause between maneuvers, he deftly and forcefully incised to the bone, ignored the spurting of the arteries, slipped in mechanical retractors, and incised the periosteum covering the bone. He held the scalpel up. The nurse took it quickly and laid the electric burr in his hand. Gently Gonzaga held it to the bone, waited for it to catch, then drove it home until it locked. Steinke moved in, irrigated the neat round hole with warm saline from a bulb syringe in the time it took Gonzaga to lay down the burr.

"Looks blue," Gonzaga said.

Steinke grunted. "Of course."

"Suction," said Gonzaga, and held the tip of the sucker to the hole as he opened the dura with a quick downward stroke of the scimitar-shaped scalpel. A gush of dark black blood tinged with streaks of red poured out of the cavity faster than the sucker could handle it. Deep in the dark hole the brain pulsated strongly. Gradually, as the blood ran out, the brain rose closer and closer to the surface until it lay just a few millimeters from the undersurface of the bone.

Gonzaga plugged the hole with a cottonoid sponge and quickly made another burr hole in a previously marked spot. Here there was only a small amount of bloody drainage.

"Looks like we got it all from the frontal trephine, Dr. Steinke."

No comment, but there was a distinct feeling of relief, even of relaxation in the room.

Gonzaga removed the cottonoid from the first hole. "The brain's almost completely expanded already," he said to no one in particular. "Better move fast, she's going to start waking up."

With the sureness born of decades of practice, Steinke made burr holes on the other side of the scalp. Reynolds was sure that it would be impossible for him to move faster than Gonzaga, but he did. Here was a master at work, Reynolds thought, and knew that if he ever had to have brain surgery he would know where to go.

The patient stirred restlessly as the last of the skin sutures were placed. "Will she be alright?" Reynolds asked, and Steinke started as if he had forgotten Reynolds was there. He looked up and nodded, his bushy eyebrows lowering.

"Unless there is too much damage already before we release the hematoma."

They changed clothes in the dressing room, slowly now in contrast to the haste with which they had gotten ready for the surgery. "Things went well," Reynolds ventured.

Gonzaga glanced at Steinke and grinned. "Anything is easy if you know how. Everything is tough if you don't."

Reynolds pondered those sage words as they descended to Ward 30. Would things go well with their brain transplants just because they knew how?

6

They walked briskly through the ward, Steinke listening intently to each new case summary, barking out a question or a comment at almost every bedside. Gonzaga wrote furiously in a small notebook as Steinke moved on to the next bed. In an hour they saw all the new patients and had settled the problems of the old ones. Miss Rogers kept pace with them, stopping to say a word to each patient after the doctors had moved on, fluffing up the pillow or rearranging the bedclothes, or perhaps merely patting the patient on the arm.

Steinke stopped at the doorway to the nurses' station. "We go now," he said, "to show Dr. Reynolds his workshop at Hektoen."

Reynolds shook Gonzaga's hand and said, "It'll be a pleasure working with you, doctor. I've got a lot to learn from you."

"I've got a lot to learn from you, too," Gonzaga replied.

Reynolds knew what he meant. It seemed obvious that no neurosurgeon would want to be dependent forever on him to monitor the enlon strands and control a vital part of the surgical technique. They would want to learn the technique themselves, and quite literally work Reynolds out of the job. That would be alright with him. He had carried the work about as far as he could, short of brain transplants. He had seen his invention used for the cure of previously hopeless cases of paraplegia and even a few cases of quadriplegia. It was time to move on to brain transplants; when he had imparted his knowledge of that field —perhaps in a year or two—he would be happy to work on something else.

They crossed under Wood Street in the tunnel again. This time Reynolds noticed the reaction of other people to Steinke. Everyone knew him, that was clear, and treated him with great respect. Reynolds knew why, after just an hour in the Operating Room and an hour on the wards. He was a genius.

When they reached the ninth floor of the Hektoen Institute, Steinke looked slyly at Reynolds and said, "Come, I show you where I live."

Reynolds thought he was joking until he was ushered into a tiny room adjoining the bare room where they had first met. It was fitted with a bed, dresser, three telephones with different numbers, a bathroom, and a small clothes closet in which hung a single suit of clothes. Unlike his super-tidy office, here his papers, books, and research journals littered the desk and the floor beside it. He wasn't joking at all.

There was just a hint of a smug smile as he waved a hand across the room. "Command post," he said, and abruptly turned away. Reynolds got a glimpse of himself in the mirror across the room and knew how callow he must look to this almost sixty-year-old Jewish refugee from a Hitler concentration camp. Steinke would see the calm face—which Reynolds' mother insisted looked benign, even gentle—and conservative white shirt and tie, and wonder if this wet-behind-the-ears youth could really live up to his advance billing. Staring at his image, Reynolds shrugged his shoulders and strode vigorously out of the room behind Steinke.

In the corridor, Steinke turned toward Reynolds and said, "Now for a little history lesson and a little inspiration."

In the elevator again they dropped quickly to the second floor where they passed the library, several small conference rooms, and the administrative offices. In a widened area of the corridor, where the walls were painted a soothing robin's egg blue, they sat on a black leatherette settee. In front of them was a life-sized portrait of a distinguished, white-mustachioed man in rimless glasses seated at an old-fashioned desk. His white linen suit with the Mao-style collar was impeccable. His long, slim fingers closed gently around a tilted glass test-tube half-filled with clotted blood.

The inscription read:

LUDWIG A HEKTOEN

1863-1951

They sat gazing at the great man for a full five minutes. Steinke didn't have to say a word, for the history lesson and the inspiration leaped out at Reynolds from that painting far better than any words could have done: a gentle man in a white suit who had had a research laboratory named after him because he knew how to extract the secrets from a tube of blood. His life had spanned one of the most exciting periods in the history of medicine: the discovery by Morton of anesthesia, the great advances in surgery by Halsted and his contemporaries, the shakeup and standardization of medical schools by the Flexner report, the discovery of penicillin and sulfanilimide and later the multitude of antibiotics, two world wars and their impact on surgical technique and laboratory analysis, the growth of medical technology which formed the basis for everything Reynolds had done and was going to do.

They continued the tour. There was one floor for the histophysical lab, cytology, surgical pathology and post-mortem room (where seven gleaming tables stood with hanging meat-market scales and bloody pans), one floor for cyto-genetics, special procedures and routine tests, and on which the Chief of Pathology had his paper-cluttered offices; one floor for microchemistry, enzyme studies, and toxicology, whose corridors were lined with dozens of five-foot tanks of helium and compressed air . . .

. . . and three other floors crowded with the people and the technology dedicated to solving the pathological problems of the human race. Engrossed as he had been for his short lifetime in the laboratory, Reynolds was still overwhelmed by the immensity of the Hektoen Institute.

They came back finally to the ninth floor. Steinke said, "Your office is next to mine. You may use it as you see fit. You may go in it only to read something you have forgotten, or to sleep when you have been up all night. Or you may sit there and direct things by memos. That is your business. As long as the work gets done. If the work doesn't get done—"

He didn't finish the sentence and he didn't need to. He doesn't need to bully me, Reynolds thought, because I'll get the work done. In a year or two, I'll be ready.

"The first human brain transplant," Steinke said as he entered the main complex of labs, "we will be doing in six months."

Reynolds flushed and raised his hand in protest but Steinke had already moved away from him. He followed numbly, humbly. He had, in fact, never felt so humble.

The entire central core of the ninth floor was one vast transplant laboratory. Along one wall was a row of battered old metal desks, gun-metal gray as if salvaged from a Navy junkyard. Each desk was piled high with journals and papers; some looked like no one had sat down at them for months.

Down the center of the great room were six work tables laden with the instruments of the researchers: glass tubes, retorts, and pipettes; computer consoles, printers, and files of software; inked drum tracings, sinks, scales and balances. On one worktable was an EKG machine, and on another an EEG machine. Lining one entire wall were shelves overflowing with pamphlets, journals and textbooks.

In one corner of the vast lab was a glass-walled operating room in which two white-clad men were working on an anesthetized dog. Reynolds moved up to the partition and watched for a moment as one of the surgeons neatly cannulated the femoral artery while at the head of the table the other was doing a tracheostomy.

Steinke stood behind him. "Your surgeons, Dr. Reynolds. A model they are preparing for your first cranial nerve implantation."

Reynolds turned startled eyes on Steinke. "You expect me to get right to work!"

"Tomorrow will the dog be ready."

"I'm ready today."

Steinke nodded and without a word moved away from the window. Reynolds watched for a few more moments and then followed him.

They stood together at the exit, watching the workers at their tasks. Steinke smiled grimly, "you will notice that it is a young man's world."

Reynolds smiled. "And a young woman's," he said, for he had noticed many young women bending with great concentration over their pipettes and calipers and notebooks. But Steinke was right about their ages. They were all young, in their twenties, thirties, or early forties. Steinke was an anachronism. He belonged to that somewhat uncommon breed of older men who maintain a youthful enthusiasm for their work. And, more importantly and linked with it, who retain contact with the frontiers of medicine into their later years.

"Come," Steinke said, "we talk."

They returned to Steinke's office. Steinke took off his lab coat, tossed it carelessly on his desk, and sat down in his revolving chair. He sat in quiet reverie for a moment, absently scratching his tattoo. Reynolds sat in the straight-backed chair, mroe at ease now, and looked out the window into the grey dusk.

"Does six months seem too short?" Steinke said suddenly.

Reynolds nodded. "I had expected about a year, perhaps longer."

"Start we cannot until you are ready. I do not hide the fact that we are all dependent on you. But *we* are ready . . . whenever you are."

"I'll try." He shook his head, and, almost to himself added, "So little time." He looked up at Steinke. "You haven't started to look for candidates?"

"No, it is too early for that. But we know what we will be looking for."

Reynolds leaned forward, the elbow of his right arm resting on his crossed knees, fingers laced tightly together. "Tell me."

"The brain we are looking for must be perfect. It cannot be affected by the illness which is killing the patient. Patients with cancer almost every one we will rule out, first of all. Even with our fifth generation CT scans, microscopic spread cannot be seen. Our chemists tell us within one-tenth of one percent error if in his body a patient *has* cancer cells, but they still cannot tell us if there are cancer cells in the brain."

Reynolds nodded. "And what a horrendously bad joke that would be to transplant a brain with cancer in it."

"Precisely. And consider them we cannot are the senile patients, and diabetics with advanced hardening of the arteries. And brains damaged by trauma we cannot use."

"What about other forms of trauma like ruptured livers, or aortas or some other internal organs?"

"We save most of them. Or they die so quickly that they are of no use. But if their original trauma they survive and go into coma from infection or blood clots, those we might use."

"Who else can you use, then?"

"Severely burned patients who have no chance of survival. Patients in terminal heart failure who are not candidates for heart transplants or mechanical hearts. Neurologic disorders like Lou Gehrig's disease. Congenital lung and kidney diseases for whom we can find no transplants. Giant aneurysms of the aorta which cannot be excised and replaced. Quadriplegics, not treatable with enlon-implants, who want a new life in a new body."

Reynolds shifted uneasily. "Which brings up the most important criterion of all: does the individual under consideration want his brain transplanted?"

Steinke was silent. Then he said softly.

"Yes, most important criterion of all."

"And the recipients?"

The fat man smiled, a smile so enigmatic that Reynolds was to remember it later under the most grotesque circumstances. "The recipient," Steinke said, "will be easy part. Dead he will already be."

"But . . ."

"Legally dead, Dr. Reynolds."

"Yes, I see."

"Most will be trauma victims, patients whose brains are shattered beyond repair, whose electro-encephalographic tracings draw straight lines on the paper, whose bodies to signals from that dead brain will never again respond. Others will be young people with spontaneous brain hemorrhages not curable with surgery, usually aneurysms of the Circle of Willis. Yes, we save most of them now. But not all. Some have too much damage to their brains from the pressure. Some patients with tumors of the brain itself, tumors that to other parts of the body never metastasize."

Later, as Reynolds walked through the still-falling drizzle to his room in Karl Meyer Hall, he mused that all of this was sort of like telling a man how the watch works when all he wanted was the time. The important thing was: they needed a healthy brain to transplant into a healthy body. Given those two things, they could create a new human being.

7

Outwardly Mercury Reynolds appeared well adjusted to the life of late twentieth century America. To the casual observer his reality seemed to be that of eastern seaboard prep school, southern country-club university, medical establishment. Those close to him—and there were not many—knew better. Beneath that veneer of reality spread thinly over the surface lay a bedrock of unreality. He himself could feel it all the time. A sense of never being able to settle once and for all into the proper niche; a feral dog never completely accepted by the wild things, yet never really at home in the ordinary affairs of the kennel; a nomad who chooses to live in a foreign country and then is never quite at home in his own land.

His name alone set him apart. Mercury. Teachers had raised their eyebrows and schoolboys had laughed outright. There just had to be something odd about a boy with that peculiar name. No one guessed just how odd.

But he was proud of it. His mother had chosen it. When he was old enough she told him why. His father was Pan, named by his foster-father (the first Dr. Reynolds) for the god of flocks and herds, the sylvan deity who played the pipes for nymphs and dryads to dance by, the dreamer who could send visions to those he loved. Pan was a beautiful youth, tall, blue-eyed, with reddish-blonde hair and beard, forever fey (in the sense of being doomed from birth), half *Homo sapiens,* half *Pan troglodytes*, half wild, half serene, his two natures warring until he met Phoebe in the mountains of Appalachia. She tamed the wild half and lived with him for a year till Mercury was born and Pan died in a rainstorm high in those haunted mountains of Arcadia and Phoebe left the hills forever.

Pan's father was Hermes, a chimpanzee, his mother Penelope, brought together by the satanic genius of Dr. John Reynolds and his wife Sylvia. A union Devil-inspired and God-damned, but rescued from Hell by a gentle black man by the name of Jed

BRAIN CHILD

Schroeder and a gentle white woman by the name of Phoebe. Phoebe considered naming Pan's son Hermes, but there were too many connotations she couldn't live with. So she settled on Mercury, the Roman name for Hermes.

Both mother and child, Phoebe and Mercury, knew from early childhood that he was different; different in a way which would lead—or push—him to greatness. In addition to superb powers of ratiocination, his ancestry had bequeathed him the ability to read nuances in the actions and words of others. In a word, he was clairaudient. Not at first a "mind-reader"—the magical power to deduce without other clues the exact thoughts of a person—yet often sensing from words, eyes and body movements what wasn't said aloud. But then sometimes—not often at first, but more and more as he grew older—he could anticipate by a fraction of a second what the speaker was going to say. It was not always a pleasant experience.

His mother Phoebe recognized this trait in his early years, was neither awed nor surprised by it. With maternal love she nurtured it, through the grades, into high school, cautioning him not to use a god-given talent for personal gain. With incredible wisdom she coached him in techniques for living in a world hostile to the unusual, in a society suspicious of the nonconformist. As soon as he was old enough to understand, she told him what clairaudience meant. When he was older still, he looked it up in the dictionary: "act or power of hearing something not present to the ear but regarded as having objective reality" Gobble-de-gook, he chuckled. Mom said it better with smaller words.

She herself was no conformist, and had proven it by living with Pan in a tent in the hills of Appalachia. Knowing that Pan was unable to live just then within the strictures of contemporary society, she accepted what he was (and wasn't) and adapted to him and his life. Not many young women could have done what she did.

Throughout Mercury's formative years she showed him how to extract from American life the important things without being assimilated bodily into the mainstream of that life. So inevitably he went to college — at the University of Virginia in Charlottesville — and began to put into practice, on his own, what she had drilled into him for seventeen years.

His roommate throughout the entire four years was Hal Forester, a jock who refused to room with the other jocks because he found their company intellectually stultifying. Six feet one and powerfully built, he was a pleasing mixture of Hercules and Adonis (in a football helmet), but with the haunting eyes, dark and piercing, of a Dostoevski. Below a spacious forehead accentuated by two deep cowlicks, stood a Roman nose which more than offset a somewhat receding chin.

One late afternoon in their senior year, Reynolds was solemnly discoursing on some philosophical conundrum. Forester cut him off, as he sometimes did, with a wave of his big hand.

"Coming to the big game tomorrow, Merc?"

"Probably not."

"Why the hell not?" he barked. "Don't you want to see your roomie make hash of that bunch of hicks they call the Crimson Tide?"

Reynolds laughed. "Not that at all. I figured to spend most of the day studying for my physics exam Monday."

"Time enough for that when you're old and grey. You're only young once, and all that bull."

They were lying on their cots in the dorm, the day darkening outside, the lights not yet on. Shadows were beginning to soften the harshness of their spartan room: two narrow beds, two desks, two chairs, and a scattering of clothes thrown carelessly about. Through the door to the bathroom which they shared with the room next door, they could hear water running as their neighbors washed up for supper.

"I guess I'd subscribe to the latter anyway," Reynolds said. "What I mean is that I *am* only young once and now is the time to get ready for when I'm old and grey. I don't want just any job. I've got a long way to go before I'm ready for what I want. A long, long way."

Forester caught Reynolds' mood, as he often did, and settled back on his bed, fingers laced behind his head. " 'The woods are lovely, dark and deep, and I have promises to keep, and miles to go before I sleep.' " Then he added, with a teasing sidelong glance at Reynolds, "Shakespeare," knowing that Reynolds would recognize Frost. In the first days of their friendship, Reynolds continually fell for the trick until he realized that Forester read as much as he did, maybe more. Forester was always doing that, coming up with a quote from the literature, surprising people who thought of him as all muscles and bone.

"Precisely." Reynolds sat on the edge of his cot, tilted his head back a little, looking through half-closed eyes, and said, "Don't you see, Hal, that I've got to prove myself in ways you'll never have to? You're captain of the football team. Letter sweaters all over the place. You make your way through life on charm and bluff. You don't mind being stereotyped. You think it's great to be a jock, and hide the other side." He smiled. "You might say you've got everyone fooled *but* me."

"I've never tried to fool you."

"I know. That's what I said."

"You know why? Because I never

could've. I knew that the very first day we met. Remember?"

Reynolds remembered. It had been a cold rainy day in mid-September. They had stood together in the registration line, inching along toward the pretty little girl who was explaining in kindergarten terms how to fill out the forms. Both the boys were seventeen. Reynolds was lost in thought, thinking about his father, who when he was seventeen had left home to live alone in the mountains of Appalachia. Pan had never gone to college, had never lived a normal life after leaving home. He'd envy me, Reynolds thought, and be proud, too, that I'm starting a life such as he had never known even existed.

Hal meanwhile was flirting with the registrar. Though several years older than he, she was charmed by this big raw-boned youth with the unsettling eyes. As they walked away from the desk, Reynolds looked at him, saw him flushed with victory, and said, "She's looking for a husband, and thinks you might be him . . ."

"He."

". . . might be he. You're looking for a night in the sack and wonder if she'll give."

Forester turned startled eyes on Reynolds. "You could tell all that from just those few minutes?" he asked.

"I could tell from the way she watched you, measuring you, toting up the bill of sale, you might say. Would you be surprised to know she didn't even see your muscles? She saw only your eyes . . ."

"But," he interrupted, "if she just saw my eyes, why did she decide to go out with me tonight?"

"She hopes she's wrong."

That was three years before. Now as he lay lazily on his bunk, Reynolds asked, "Whatever happened to that little girl?"

"She left her job a few months later and I never saw her again." He grinned. "Way with most of my girls, if you've noticed."

"She really wanted to marry you."

"I wasn't ready. Not ready, even now. Too many things to do, too many other girls in the world. I decided years ago that either I had to stay single a long time or have a series of wives."

He glanced at his watch, swung his legs to the floor and stretched. "Skull practice. Boring damn stuff. I know every defense Alabama can throw at us. And I've known our own plays better than the coach for years."

His cheerful whistle faded down the stairwell, then reappeared outside the window. Reynolds parted the curtains and watched him go. With the long easy strides of a farmer crossing a furrowed field, he passed everyone on the sidewalk without seeming to hurry. Girls stopped in mid-sentence, tossed their hair in animal joy and stared bemused. Boys unconsciously threw their shoulders back, pumped their arms a little harder, caught their weight with knees slightly bent, emulating their Saturday hero. Reynolds tapped a tattoo on the windowsill with his pencil, envying Forester for his perfect body, his ingenuous power, his charisma.

In a way he envied his mind, too. Not for his intelligence—he was aware of his own prowess there—but the ability he had to utilize it in such a vastly different way on the football field. In the library, in their study-room, Forester was able to carve niches for Frost and Shakespeare, then leave them on the shelf when he put on the pads. Reynolds knew few people who could do that—certainly not many football players.

And neither could Reynolds. His brain stuck to its usual channels—Forester called them ruts. He knew he had a physics test Monday. *Ergo,* he must study for it that night, the next day, and perhaps most of Sunday. He knew that some people called this perseverance, or dedication. Others, who knew better, realized that the poor trapped soul couldn't conceive of anything else. His problem was just the opposite of most athletes: they couldn't get themselves to study; he couldn't quit.

But the next day he sacrificed three hours of study time to watch Hal star in the game. Forester went on from there to all-conference and finally all-American honors. The Philadelphia Eagles picked him up, very high in the draft—third round—and he played first-string right up to the time of his accident.

Through the rest of the school year Reynolds went to every game he could, even though he knew very little about the nuances of play. But he recognized a great run when he saw it, and appreciated the magnificence of an over-the-shoulder catch of a ball thrown fifty yards through the air. Forester could "do it all," the coaches exclaimed. "Great hands," they'd say, or "Perfect timing."

So Hal Forester took his superbly conditioned body to the Philadelphia Eagles, where he became famous. Mercury Reynolds took his superbly gifted mind to graduate school where he got his doctorate and became famous, and then to Cook County's Hektoen Institute, where he was to become more famous still.

8

Just a few days after Reynolds arrived, Steinke asked him to speak to the entire Hektoen research staff. "A big boost they will get, Dr. Reynolds, if you give them a little talk on your enlon strand."

Reluctantly he agreed. It was not his favorite pasttime. Two days later he found himself standing in front of hundreds of scientists, technicians, and a handful of medical doctors working in the transplant field. He was embarrassed by the thunderous applause. Several people stood up but Reynolds was relieved to see that the entire audience did not follow suit. That would have been too much.

He leaned nonchalantly against the podium, apparently at ease, churning inside with fear. "As with every major advance," he began, "one scientist builds upon the work of others. Copernicus, Harvey, Lister, Pasteur, Schick, Fleming, Salk, even our own Ludwig Hektoen—and literally thousands more—all made startling discoveries. But they made them by building on knowledge recorded by others. Don't ever forget that. It will keep you humble.

"I mention this because the enlon we use is worthless without the micro-silicon chip, the depolarizer, the CT scanner, the sensor apparatus. I myself did not invent any of those. I merely saw a way to use them to stimulate nerve growth.

"Enough philosophy." He smiled now, and could feel the entire audience relax and literally sit back waiting for him to continue. "The enlon strand. What is it? How does it work? Here is a diagram of a cross section. In the center is one wire, one-tenth of a millimeter in diameter, which is used to carry the transmission signal. This is surrounded by plastic insulation two-tenths of a millimeter thick. On the outer surface of the insulation is a non-conducting sheath one-tenth of a millimeter thick. The inner surface is coated electrolytically with shielding material that also acts as a ground wire. On the outer surface are etched eight conducting strands. One supplies the power source. Five provide addressing information so the transmission of any one of up to thirty-one depolarizers can be controlled by the computer or someone at the computer console. You will recognize that all leads are zero if none are accessed.

"The remaining two etched leads will determine the function of the depolarization node by a pulsed encodement: 00, do nothing; 01, increase transmission; 11, on/off pulse; 10, decrease transmission.

"The depolarization force is a micromagnetic wave one-point-one millimeter in length, that is 2.7×10^{11} Hertz.

"Now, how do we know what's going on and how do we react?

"We have constructed a soft, floppy skull cap which has an imbedded sensor for each square centimeter of the skull—about six hundred of them. We have developed a vest-like garment with sensors covering every two square centimeters of the back to pick up the entire spinal cord—about 1,000. Some of you will have a chance to work with these. They're ridiculously simple. Now." He smiled broadly and the audience laughed. "Oh, and along the sides of the vest are two calibration enlon lines which we will use at least once a day to check on things. On the way from surgery, the patient will have a total head and body CT scan to accurately pinpoint every depolarizer. This is extremely important since this will allow the computer to superimpose the results of the sensors onto the computer image from the CT scan. This will give us a visual picture of everything that is taking place.

"The sensors will pick up the continuous transmission from the depolarizers, one by one, as they are activated by the computer, which is programmed to handle most adjustments in voltage. We'll activate the sensors once every twenty minutes for the first month, for one minute. Since we expect approximately 200 bytes of information from each sensor during that minute, simple arithmetic—I see some of you doing it in your heads already—gives us 14,400 bytes per sensor per day, or 432,000,000 bytes for the spinal cord and 259,200,000 for the skull, per month.

"All this information will be stored permanently on a billion-byte laser diskpack. I think all of you are familiar with that technology. The rack will be kept in my office.

"Questions?"

A hand shot up in the second row, a junior neurosurgery resident from Ward 30. "How do you know how fast the nerves are growing?"

"Good question. Because of absorption peaks in the sensors, the computer will be able to detect exactly where growth is taking place—almost to the micron, though we don't need that much definition."

"That assumes," the resident said, "that the greatest absorption of the micromagnetic waves takes place at the point of growth."

"Correct. In any one cube, the amount of the absorption peak will identify the number of cells actively growing."

He answered questions for almost an hour and then said, "I think that's about enough for today. I'll be available to talk to any of you who have other questions as our work progresses."

He waved a hand in farewell and started down the aisle toward the door. Now everyone was standing, turning toward him, clapping furiously. He waved again, his face flushed. He hoped they would still be clapping in six months.

Sensing the impatience of the neurosurgeons to get moving, yet determined to be fully prepared for every emergency, Reynolds drove himself and his co-workers to the limit of their endurance. He had planned to spend a week just wandering around the labs, taking inventory of the physical and mental capacities of his assistants. Within two days he came to the obvious and very pleasant conclusion that (1) the material was incredibly complete, and (2) the laboratory personnel were incredibly well trained.

So starting on the third day he held a

five o'clock meeting every day except Sunday. He did not need to make attendance mandatory. Everyone in the whole building would have been there if he had allowed it, but he restricted it to a dozen members of the staff who would be involved in the actual experimental brain transplants. Steinke and Gonzaga were included even though they already knew their roles. They had done neural anastamoses and enlon implants in other circumstances, and did not need to practice that aspect of the surgery, but neither had ever done implants of enlon strands in the cranial nerves or the brain stem.

Reynolds himself opened the ninth floor lab each morning about seven. He sat in his office, feet up on the desk, coffee cup in hand, eyes half-closed, reviewing the past day and anticipating the present day. Like every good researcher, he was methodical to a fault. He divided up the day into neat sections, and unless something happened to disrupt his plans he knew where he would be and what he would be doing every moment. Sometimes he made notes to himself, but usually his internal clock kept him on schedule.

At eight o'clock the other members of the team arrived. Each would pop his head in the door to say good morning and ask if there was any change in plans for the day. Sometimes they would sit for a moment to discuss some aspect of the day's work which they were unsure of. Reynolds cherished that hour from eight to nine, because it was then that he got to know his people, learned what their strengths and weaknesses were. They in turn began to comprehend the genius of this young researcher who had already put his name in history books as the discoverer of the "magic thread of life." They began to see their various roles in the coming drama of a brain transplant in a human being.

Reynolds himself sometimes shuddered at the awesomeness of the undertaking. He recognized an ambivalence in his feelings: he knew he must remain didactically neutral, must ritualize his work in steady progression from dogs to primates and then finally to humans. But someday, in a future that was creeping closer and closer upon him, he would go to Ward 30, or to some other ward in the giant hospital, and witness the selection of two people who would be the first humans in the world to have a brain transplanted. He would have to talk to a person whose body was being destroyed by some fatal disease, and who would be willing to give up that body in order to continue to live. And then he would go into the room of someone who was dying, probably in coma, and watch Steinke make the final decision as to the "suitability" of that body to accept another person's brain.

He wondered, if at that time, he could

maintain the necessary researcher's cool detachment. Then he knew he could, because he knew he must.

9

He visited his mother in Charlottesville in early July, two months after he had moved to Chicago. He almost never went back to Standing Oaks, the country home where Pan had been conceived and born. The associations, the vibrations he received, the total ambience of the place haunted him and made him very uncomfortable. Phoebe had been able to move back there when the Reynoldses both died because she had wiped the slate clean with her indomitable will and powers of reason.

So he stayed in a hotel in town and she moved into a room in the same hotel for a few days. He found, partly to his dismay and partly to his amusement, that the press had not forgotten him. His move to Cook County Hospital had been well publicized only a few months before and they still ran an occasional feature story in the local papers about Charlottesville's most illustrious citizen since Thomas Jefferson.

A few hours after he arrived he took her to dinner in one of Charlottesville's nicest restaurants. Even when he lived there, he had rarely eaten there, but to his surprise the maitre d' recognized him immediately. Not so subtly he led them through the crush at the door to one of the best tables. A few heads turned in their direction, for it was a smallish town, and Reynolds could hear whisperings around them as they sat down. Curved leather seats protected them from curious eyes and he was grateful to the maitre d' for his sensitivity.

"Everyone's looking at you," Reynolds said to Phoebe.

"Nonsense," she countered. "They're talking about you."

They giggled conspiratorily. It was the first brush of notoriety for them both. As they unfolded napkins in their laps, he said, "Well, they *could* be talking about you."

Phoebe was forty-eight, and as beautiful in a more mature way as she had been when she and Pan lived together in the mountains of Appalachia. Tall and svelte, she still moved with the fluid movements of a young woman. Her ebony hair, streaked now with scattered strands of white, no longer fell in schoolgirl waves about her face and neck, but it was thick and as glossy as a curried racehorse. She emanated an aura of freshness and youth that belied the little lines beneath her eyes and at the corners of her mouth.

She had never remarried. Reynolds never thought it odd when he was growing up; little children don't think much about their parents' love life even when they see signs of it. And when there is no obvious evidence, they consider it even less. But as he grew older, he did wonder why there was no man in her life. With the ingenuousness of a child he had asked her about it one day. She had stroked his head as he stood beside her at the kitchen stove, and said, "Mercury, you've got to grow a bit to understand it all, and then you may not have to wonder. Just for now, let's leave it that once you've had a god for a husband, it's not possible to take a mere man into your heart."

That was good enough for him then, and adequate even now if he expanded it to mean that it was impossible for her to take another man into her life—and into her bed—once she'd had the great god Pan there.

"You're making quite a mark for yourself, Dr. Reynolds," she said now as she gently waved the cocktail waitress away.

"I've been lucky."

Her smile was tender, loving, with a hint of motherly pride. Highlights glinted in her hair and in her eyes.

"The right person in the right place at the right time?"

"Exactly."

"Modesty will get you nowhere in this world."

"But in the next?"

"We'll know when we find out, won't we?"

Neither of them had ever been very religious, at least not with the devout Christian's belief in a "next world," but he had often heard her speak of Pan as someone she expected to see again. He had always thought that she meant she expected to see Pan in him some day.

"Perhaps," he answered.

They ordered and as the waiter left he cocked his head slightly as he took the menu from Phoebe, as close to a bow as he could manage without becoming too obsequious in this hurly-burly society. Phoebe giggled and Reynolds said to her, "He recognizes royalty when he sees it." To Reynolds she did seem elegant, sitting there with the red velour of the cushions accenting her dark loveliness. He felt that he should be wearing a tux rather than a conservatively cut blue suit and plain tie.

She leaned across the table, fingers laced under her chin, eyes luminous, full lips quivering sensuously.

"What *is* it you've discovered, Mercury?"

"Ah, sweet mystery of life, at last I've found you," he teased.

"You're in a strange mood," she said, and sat back.

"Happy."

"I wish I had your father's insight," she said, a faint smile tugging at the corners of her mouth.

"You used to. Spanked me many a time when for the life of me I couldn't tell how you knew what I'd done."

"That's a mother's prerogative."

"When a kid's pejorative, his mother has prerogative?"

"Something like that. Now be serious. I know in general what you've been doing. You went up to Chicago to work with Victor Steinke on experimental brain transplants. Now the papers say you're going to do them in humans."

He sobered immediately. She really wanted to know. And he really wanted to tell her.

"Yes, we are."

"Science fiction."

"No longer."

"Are you serious?"

"Deadly serious."

"The implications of that are as great as genetic manipulations."

"I know."

Her staring eyes unfocused and she

looked through him into another world. He tried to read her thoughts and found that somehow she was shielding them from him. She knew him, and his powers, and could override them. The moment passed, and she returned to the present. But she had left the tag end of her thoughts in full view and he knew she was thinking of Pan, and how he had been created by a scientist who was the world's foremost authority on genetic manipulations until he lost control of himself.

"God," she said. "I wish your father could hear this. He loved life, and was so in tune with it that he never held a grudge against old Dr. Reynolds even after he found out what he'd done. He would have loved to know that you're working *with* people, not against them."

The waiter poured a bit of wine and stepped back a pace expectantly. Reynolds tasted it and nodded acceptance. When the waiter had poured the wine and left, Reynolds whispered to Phoebe, "Someday I'm going to shake my head and say that's not what I had in mind at all."

"A noble objective." Her eyes glinted with silent laughter.

"He'd need a brain transplant to recover," he said, and her laughter bubbled out and reminded him of his childhood when they laughed about everything.

The dinner was served and they talked about less significant things, knowing how hard it is to really enjoy a good meal and discuss the deeper things of life.

"Some B & B, mother?"

"Love it."

As she sipped the golden liqueur from the tiny glass he could hear a question forming in her mind. He slumped in the seat, lay his head on the back of it, and regarded her through half-closed lids.

"What happens," she asked, "when you take a brain from one man and put it into another man's body? Who is he?"

"Who is he? I don't know."

"Hadn't you better find out?"

"Yes."

"It's not exactly like transplanting a kidney or an artery."

"I know."

Her eyes widened in awe as she contemplated the magnitude of his project. "One man, we'll call him Joe, has an incurable disease, but his brain is very much normal. Another man, Frank, has his brain blown away by a hermorrhage or a bullet, but his body is as strong as ever. So you cut out Joe's brain and put it into Frank's body."

"That's the essence of it."

"Who is the man, Joe or Frank?"

"The ethics committee is working on that."

"You'd better start thinking about it yourself."

"I have."

"And what did you decide?"

"Either one would have an awful time getting a passport."

"Oh, you're impossible." But there was understanding in her eyes, for she knew him too well to think he'd joke callously about such a thing unless he had it pretty well worked out in his own mind.

A strobe light went off a few feet away, and the photographer said, "Thanks, doc, I'll see you get a copy of this to give your girl. Or she can cut it out of the morning newspaper."

"She's not . . ."

But he was gone, and Phoebe was laughing, her face flushed and tears coming to her eyes. "It was worth the price of admission just to hear that."

People were watching them, a few wondering who they were and what they had done to deserve such notoriety. Reynolds felt acutely uncomfortable. This wasn't the first time this had happened. Was this to be the story of his life from now on?

The next day he called Steinke and told him he was going to stay in Charlottesville for several more days. They walked in the hot summer sun through the old city. The population of Charlottesville was under 75,000 people but still growing rapidly because it was centrally located and only seventy miles from Richmond. They strolled through the campus where he had done his undergraduate work in the classrooms and his graduate work in the labs.

"Thomas Jefferson founded this school, way back in 1819," he reminded her. "For men only."

She smiled. "Hasn't kept the fellows too restricted, has it?"

"Mary Washington is only twenty-five miles away."

"You haven't found the right one yet?"

"There's a cute little girl does my EEGs." But the tone of his voice belied any real interest and she let it go.

They climbed the hills overlooking the town and sat on a bench in front of Monticello, admiring again the clean lines of red brick, white porticoes, and imposing dome.

"The inside is filled with Jefferson's inventions," he said.

"Nothing compared to what you've done."

He grinned. "My son, the inventor."

But she was serious. "Do other people know what you know about enlon and its potential?"

"It's written up pretty thoroughly."

"Could others duplicate your work?"

"Yes, certainly. It would be scientifically worthless if they couldn't."

Her brows knitted and her mouth worked a little. "What precautions have you taken to guard it?"

"Guard it?"

"Guard it. It's the responsibility of the inventor to shield his inventions from immoral and unethical uses. If the inventor..."

"Like John Reynolds..." he interjected, knowing what she was driving at.

She winced, continued, "If the inventor himself can't see all the implications, perhaps someone else will." She stood up, turned toward the monument. "Don't you see, Mercury, that you of all people should weigh the possibilities for good and evil in your discovery? Nothing is in itself good or evil."

"Nothing?" he asked.

"Nothing. 'For there is nothing either good or bad, but thinking makes it so.'"

He laughed. "One Hal Forester in this world is enough."

"But it's true."

He sobered. "Nothing?" he asked again.

"Nothing."

"Rape?"

"Sex, which is in itself good, perverted."

"Murder?"

"The misuse of basically amoral things: a gun which in itself is not evil, a knife which can save a life if you call it a scalpel, poison which is merely an overdose of an otherwise useful drug."

"Invasion of another country?"

She had to think about that one. "The misuse of the territorial imperative. Each person, each country, has his own place in this world, and tries to expand it. This becomes wrong only if that expansion abridges the rights of another person or country. My rights end where yours begin. If I come up to a redlight, and feel that I'm so important that I don't need to stop, then I'm infringing on your rights if you're trying to cross on the green."

"I'm convinced."

"It wasn't hard, you know. You're basically a moral person."

"Despite my heritage?"

She hesitated. They didn't talk about that much. "*Because* of it. You've inherited from Hermes and Penelope—through Pan, your father—the best of two worlds, not the worst. Oh, the possibility for evil exists, as it does in every man. But you have no more potential for evil than any man. Maybe less."

"Besides, I have half your gentle genes."

She bowed her head. "You know, Mercury, there were times when you were a baby that I could have wished you'd never been born. But I never did. Never, during the two years I lived in that shack of Jed Schroeder's before my mother found me. And never later, when John and Sylvia Reynolds died and left Standing Oaks to you. And certainly not now—decidedly not now—when you've proved to the world that your brain is as normal as anyone's."

"I never felt I was trying to prove anything."

"I know you didn't. Neither did your father. But nevertheless it was implicit in everything he did and you do. John Reynolds kept watching Pan to see if there were signs of reduced intelligence. He never found any. When I first met Pan I didn't know anything about his interspecific heritage, so naturally I didn't look for anything. I just knew I loved him. From the very first. Oh, I've told you all this."

He touched the back of her hand with his fingertips and then said, "Yes, you've told me. And always with at least a hint of apology for what my father was. But you don't have to explain anything away. My father was a real man. *Homo sapiens*. The fact that half of his chromosomes came from *Pan troglodytes* means nothing. John Reynolds saw to that when he did the micro-surgery and corrected the translocations and inversions. The fact that a fourth of *my* chromosomes come from a chimp doesn't mean I'm one-fourth chimpanzee! The chromosomal differences were corrected. I give John Reynolds credit for his genius there. The *genes* that those chromosomes carried did affect my father and they affect me. We *are* different. But we're not bestial."

"Now look who's protesting too much."

He grinned. "Shakespeare again. Hamlet's mother, and she was right. And I guess you're right. I was just trying to convince you that I don't ever think about it."

"You'd have to be an idiot to never think about it."

"Agreed."

"Do you wish I'd never told you?"

"There were times when I wished exactly that. Usually when things weren't going right, and I wanted to blame my shortcomings on someone or something else. Slowly I began to realize that sometimes I myself was the culprit when things went wrong."

"Adults call that maturing, or growing up."

"And children hate them for it."

She smiled, then grinned. "Let's go eat at that nice place where the photographer thought I was your girl."

"Done."

Two hours later, just as they were finishing dinner, an explosion of greeting came to them from across the room. He looked up and even in the dim light could easily make out the origin of that preemptive, "Yes, it is! Hey, Merc!"

There, with his arms draped languidly over the shoulders of two pretty young women, was Hal Forester.

10

Hal Forester hadn't changed much. He still combed his long reddish-brown hair back along the sides of his head, and the proud Roman nose still ruled his face. His eyes looked black in the dim light, but they caught glints from the candle on the table and flickered like will-o'-the-wisps in a Florida swamp.

Reynolds smiled benignly, knowing that he himself would have looked outlandish in Forester's clothes; on Hal, they merely emphasized his uniqueness: faded blue denim pants with a large silver-eagle buckle, open-necked yellow shirt, light brown gabardine jacket. In button-down

Charlottesville, he was as refreshing as a cool shower after a day in the saddle. In fact, he looked like a working cowboy on a Saturday night date.

The obvious pleasure he took from their friendship always amazed Reynolds. Superficially their lives were disparate in so many ways: Forester the heavy-handed jock, Reynolds the retiring lab recluse. But Reynolds knew that these differences *were* only superficial. On deeper levels they were much alike. Forester was not all meat and bones and Reynolds was not all brains and guts. They both loved classical literature, and both were athletically inclined.

Reynolds thought of this as Forester surged across the room, hands outstretched, fingers splayed as if he were rushing an oncoming halfback. The two girls trailed in his wake like canoes towed by a speedboat.

"By the sacred caduceus of Hermes," he said, "if it isn't the precocious Greek god of trickery and cunning. Stolen any of Apollo's cows lately, Mercury?"

"Put them in the Augean stables for you, Hercules."

Forester roared with laughter as he reached across the table and almost broke Reynolds' hand with his grip. "Never could catch this guy." He turned to Phoebe and gently took her hand. "And Mrs. Reynolds, how do?" She beamed with animal pleasure as he bowed low to peer into her eyes. For a moment it looked as if he were going to kiss her hand. It would have seemed perfectly natural.

"I do fine, Hal. Good to see you in the flesh."

"You see me on TV?"

"I'm almost as avid as your old roomie. Never miss a game you're in."

He backed a step and threw his arms over the shoulders of the two girls. "Want you to meet the two prettiest girls in Charlottesville. Maia and Britt Reardon. Phoebe Reynolds and her illustrious son, Dr. Mercury Reynolds."

Like a mother coaxing her daughters to do a dance number, he pushed the girls forward so they stood above Reynolds and Phoebe. Britt shrugged off Forester's hand and slid into the curved seat beside Phoebe. There were glaciers in her blue eyes, *haute couture* in the lissome grace of her body, sullenness mixed with vulnerability in the tilt of her head. She was not under Hal Forester's spell. If anything, was cold to him. Reynolds wondered why. Years later, when it hardly mattered, he found out. If he had known in that restaurant that day the reason for Britt's surliness to Hal, huge chunks of his life would have gone differently.

Maia Reardon was perfect counterpoint to Hal's bounce and Britt's icy contempt. She laughed quietly in response to his introduction, eyed Reynolds candidly, and slid into the seat beside him. Her hair was as blonde as Britt's, but much shorter, and her eyes as blue. There were obvious signs of sisterhood in the bones of their faces and the slimness of their figures. But there the resemblance ceased. Maia was relaxed, casual, and had that certain air one sees in modern young nuns who have completely adjusted to their vocation: an honest, open face, enthusiasm for life, a lack of guile. Odd, Reynolds thought, it's she, not the proud Britt, who is Hal's companion. Perhaps—a stab of envy pierced him—his love-of-the-month.

Forester pulled up a chair from a nearby table, turned it around so that he could rest his arms on the back. He took Maia's hand casually and the ice in Britt's eyes turned to white fire.

One of Britt's perfectly arched eyebrows rose almost imperceptibly when Hal leaned forward against the seatback and said, "Now before anything else, tell us what the hell gets you so famous all of a sudden."

His black eyes softened as they gazed directly into Reynolds'. For all his bluff and bravado, he was very proud of his old roommate. Reynolds sensed that it was neither the time nor the place to give Forester and the Reardon sisters a curriculum vitae, so he tried to dodge the question. "Just some research I've been doing."

Britt, too, leaned forward across the

table, blue eyes now wide, ingenuous, lavender-colored in the darkness. Her long blonde hair framed her face. Phoebe, watching her son's expression and recognizing it, felt a stab of maternal pain for she was sure that he had fallen in love at that very instant.

"I've made the connection now," Britt said. "The papers said you'd found a cure for paraplegia and now you're working on brain transplants . . ."

For the next half hour Reynolds was the focus of their attention. Britt plied him with question after question. Forester, in his unaccustomed role of bystander, glowed with pride and grinned maliciously as he saw what was happening. Reynolds, still blissfully unaware, unconsciously blocked out everyone but Britt. Later, alone with Phoebe, he listened in awe as she gently chided him for being so rude to Hal and Maia. Then he laughed and said, "I can't think of anyone who'd understand better than Hal Forester."

When Phoebe left for Standing Oaks later that afternoon, Reynolds called Britt, wondering what kind of reaction he'd get. The slight intake of her breath told him. They met for dinner that night in an old-fashioned nightclub and danced till the orchestra packed its strings and horns. If she carried a torch for Hal Forester, as Reynolds had at first assumed, she hid it well. She never talked about him, odd in itself, but Reynolds didn't notice then. He was too much in love.

He returned to Chicago the next morning, dazed with the realization that he could not forget her. Did not want to forget her. He called her every night from his monk's cell in Karl Meyer Hall and each time when he hung up he gazed around him in disgust. This was no way to live.

She came up to Chicago for a long weekend and he flew down a month later to be with her. He spent an afternoon with Phoebe and for the first time begrudged every hour. Phoebe understood all too well and smilingly told him not to worry about it.

Then Britt got a part-time modelling job in Oak Park and moved into a small apartment on Euclid Avenue. Now he could see her whenever he could break away from the lab with a clear conscience. He had already concluded that he had completely misjudged her on their first meeting. Vivacious, outgoing, she thrived on action. Tall, slim—almost skinny—she moved with the langorous vigor of youth through the crowds, long blonde hair swinging free, talking gaily with the enthusiasm and zest of a ten-year-old. She dressed beautifully, although her family was not rich and her modelling jobs sporadic. She knew how to stretch her dollars, buying clothes and accessories which could be worn in seemingly endless combinations.

Not so subtly, she began to draw him out of his hermit's cave. He came willingly, not knowing yet whether he liked it but wanting to be with her. Before meeting her, he preferred to share a bottle of wine with a girl in a quiet supper club. With Britt he found himself in all kinds of new arenas: cocktail parties, picnics, every kind of group where people gather to drink, gossip, and chatter.

He still had most evenings free to read and work on his research, and did not change his daily routine at all. The laboratory was still his master. It had to be. In three short months they had learned all they could from their dog work. Gratefully, with trembling spirits, they turned to primates, Rhesus monkeys at first, later to chimpanzees. At first all the animals died, or the arterial anastamoses failed, or the enlon implants pulled loose, or some other disaster drove the researchers nearly frantic with frustration. But gradually success became more common and then routine. Reynolds was able to say to Steinke one day, "We'll be ready after three more chimps."

Steinke sat stiffly in his revolving chair and thoughtfully scratched his tattoo. Reynolds was standing over him and for the first time made note of the number itself on Steinke's arm—37101. He shivered. Steinke said, "Three weeks, then, you will be ready?"

Reynolds nodded.

"I come see you in two weeks."

Reynolds smiled inwardly as he turned and left the room. Except for the daily five o'clock meetings, Steinke stayed out of Reynolds' end of the lab. A far cry from his threat to supervise every facet of Reynolds' work. Not that he had lost contact. Far from it. He pored over the data emerging from the work, made furious notes in the margins, probed each failure deeply for its error, searched each success for its causes.

Hal Forester began to pop up from time to time, usually for just a day or two. He seemed to enjoy getting a firsthand report from Reynolds about the conduct of the experiments. And he was in great demand on talk shows and at high-school and college letter-award banquets. Reynolds could see why. He was tall, handsome, a successful professional ballplayer, and at ease in front of the zoom lens and with boys and coaches and fathers. Later in the fall he stopped en route from one game to another. How he avoided the charter flights with the other players, Reynolds never knew, but supposed that superstars didn't have to be shepherded around, or didn't allow themselves to be. Maia was always with him.

He usually stayed in a hotel although he knew Reynolds' room was open to him. Reynolds didn't push him to stay with him because he supposed Forester wanted to have some time alone with Maia. Forester liked to go out to Britt's apartment when Reynolds was there, for a drink and whatever food Britt could put together. Sometimes he brought a bucket of chicken or a package of steaks. Always he brought Maia.

Britt was always more subdued when he was there. Reynolds had the feeling that someone should tell him why. Maia, perhaps. Much later he was sure of it, but she didn't, and he could only wonder if perhaps Britt and Hal had been closer than she let on. She did drop a hint once to that effect, but didn't elaborate and Reynolds didn't crowd her.

One thing he did notice were the sharp differences between the two sisters. Britt was so different from Maia that he suggested once that one of them was a changeling.

"A changeling?" Britt asked.

"You know, left on the doorstep or switched in the crib or something."

Her laugh was short, bitter, her eyes smoldering with some deep emotion. "Are we that different?"

"You know you are. There's something in Maia that runs deep . . ."

"And I'm superficial?" Her reaction to his casual comment seemed inappropriate. He backed off.

"No, I didn't mean that at all. But

you're more outgoing. You like crowds of people around you. She'd rather spend a quiet evening curled up in front of the fire with a book."

"And how do you know all this?"

"From Hal."

She shot him a startled look. "Does he talk to you about us?"

"Not much. Mostly about Maia."

She relaxed. "But she's no shrinking violet, you know, even if she *is* a librarian."

"Oh, I know. She wouldn't be going out with Hal Forester if she were."

"Sometimes I think you'd rather curl up with a book than go to all these parties I drag you to."

"I want to do what you want to do."

"You're sweet."

She was like that. Volatile. Emotions changing in moments. From sadness to gaiety. Concern to disinterest. Like to dislike and back again. He could hardly keep up with her pendulum swings.

He leaned forward and said, "Say that again." As her lips puckered to say "sweet" he kissed her, felt her whole body soften, and wished they were going to be alone that evening. But then she broke away, saying, "Hey, there, I spent an hour at the beauty shop today just for this party, and you're not going to mess up my twenty dollars in two minutes." She was laughing, but she meant it.

They were waiting in her apartment for

guests to arrive for one of the big dinner parties she loved to give. He didn't feel at home there. It was too modern, glass and wrought-iron chairs and tables, lighting fixtures right out of Star Wars, artificial flowers, twisted glass and aluminum figurines.

As she moved swiftly away to fiddle with the table settings, he watched her longingly. She was particularly beautiful that night, although as usual, slightly too made up. She could handle that, however, he mused, with her angular face, high cheek bones, wide mouth, and wideset blue eyes. She looked every bit the high-fashion model and he felt she could easily have moved on from two-bit posing in Chicago to a top agency in New York. Or at least so he thought then.

He slumped back in the sofa, wondering what this alluring woman could see in him. Physically, she was so perfect, while he had a curvature to his spine and a drag to his left leg. She had once asked about the leg, but when he said it was congenital, she just said, "Oh," and never mentioned it again. He wondered now if she might be attracted to him more as a personage than as a person. His fame was certainly spreading. The discoverer of the "magic thread of life" was redhot. Science magazines, Sunday supplements, women's magazines, talk shows, all were after him for interviews. He gave all of them short shrift except the real science sheets, but somehow they were able to come up with pictures and enough material to do stories without his help. He was not playing hard to get. He *was* hard to get. He hated the thought of cheap sensationalism. Unfortunately, his reclusiveness only served to fan the flames higher.

Britt came over and stood in front of him, hands on hips, a DI reviewing a band of ragged recruits. "Tonight," she said, "I don't want you hiding your light under a bushel. When people compliment you on your work, and ask you about it, tell them." It was an order.

He smiled. "You don't know how tough that is. I don't like to talk shop all the time."

"I know that. And you don't have to, all the time. That would be boring. But you don't talk enough about your work. People are really interested."

She knelt in front of him, the long skirt swirling around classically beautiful legs, hands on his knees, low-cut blouse falling away from her shoulders and exposing the upper half of her breasts. He leaned forward and kissed her on the side of her neck. She shivered and got up, throwing a glance over her shoulder which he interpreted as a promise.

After the guests had come and gone, she delivered on that promise.

They were married in November, in her parents' home in Charlottesville. Maia was her maid of honor and Hal his best man. Phoebe came up from Standing Oaks, radiant and beautiful, happy for him. She didn't know Britt at all well so her heart held some misgivings about her only son reaching this milestone in his life. But she hid it well and showed only the customary tear as they came down the aisle. She didn't have much chance to talk with her illustrious son, but she knew one never does at a wedding, which she thought a shame, for it is then that deep thoughts come and should be expressed.

Stunning was the word for Britt as she moved with beguiling grace through the ceremony and the reception afterwards. Reynolds' pride was limitless as he saw their lives interweaving far into the future: ten, twenty, thirty years and more, each of them bringing to their marriage distinctive qualities which would merge into one perfect whole as they grew in each other's love.

Only one incident marred the otherwise flawless day. It happened so quickly that later Reynolds wasn't even sure it had really occurred. He was talking to Britt's mother and saw Hal approach Britt across the dance floor. She stood stiffly, expectantly, and although Reynolds couldn't hear what she said, he could feel the hatred and knew she was refusing to dance with Hal. Hal stood immobile for a moment, smiled in resignation, and turned away.

BRAIN CHILD

They spent their honeymoon on the white sand beach of Grand Cayman. Hal Forester's wedding present to them was a week in his condominium just outside of Georgetown. Britt's obvious contempt for Hal didn't prevent her from accepting it. It was perfect for Reynolds but Britt fretted at the lack of social contacts. So began a series of adjustments which would plague their marriage for years.

During the day they slept and read and made love. In the evenings they rented a mini-moke and drove to one of the resort hotels which dotted the southeastern end of the twenty-two-mile-long island. With her deepening tan and swinging blonde hair, she was captivating in a white dress and navy and white polka-dot scarf knotted loosely around her neck.

He made her promise not to tell anyone who he was. She laughed and said, "Why, Merc, my love, you could be the most exciting visitor these islands have had since Columbus landed here four hundred years ago."

He grinned. "I prefer to remain anonymous. Let's go look at the turtles."

"I hate turtles."

So they made love instead and later sat on the little lanai outside their room and watched the sunbathers on the beach until the sun went down. He wondered again if he should have told her about his mixed-up chromosomes before they were married.

Wondered, too, if this was the time. And decided against it. She didn't want children now. He could read that in the way she talked about other people's children, and from the dreams she told him about.

He had always been able to interpret dreams, a legacy of the god Hermes, bequeathed him through his father Pan. His mother had told him about the god for whom he was named. Hermes—or Mercury—functioned in many ways, but never as strongly as when he was a conductor of dreams for earthbound mortals. Even Aeschylus invoked Hermes, along with Earth and Hades, in summoning a shade from the underworld. Hermes was Jupiter's messenger, then, of gentle mien, often portrayed with winged cap and shoes, bearing a rod entwined with two serpents—the caduceus. The young messenger had invented the lyre, fashioning it from a tortoise shell and linen cords, nine strings in honor of the nine Muses. But he gave up the lyre to his brother Apollo in exchange for the caduceus.

Now Reynolds had also given up the lyre, symbol of gentle music and gracious living, and had accepted the caduceus as his token. He carried it proudly in his heart, the symbol of healing for three thousand years. Though not a medical doctor, he was in that milieu for good. This he knew as surely as he knew that his heart would beat once every second for the rest of his life. He could not foresee what that life would hold, but whatever it was, it was going to be dedicated to the preservation or restoration of useful life in diseased bodies.

And Britt was going to be there to help him. Forever.

11

Long before their honeymoon was over, Reynolds began to fret over his protracted absence from Hektoen. He almost cancelled their planned stop-over in Charlottesville to see his mother, then decided she would be too disappointed and one more day would not change anything.

The immense green bowl surrounding Charlottesville looked almost flat from 10,000 feet, but as they settled down for the landing, they could see the foothills beginning to take shape. Off to the west, dark and forbidding, were the Blue Ridge Mountains themselves, merging north and south with the rest of the Appalachians.

It was there in those mountains that his father had lived for five years before he met Phoebe, then with her for another year before he, Mercury, was born. He had lived there, too, with his mother, in old Jed Schroeder's shack for the first two years of his life. When Phoebe talked about it, which was seldom, she used Arcadia and Appalachia interchangeably. He wondered about that until he was in high school, when he read that the god Mercury had been born on Mt. Cyllene in Aracdia on the fourth of the month. Mercury Reynolds was born on April 4th, high on a mountain top in Appalachia.

As he grew older, he often pestered his mother to take him into those mountains to show him where she had lived, and where he had been born. The answer was always, "Someday . . ." Her memories were too poignant, too interwoven with heartache and despair, too tightly locked into a part of her mind that she didn't want to reopen.

Old Jed Schroeder was dead. She had heard that from Jennifer, her camping companion when she met Pan, and whose mother still lived in the village a two-hour walk from Jed's cabin. Perhaps if the old black man had still been alive, Phoebe might have at least taken Reynolds that far, if not up onto the mountain-top where everything had happened. Some day he would go and she would go with him, he was sure of that. But what he couldn't know were the horrible circumstances that would force that trip.

The 757 swooped in with the grace of a Canada goose, jet engines almost inaudible until they reversed to slow it down on the runway. Reynolds reached for Britt's hand and together they peered out the little window at the mountains behind the terminal. Someday, he thought, he must tell her what those mountains meant to him.

There was so much about him she didn't know. But, he mused, that was always true with married couples, especially at first. They selected out what they thought the other should know: the honors, the triumphs, the positive aspects of their lives. They didn't necessarily try to hide the skeletons in the closet, but they just didn't talk about them and the bones remained unfleshed. In general, there was nothing wrong about that. He didn't really want to know all about her previous boyfriends, about the years she wore braces on her teeth, about the stupid things she did while she was living her life without him. Let her childhood remain in her memory; let her tell him slowly, over the years, just what she wanted him to know.

Phoebe met them at the terminal and whisked them through the late evening traffic to their hotel.

"We're leaving again early in the morning, Mother," Reynolds said when they met later for dinner.

Phoebe sighed and smiled, "I thought you probably would. I'd hoped to see more of you than that. But I understand."

Britt laughed and said merrily, "He can hardly wait to get back to his chimps. This past week he talked more about them than he did about me. Just so he doesn't decide to marry one of the pretty ones!"

Reynolds chuckled and almost said, "One in the family's enough," but caught himself in time. Phoebe flushed and changed the subject. "Maia tells me the Eagles won their division and start in the play-offs next week. So Hal may be in the Super Bowl yet."

"Great!" Reynolds said. "I didn't even know they were contenders this year."

"You really are the absent-minded professor, aren't you?" Phoebe said. "But then you've had a few other things on your mind."

"You know," he said, "She really ought to marry that guy."

Britt stared straight ahead. "He's not ready yet."

Phoebe said, "Will he ever be? A guy like Hal?"

"I doubt it," Britt said. "Guys like Hal Forester never are. They're just looking for . . ."

Later in their room, he continued the conversation, anxious to penetrate a little into the mystery of Britt's obvious dislike of Hal Forester. "What does Maia see in Hal?" he asked as he flopped down on their bed and pulled both pillows under his head.

She sat on the bed and looked at him askance. "My God, you should be able to answer that. What do you think she sees?"

"Well, he's big and handsome and a pro football star. Maybe that's what she sees. What she needs."

"She needs a guy with depth, and Hal Forester is shallow."

"Oh, but he isn't. You don't know him well or you wouldn't say that."

"I know him well enough."

He waited for her to go on but she didn't and he was afraid to pursue it. "He's more than just another jock," he said finally. "Haven't you heard him quoting Shakespeare and Locke and all those others I've never even read? Where do you think he gets all those quotes? From the comics?"

"I know he reads," she said emphatically.

"All the time," he said, "when he's not studying plays or actually at practice. He soaks up literature like a sponge. And never forgets a line once he's memorized it."

"That doesn't prove a damn thing," she said, eyes blazing. She tossed her hair impatiently, then said, "But maybe that's what Maia sees in him. She is a librarian, you know."

"OK, smartypants, what does *he* see in *her* then?"

"Peace and quiet."

He peered at her through half-closed eyes. "Why would a guy like that want peace and quiet?"

"It's the contrast between his life on the road and what he finds here in C'ville. She's a leavening influence, and he recognizes it."

"Enough to marry her?"

"Hell, no!" Her voice was an axe chopping each word at the roots.

She had finished unpacking their overnight things, so he got up and started to undress. She lay on the bed and curled a finger toward him. "Come here," she said. He lay down sideways on the bed and rested his head in her lap. "I'm sorry if I'm so sharp about Hal Forester. I know he's one of your best friends."

"You've a right to your opinion. But I just don't understand it."

And you never will, she thought. Out loud she said, "Did I ever tell you that I love everything about your face?" She ran sensitive fingers through his hair and across his nose and down his cheeks to his beard. "I like the reddish-brown tints in your hair, your bushy eyebrows, your beard, even your freckles."

"Mother says I look a lot like my father, only smaller. He was a big brawny guy, over six feet, with a shaggy mane of blonde hair and a bushy beard."

"You've never told me much about him, except that he's dead . . ."

"I will, someday," he interrupted.

Her fingers stopped their sensuous movements for a moment, then continued. "Alright, when you're ready." She bent and blew in his ear. "I like the way you crop your beard. Sort of looks like a van Dyke, yet not so tailored. And I like your ears . . ."

He wriggled around and buried his nose in her bare belly. He laughed then, looked up at her mischievously, and said, "You know what a belly button's for?"

"No, what?"

"To put salt in when you eat celery in bed."

She giggled and pulled his lips to her breasts. She began to sing softly, "I'll taste your strawberries and drink your sweet wine . . ."

Later, when their passions were under control again, he looked up at her and said, "You know, people have told me I picked the wrong sister. And you picked the wrong roommate."

"Oh, no," she said emphatically, "you're the one for me. Hal Forester repels me. So very big and so very handsome and so very sure of himself."

He almost said that that sounded like sour grapes, but bit it back. If it really were, he didn't want to know. Not yet, anyway. "Maybe Hal does come on too strong for some people. But he's always been a hero to me. My opposite in so many ways. I've never been comfortable in the spotlight, but he just blossoms when the crowd roars. Have you ever seen him raise his right fist in the air, like a black power salute, whenever he's scored a touchdown or made a long gain?"

She nodded. "Yes, I've seen that."

"I'd at least like for you to be friends," he said.

She shook her head. "We'll never be friends. But I'll try to be civil. If he keeps his big paws off me, and as long as he treats Maia right."

"You think he might not?"

"Yes, I think he might not. I wouldn't trust him any farther than I could throw him."

"Whatever Hal Forester might be, or might not be, he's not untrustworthy."

She made no comment, just looked at him archly and then turned her head aside.

12

They had found an apartment less than half a mile from Hektoen, on Harrison, near the Circle Campus of the University of Illinois. It was an easy walk, or would be most days in half-decent weather. When howling January winds made Chicago just slightly less fit to live in than Nome, Alaska, he would be able to jump on a bus at the Burger King across the street.

Rather than feeling caged, he had a sense of space when he stepped out onto the street from the little cluster of two-story, brick apartment buildings. On both sides of the street, wrecking crews had levelled three blocks of slum to the east and two blocks to the west. On clear days he could see the Sears Tower in the Loop, a black pile of glass blocks swaying in the gale off Lake Michigan. To the west lay the great jumble of one of the largest medical centers in the world: Cook County Hospital, St. Lukes-Presbyterian, the University of Illinois professional colleges of medicine, dentistry and pharmacy, dozens of other piles of stone serving the gods of healing.

At first the openness pleased him. Then it saddened him, for the wide open spaces had been created at the expense of trees. There were none, and precious few shrubs and weeds and grass. Concrete and bricks and asphalt had replaced them. Steel ribs of still more concrete and bricks had sprouted where once oaks and elms and prairie grasses flourished. And there was the noise. Buses grinding gears, car-tires screeching, the constant roar from the Eisenhower Expressway a block north, sirens, airplanes overhead, horns honking. The din of the big city which long-time residents didn't even hear any more.

It sure wasn't Charlottesville, he mumbled, but it wasn't the ghetto either. He knew he could adjust, but could Britt?

Britt was caught in a classic urban trap. She didn't know her neighbors, was reluctant to invite them in, thinking it was really their move as established tenants to welcome the newcomer. But they all had their own lives, friends, activities. They came and went, passed her in the street without so much as a nod, not knowing who she was either, and not caring. In Charlottesville, Britt had been a queen. In Chicago she was nobody.

She had quit her job in the Oak Park modelling agency, and tried to find another one in the Loop. But everywhere she went she was told, "We'll call you," and so far they hadn't. She settled for a part-time job as a clerk in Wieboldt's department store on North Ashland. It was demeaning for her. For the first time Reynolds realized that she wasn't as secure as he'd thought. The appearance of strength and hauteur, which captivated all of them, was a facade that depended to a large degree on the constant awareness of her beauty by others. She had traded on her looks for so many years that she became unnerved when they got her nowhere. At Wieboldt's the ugly ribbon-clerks made as much as the pretty ones. Reynolds was surprised when he detected this trait, and then knew he shouldn't be, musing that no one, no matter how highly placed, is free from the bogey-man of self-doubt.

He knew he wasn't much help, especially at first when he was not only too busy to take her out but also not fully aware of the state of her mind. But she kept busy, too. The apartment began to look like a home. She kept a neat, if not immaculate, house. Whether or not she wished for the latest in Danish-modern furniture he never knew. But she took down the curtains at the front windows and hung drapes. She salvaged a beautiful old coffee table from a junk store on Maxwell Street, set it in front of the fireplace, and laid out a few of the right magazines: Time, Mademoiselle, National Geographic, and sometimes the New Yorker if she'd worked a few hours overtime and felt like splurging. Her under-lying insecurity showed itself in little things. She dressed up each morning as if she were going out on the town. When Reynolds was home she never wore curlers or a headscarf. She turned on every light in the house because she wanted any chance visitor to see her at her very best.

She didn't complain about her enforced leisure. She understood when he came home tired, didn't push him to go out. She smiled, turned on the TV or pulled out a book, and curled up on the sofa in front of the fireplace, whether or not they could afford to burn a few logs that week.

But she was like a little girl going to a party whenever they did go down to the Circle Campus to a play, or invited some of his colleagues in for a drink and some bridge. This more than anything tipped him off to the deadly dull, alien world in which she lived while he was at the lab all day. To break her monotony he suggested that she ask Maia to visit for a couple of weeks. She leaped at the idea as if she had been waiting for him to mention it.

Maia arrived on a late evening flight at O'Hare. She came up the enclosed gangway from the plane carrying only a book, easily the prettiest girl in the airport except for Britt. Britt, of course, stood out like a rainbow on a stormy grey day.

The two sisters embraced as if they hadn't seen each other for ten years. The conflict between them which Reynolds had sensed in their first meeting, and for a while afterward, was definitely muted. Whatever had caused that rift seemed to be smoothed over now. Maia let him peck her on the cheek and then dashed off with Britt.

He took her claim checks and went for the luggage, pondering again the immense difference between the two girls. Britt so poised and worldly, Maia so demure. No, not demure, tranquil. But in this peaceful dormancy he sensed a latent seiche waiting to sweep across a quiet lake.

He left them chatting happily on the lower level and brought around the little Toyota he had picked up in a used-car lot. Off to the west he counted the lights of six giant planes lined up in the air, one behind the other, about a half mile apart on the approach to the runway. O'Hare was still the busiest port in the world, averaging a landing and takeoff every minute. The air was damp and cold, the sky overcast. Winter had sneaked up on him. In Charlottesville he had watched the seasons change, spring turning the birch trees a fiery green along the streams, fall transforming the maples into huge exploding orbs of flame. But in Chicago he would reckon the changing seasons by the decorations in the store windows.

He settled into his seat and let the girls chatter in back. He felt like a chauffeur and almost asked if they wanted the Palmer House. Then, without conscious effort, he wandered off into his own world, back to the lab where his real life was lived. His heart thudded slowly in his chest as he recalled a conversation in his office earlier that day. Victor Steinke had come in, bustling as usual, white coat flapping. He settled on one of the two straight-back chairs and looked around as if he hadn't ever been there before. Reynolds knew he approved of the austerity: a large steel desk with a wood-grain formica top, a few books (Stedman's Medical Dictionary, a PDR, Gray's Anatomy, Joe Tobin's Textbook of Psychopharmacology), a few papers and journals, an old L.C. Smith manual typewriter his mother had given him years before. No IN and OUT boxes, no pictures, no fancy paper weights.

His little pig eyes stared at Reynolds as he ran a hand over his bald pate. "When will you be ready, Dr. Reynolds?"

"I could go any time," he answered, "if I had to. But I'd like to do one more animal simulation. Another week?"

Steinke's eyes narrowed even more and he scratched the tattoo on his arm. "Then, a week from Monday, we choose the donor."

Reynolds gripped the edge of his desk and felt sweat break out in his hands. "Alright," he said.

Steinke had already chosen the recipient. Gerard Houston, a 47-year-old carpenter who'd had a brain hemorrhage two weeks before, lay legally dead in Room 3007. Gonzaga had operated on him, found so much of his brain destroyed that he could do nothing except clip the bleeding blood vessel and back out. For over a week now his EEG had been flat. He was one of the classic candidates that Steinke had talked about six months before. Under ordinary circumstances someone would have pulled the plug and let him die days before. But with Reynolds' work so close to being ready, Steinke had vetoed that. They fed a Schwann-Ganz catheter through his right brachial (arm) vein into his right lung to measure the blood gases and pulmonary wedge-pressure. They threaded another plastic catheter into his left jugular vein to give him high doses of glucose to prevent him from auto-cannibalizing his own proteins. The surgeons performed a tracheostomy to ensure that his lungs and trachea would remain free of drying mucus and pus. Like strings on a marionette, tubes and wires gave life to a body bereft of a brain.

Reynolds saw all this as he sat in that speeding car, saw himself as the puppeteer. His strings were thin strands of enlon placed between the living brain of one man and the living body of another.

A hand on his shoulder, a voice breaking through. Maia. "How's the work going, Merc?"

He grinned back at her. "Thought you'd never ask. We're just about ready for the big try." He glanced back at her again as she said, "Really?" Her eyes were wide in the sudden light of a passing car. "You mean you're actually ready to do a brain transplant?"

"A week from Monday we start looking for the donor."

She was silent for a moment, then said almost in a whisper, "I just know it'll be successful."

He wasn't so sure. He remembered a dream he'd had only a few nights before. A nightmare, actually. He sat in a subway train, late at night, a large group of people crowded around listening to him talk. They stopped at station after station, and at each one a few passengers got off. He kept looking at the fat conductor for a sign that he too should leave, but the conductor just shook his head solemnly. Finally the last passenger got off, followed by the conductor. Reynolds leaped to his feet and ran for the door, but his legs wouldn't move and it closed in his face. At the same time the train started up again, throwing him to the floor. He lay there in surprise and terror as the train roared through the dark tunnel. Then to his horror the whole train began to collapse in on itself until finally he was confined in a tiny replica of the once roomy car. The engine stopped, the lights went out, and there was total silence.

The meaning was all too clear. The conductor was Victor Steinke. Reynolds was the transplanted brain. The passengers were the doctors and nurses and technicians who had brought him to that place. Then they all left him there, alone. The imploding walls were not steel but bone, trapping him in the total isolation, barring communication with anyone, anywhere.

13

The entourage snaked through the internal-medicine ward, in and out of each private room, an asp stalking a victim. Victor Steinke was the head of the viper, forked tongue darting to and fro, nostrils flaring, hooded eyes searching, searching . . .

Behind him trotted Miss Helen Rogers, a stack of charts balanced on her arm and clutched to her breast. Alfredo Gonzaga, who with Steinke would do the actual transplants, followed her with his notebook and ballpoint at the ready. Occasionally he turned to Jonathan Kettering, the senior medical resident, asking a question or making a comment. Following in total silence came the junior neurosurgical resident, the interns, and two medical students. Reynolds trailed in their wake, listening, somewhat out of his element.

They stopped at the beside of a thin, wiry black man who sat propped against the headboard with several pillows. Each breath was torture, all the muscles of his chest and neck tensing rhythmically with each gasp, his gaping mouth exposing a dry, red, shrivelled tongue. A green oxygen catheter was taped to his nose. His eyes, however, were alight with intelligence and understanding, a white *arcus senilis* ringing each black pupil.

Steinke stood at the foot of the bed, hands stuffed in his lab coat, head thrust forward almost menacingly. Reynolds wondered if he realized how fierce he looked, bald pate gleaming, mustaches drooping, little pig eyes almost hidden by fat. Very few people sensed the warmth hidden behind that ferocious facade.

"Good morning," he said.

The black nodded.

Steinke turned to Jonathan Kettering, who stood with his hands deep in the pockets of his long white coat. "You have talked to him?" he asked.

"Yes, sir."

"He is fully aware of what we want to do?"

"He is."

A faint smile ghosted across the black face. He spoke in a whisper, sucked in a deep breath of air after almost every word. Everyone leaned forward to hear, the effect predatory. "I know . . . what . . . you want . . . to do . . . ain't . . . nothing . . . to lose."

One of the medical students stepped forward half a pace. "Dr. Steinke?" he said.

Ponderously Steinke turned toward him as if the student had broken wind. "Yesss?"

"Has a heart transplant been offered to this patient?"

A growl rumbled in Steinke's throat. "Tell him, Alfredo."

Dr. Gonzaga riffled the pages of the chart to the laboratory sheets, then handed the chart to the student. "He's been thoroughly worked up, doctor. He suffers, as you can see, from the advanced stages of mitral valvular disease in severe decompensation. But the immunological tests show that his body would never accept another person's heart."

"Even with massive doses of immunosuppressive drugs?"

"Even with everything we could throw at him." His eyes darted around the circle of people as if for support. Steinke and Kettering nodded.

The student persisted. "But won't he reject a brain transplant, too, then?"

Patiently Gonzaga explained that for some reason brains were never rejected, at least in experimental animals. "That's well documented," he said, "beginning with Dr. Robert White's work in Cleveland as far back as the early sixties. Many others, including Dr. Steinke, have confirmed it."

The student handed back the chart without a word. Gonzaga's smile was sphinx-like, the arrogance of the always-right neurosurgeon written in plain English across his face.

The snake twisted out of the room into the corridor, its head stopping just outside the black's door.

"I don't like it," Steinke said. "A black man's brain in a white man's body. *Mein Gott,* it's like putting a Jew's brain in a Gestapo's body."

Reynolds had already talked at great length with the black man. The man knew he was dying, knew nothing could save him except a clearly contra-indicated heart transplant. He accepted a brain transplant as a last minute reprieve from the gas chamber. When Reynolds had asked him what he thought of spending the rest of his life in a white man's body, he said, "Well, now, I think that would be the biggest joke since Massa Tom Jefferson's black grandson passed off as a white in Boston."

Reynolds had left him then, admitting to second thoughts about sending into the streets of Chicago a black man's brain in a white man's body. He couldn't help thinking about the odd mixture of chromosomes that the first Dr. Reynolds had re-arranged in the brain of his father Pan. Pan had fought that battle for six years and finally lost it when he lost his life. And Mercury Reynolds was still feeling the shock waves, even though he had managed—with his mother's sensitive and brave help—to get where he was that day.

Victor Steinke waited imperiously in the corridor, scratching his tattoo. Dr. Gonzaga stood beside him, short and stocky, dark black eyes exposing to view the brilliant mind behind them. Steinke spun toward Kettering. "Is there no one else?"

"Perhaps. Come."

He led them further into the ward, past the flotsam and jetsam which had been washed up on the shores of Cook County Hospital.

At the far end of the ward was another pair of private rooms for the terminal care of patients who were considered beyond hope. Through the open door of one room they saw the bloated body of a comatose woman. An IV hung from a metal standard, yellow fluid dripping slowly into her arm. A frothy pinkish liquid thickly coated her lips and bubbled in and out of her open mouth with each breath. She was dying alone.

They turned into the other room.

On the bed lay a yellow man, jaundice so deep that he was almost orange. His yellow eyes followed them as they crowded in. Dr. Kettering nodded a greeting and then pulled the sheet down to expose the tense skin stretched over the fluid-filled belly. Large, tortuous veins converged on his navel like the tentacles of an octopus. His arms and legs were spindly, sticklike. There was no hair on his torso, even in his armpits, and the pubic hair was scanty and shaped like a woman's. Tiny spider-nevi were scattered at random all over his face and body.

From his nose issued a thin plastic tube sucking bright red blood from his stomach. Only his yellow eyes were alive, and they were clouded over with a thin film.

Even Steinke was struck dumb for a moment. Then, "What is this, Dr. Kettering, a joke?"

"No, sir. He's dying of cirrhosis of the liver, bleeding steadily but rather slowly from esophageal varices."

"He has been operated on?" Steinke asked.

"No, sir. We didn't even call the thoracic surgery service. They'd never touch him. And he's certainly no candidate for a shunt."

Reynolds knew in general what they were talking about. In cirrhosis, the scarred liver shuts down the flow of blood from the abdomen, backing it up into the blood vessels of the bowel. The liquid fraction of the blood then seeps out of the blood vessels into the free abdominal cavity, filling it with gallons of sticky yellow fluid. Around the lower esophagus the veins engorge in a futile attempt to carry off all the blood which normally passes through the liver. When those veins burst, they cause a massive hemorrhage into the stomach. Usually the bleeding can be controlled temporarily with a triple-lumen, double-balloon tube invented by Sengstaken and modified by Blakemore, readying the patient for the thoracic surgeons who can tie off the bleeders. Then later, abdominal surgeons reroute the blood supply from the bowel through the splenic or portal veins directly back into the vena cava, thereby shunting the blood back into the main stream. The chance of success was very slim.

But on this poor soul, James Abernathy, they had given up before they started.

"He is an alcoholic?" Steinke asked.

Kettering nodded, as if to say "what else?"

"You want I should take his brain?"

Kettering shrugged, said, "That's your decision."

As Steinke deliberated, Reynolds remembered a conversation only a few weeks before. He, Steinke, Kettering and Gonzaga had remained behind in Reynolds' office after the five o'clock meeting. "What do we do," Gonzaga had asked, "if the donor is an alcoholic?"

Steinke had turned to Kettering. "What is the latest, doctor? Is alcoholism transferred genetically?"

"We still don't know. If it is, your new man will be an alcoholic, too."

"Perhaps not," Gonzaga had said quickly. "The total mass of his new body might overwhelm the alcoholic gene."

Steinke had sat Buddha-like, eyes shifting from one to the other. He asked, "And if it is not genetic, he will carry with him all the traumas of childhood, the memories of parents and schoolmates and whatever else made him what he was?"

No one had answered.

Steinke said now, "I don't like it. But I like that Jew's brain in a Gestapo's body even less."

Reynolds stepped forward. "What did he say to you about a transplant, Jon?"

Kettering inclined his head. "I haven't talked to him about it. I'm not sure he'd be capable of a rational decision."

"Any relatives?" Steinke asked.

"A sister in Ohio somewhere. We've tried to contact her. No luck. They haven't been in touch for years."

Steinke spoke, his high voice penetrating the small room like a stiletto. "Dr. Reynolds, try now to get through to him."

Kettering stepped back a pace and shoved his hands deeply into his pockets. As Reynolds moved up to the bedside, he nodded his head as his mind crossed with

Kettering's. Reynolds knew that Kettering had considerable misgivings about the entire project. He reminded Reynolds again and again of the unanswered moral and ethical problems involved, not to say anything about the legal aspects. "Merc," he had said just a few days ago, "you know this isn't the same thing as taking a man's heart and putting it into another's body. Maybe the ancients would have thought so, but I don't."

Reynolds knew he was right. But he himself had thought it out pretty well. He knew they just couldn't resolve to stay out of the water until they learned how to swim. Besides, the law was clear. The "brain man" would be the legally living person. He lived on in a body whose brain was dead. The "body man" was legally dead, no longer having a wife and family and house and insurance policies. Was, in fact, *dead*. Except that his body continued to *exist* and now was the home of the "brain man."

But Kettering was right about the unsolved ethical dilemma. And Reynolds did not have all the answers. They were breaking new ground.

So now he moved to the bedside and stood there for a moment looking down at James Abernathy. For just a split second his dream on the train came back to him and he had an almost overpowering urge to say, "Oh, what the hell, let's get out of here." Then the scientific side of his brain took over from the emotional side and he said, "Mr. Abernathy."

The yellow eyes stared at him and there was a slight but distinct nod of his head.

"Your doctors tell me you have just a day or two to live." Again the feeble nod. "Your body's all worn out and there's no way anyone can put it back together again."

Reynolds looked up at the circle of white-coated doctors. Steinke stood immobile, his face and eyes hiding anything he might be thinking. Kettering faded into the background, eyes gazing blankly at the floor, hands inert in the pockets of his lab coat. Gonzaga watched Reynolds like a hawk, his eyes pleading, "Go on, don't quit now." The medical students stood spellbound, gripped by the drama, and Reynolds knew they were wondering if they would ever have the guts to stand at a man's bedside and tell him he was dying.

He searched for the right words, words which this forlorn hulk could understand, words which would make him understand they were trying to save his life, not just trying to use him in an experiment.

"You see, Mr. Abernathy . . ."

"Call me Jim," he said, his voice just barely audible.

Reynolds glanced up at Kettering and told him with his eyes there was still a man behind those glazed yellow eyeballs. Kettering caught his meaning and the deep furrows creasing his brow faded just a bit.

"You see, Jim, we think we've perfected a way to take your brain and keep it alive in another man's body."

Reynolds watched the wheels turning slowly in Abernathy's head. He knew just what he was thinking, and it didn't take any powers of clairaudience. Jim Abernathy had lived in that body for fifty-seven years, had seen that face in the mirror every time he tied his tie or shaved, had bought clothes to fit the frame that they were dooming to the fire without his brain in it, had cut the toenails on those feet and knew every corn and bunion. They were asking permission to take him away from all that, to take all that away from him. And at the same time keep *him* alive.

Reynolds read the answer in his eyes before Abernathy said anything and had already turned away when Abernathy said in a hoarse whisper, "Ok, doc, she's all yours."

As Gonzaga moved to the bedside with the simple operative permit, Reynolds strode out of the dark room into the light of the morning sun streaming in through the dirty windows. Never again, through all the dozens of times he would reenact this scene, would he have the same glow of satisfaction of a mission accomplished.

They had a body, the carpenter, Gerard Houston. They had a brain, the alcoholic,

James Abernathy.
Now all they had to do was put them together.

14

Maia was just what Britt needed. They shopped together, went to a few movies, sat at home and talked endlessly. Reynolds caught snatches of their conversation and was a little surprised to hear them talking about really serious subjects: Chicago politics, the transplant work, the problems of their country. Reynolds had known for years that with some exceptions women talk about people, men talk about ideas. Perhaps he had sold both sisters short, his wife most of all, since he had never really probed the depth of her knowledge and interests.

From the very first he and Maia recognized an odd rapport which they felt more strongly as the week passed. There was no hint of erotic love. She was a very pretty girl in a quiet sort of way, but his love for Britt ruled out another woman then.

No, he thought, it was more an interplay between their minds. They scarcely had to verbalize their thoughts for they knew beforehand what the other was going to say. His mother and he often caught each other's thoughts, and there were others with whom he sensed this awesome phenomenon, but seldom to the degree that he did with Maia. On one occasion he had had a particularly trying day and looked forward to a drink before supper, something he didn't often have. She met him at the door with a Scotch and water. Another time, when Britt was working late, Maia woke him from an after-supper nap for no apparent reason. He remembered then that he had to call the lab. He was dumbstruck by her clairvoyance.

One evening after supper, as they sat reminiscing about Charlottesville and how their lives had changed since they left, Maia asked him how "his famous enlon strands" worked.

"He's pretty close-mouthed about that," Britt said with an embarrassed giggle. "He's hardly even told his own wife about them."

Reynolds sat quietly for a moment, not relishing the job of explaining such a complicated subject, but on the other hand anxious that both women should know a little of what he was doing.

"Alright," he said finally. "I'll try to give you a run-down." He smiled wanly. "If you get bored, just yawn or something. Or get up and leave."

He went into his study, left leg dragging and shoulders drooping slightly more than usual, accentuating his mild hunchback. In a few seconds he returned with a square of plastic about an inch across and an eighth of an inch thick. He handed it to Maia. "Britt has seen this but she might want to look at it again. But before we get to that, let me back up into a little basic anatomy and physiology." He sat across the room from them, stretched out on his spine, eyelids half-closed. "First of all, a nerve fiber is just a delicate thread of protoplasm extending out from its parent cell and depending on it for nutriment. If you cut the nerve, the part separated from the cell body dies, all the way to its endplate in skin or muscle or whatever. If the two ends of the nerve are still in contact, *and* if the nerve is 'myelinated'—that is, covered with a thin sheath of Schwann cells —the nerve can regenerate all by itself. This doesn't happen very often, especially in big nerves, and it never happens in '*un*myelinated' nerves.

"Still with me? Good. Some nerves— like the optic and olfactory—and the spinal cord—don't have these essential Schwann cells to stimulate and guide the new nerve growth.

"Now we know that some lower animals can regrow parts. The lizard can regrow its tail, crabs and spiders can actually regrow legs and antennae. Most interesting of all—to me at least—is the sea cucumber, which sloughs off—autotamizes—its entire insides and front end and then can regenerate an entirely new animal from the nearly empty hull of skin and muscles.

"We know that in these lower animals the new growth comes from 'neoblasts,' cells which have been set aside in the embryo for this purpose and have never differentiated. They're scattered throughout the body and migrate to the cut surface and form the chief source of the new leg or tail or whatever.

"We, as humans, have these neoblasts in our body. If we can find a way to utilize them, we can regrow parts, too. Specifically, in my work, we can regrow unmyelinated nerves. That's what my enlon strand does."

"How?" Maia asked, wide-eyed.

"Look at that plastic square. If you look closely you can see that there's a whorl in it that looks like a hair curled on itself. That's the enlon. That piece is forty-five centimeters long—17½ inches—the average length of the spinal cord in an adult male." He described for them the construction of the enlon strand.

Maia, her eyes still wide with wonder, asked. "All that in that little hair?"

Reynolds laughed. "And it could easily hold a lot more. That technology is ancient —almost twenty years now. I modified it by placing at regular intervals what I call a 'node,' for want of a better term. Each node contains two things: a micro-silicon chip four tenths of a millimeter in diameter, and a depolarizer. I don't need to tell you about the micro-silicon chips. That's also ancient history. It's the heart of our control system, obviously. The depolarizer is what draws the neoblasts to the site by changing the alignment of electrical charges on the individual cells in its immediate vicinity through a form of micro-magnetic waves. Through it we can direct growth with a directional transmitter . . ."

"You just lost me," Britt said with a laugh.

"All that means is . . ." He stopped for a moment, closed his eyes, then opened them again. "I guess I've got to explain something else first. OK, we've got the spinal cord cut, either by injury or in a brain transplant by the scalpel. The surgeons insert, under direct vision, four enlon strands along the front of the cord, all the way from the cut to the end of the cord, the *cauda equina.*

"The placement doesn't have to be

exact. That's where the computer comes in. Five of those copper wires are the 'addressing' wires. They designate the address—or location—of the node on the enlon strand that is currently being changed. Sensors can then pick up changes in activity and allow us to tell within ten microns—that's about the size of a red blood cell—what's going on. More than close enough.

"Once the nodes are in place, we program the computer to control the growth of the spinal cord nerves within reach of each depolarizer. Does that make some sense now?"

"Yes," Britt answered and looked at Maia, who nodded. "But what about the cranial nerves?"

"A somewhat different problem. But with the same basic solution. The enlon strand is only one-half millimeter—that is, two-hundredths of an inch—thick. The micro-silicon chips are smaller, too. The depolarizers are placed every one-half centimeter, two-tenths of an inch. And we're only going to place them in the pure sensory nerves, numbers one, two, eight, and the mixed nerves, three five, seven, nine and ten. The pure motor nerves, numbers three, four, six, eleven and twelve, would be difficult, and impossible for long nerves like the vagus, which is the longest nerve in the body, fifteen to twenty feet."

"Whew," Britt said and looked at Maia.

BRAIN CHILD

"Well, I guess we asked for it. Do you understand everything he said?"

"No," Maia said, "but enough to know what's going on. But what about that little black box, Merc?"

He got up, went back into his office, and came out with a small box, which was indeed black, and smaller than a loaf of bread. "This is," he said with a smile, "the little animal that collects the data from the enlon strands and passes it on to the computer. Which in turn digests it, makes certain decisions on its own, or stores information for retrieval by the surgeons and me. The enlon strands come into it via a cable at one end. At the other end is a simple electric cord which plugs into house current."

"What about the computer?" Britt asked. "Where is it hooked up?"

"It isn't. Information from the patient and instructions from the computer are transmitted by radio. There's no direct connection. Here, let me show you. It opens like some suitcases, a three-number combination." He grinned. "It just keeps the honest people out. Anyone could get into it if they really wanted to. This one's set on Britt's birthday so I won't forget it, the eighth of December, or 128."

Britt giggled. Reynolds opened the box to reveal the electronic hardware inside.

"What are those little switch-like things?" Maia asked.

"We're going to be monitoring many people at the same time and have to have some way to keep track of whose information is currently being monitored. Each transmitter will be set to a unique code with those five switches, which gives us the capability of monitoring thirty-two patients."

"They're in pairs," Britt said.

"One for receiving and one for transmitting."

"Incredible," Maia breathed.

Reynolds shook his head. "Huh-uh. Incredible means it can't be believed. I believe this. Believe *in* this."

Both Maia's and Britt's heads were bobbing up and down almost in unison, mesmerized, despite what Reynolds had said, by the incredibility of the entire schema.

In the evenings he moved restlessly about the little apartment. He could feel their eyes glancing at him from time to time. Almost furtively Britt would ask him if he'd like some coffee, or a little brandy. He knew he was a little on edge during those last ten days before the hammer would fall. Everything was going well, and, as he had told Steinke, he was actually ready to go any time. But there were the little things that had to be tied together, routines to be honed, interns and residents to confer with. In the dark night he reviewed the hundreds of little steps which had to be taken once they moved into the actual transplant. He went to sleep at night with his eyes firmly fixed on the computer screen which would be his radar, monitoring each of the electrodes just as surely as an air-traffic controller watches his blips.

There was an unreality about those last days. His mind was inordinately alert, sifting and weighing his own thoughts and words as well as those of his associates. He tinkered in the lab, Steinke hovering like a giant moth about his flame, playing with the console as if it were a color TV. Once Reynolds ordered him out, impatience overriding his pledge to remain in his command. To his surprise, Steinke left without a word.

He could feel the pressures building subtly in the entire lab, even in those people not directly connected with their project. The usual comaraderie was missing, at least when he was around. They all paid him a certain deference which added to the air of monasticism. He was indeed Mercury of the ancient legends, a messenger of the gods, the "ram-bearer" of the myth of Argus and Io. He gripped his staff with the serpents entwined and hoped he would not become, as Mercury had in the Odyssey, the conductor of the dead to Hades.

# PART TWO

15

Now both Jim Abernathy and Gerard Houston were dead. As Reynolds sat dazedly in the old easy chair, Jim Abernathy's face hung before him. Britt had said, as she left him there hours before, "There'll be others, Merc." It had been consolation of sorts. But he didn't want "others." He wanted Abernathy, who, though not young, was too young to die.

Reynolds had been so sure they were going to show the world success; it would now see only failure. He was so obsessed with this thought that he was amazed the next day to find that the scientists and technicians in the laboratory considered the transplant team heroes, not goats. Hardly anyone felt that they had really failed; it was almost as if they were expected to fail the first time. The response was, in a way, disheartening because they had been so sure of success, but encouraging because they felt an impetus to continue.

So they did. Six weeks later, their wounds nearly healed, they found a donor in the dialysis ward, a young woman of twenty-five whose kidneys had failed and who had already had two kidney transplants. The first kidney had been rejected almost immediately, the second after a year. She came in for dialysis three times a week, and perhaps could have been kept going for some years. But at twenty-five, she pleaded with them to do the brain transplant if they thought she could be saved from a lifetime of slavery to a machine.

Reynolds was honest with her. "You're aware that our first attempt failed?"

She nodded, and grinned. "You didn't do anything wrong, did you?"

Reynolds shook his head emphatically. "No, everything was going super up until his arrest."

"OK, so that could have happened on the tenth one or the hundredth, right? So, it's tough luck for the old guy."

The recipient was a twenty-year-old girl who had been thrown off the back of a speeding motorcycle. Within two days her electroencephalogram (EEG) was flat. Her brain was mush.

So with more than a little anxiety they started the entire procedure again. They had learned a lot from Houston and Abernathy. Czrza was confident about clipping the vertebrals. Reynolds felt more at home in both the monitoring situation and the operating room. He had not had a chance to work with the enlon implants, but that was really a minor matter for he had done it so many times in paraplegics and in lower animals. Steinke was more lenient with Czrza, and excused him from the scrub during the hours of boring work with the nerves and spinal cord. They had found that Steinke was right about the excessive cooling: it had not had any effect on Abernathy's brain. They could not tie it in with the cardiac arrest. Gonzaga had learned to take the sixth nerve before the fourth to aid in the dissection.

Besides, they had faced the psychological barrier of that four-minute mile. Never again would they feel quite the same awe at the moment of exchange. Not that they would ever be blasé. Not ever. But the soul-wrenching trauma of carrying a human brain from one room to another had been done once. They had ridden the bicycle without training wheels. They had soloed. They had published their first novel.

All these things they had done, and

more. They had transplanted a human brain.

The second transplant went without a hitch. Fourteen hours after the incision was made, it was sutured shut. Alfredo Gonzaga stood back from the table and closed his eyes for several seconds. Then he sprayed collodium on the wound so that a bandage would stick to it without a roller gauze. He glanced around the room, but nobody had anything to say.

Without breaking the silence, the surgeons left the room, single file, exhausted, gloves and masks and gowns falling to mark their passage.

In the cathedral stillness, the clock clicked as its hand jumped forward a minute.

Within a few weeks they settled into a routine of bi-monthly transplants which would not vary except in minor details for the next six months. The only changes made were relatively unimportant and usually designed to speed up the work without sacrificing quality. By the end of six weeks they had shortened the operating time to about eleven hours from "skin to skin," skin incision to skin closure. In three months they took nine hours, which was considered an irreducible minimum.

In September, five months after the first successful transplant, Hal Forester came to visit Reynolds after a long absence, a sheaf of tickets poking out of the pocket of his suede sports jacket. He flipped them out with his customary flourish and said, "Fifty-yard ducats, Merc. At Soldier Field on Sunday."

Reynolds grinned and asked the obvious, "You're playing the Bears Sunday?"

"You don't read the papers much, do you?"

"Not much, not lately. I do follow your exploits in the paper, but the Eagles aren't on TV here very much. I watch every one I can."

"I'd heard you'd been busy," he said with a grin.

Britt said quickly, "That's the understatement of the century."

"Well," Reynolds said, pulling at his beard, "at least the decade."

Reynolds fixed Forester a drink, his usual brandy Manhattan, and flopped down in a chair across from him. Britt left them to putter around in the kitchen. Hal crossed his ankle on his knee and slid down on his spine. His powerful thighs bulged the material of his slacks.

"You're really doing it, aren't you?" he said finally, "real honest-to-God brain transplants?"

"Nine now. Ten actually. The first one bombed."

"Didn't make it?"

Reynolds nodded, mute. Forester was

being kind. He must have read about it in the paper. Everyone else had. Now Reynolds smiled as he felt Forester's long mental fingers searching the literature. A wicked smile tugged at Forester's handsome, sensual mouth as he found what he was looking for. " 'Nature,' " he said, " 'with equal mind, sees all her sons at play; sees man control the wind, the wind sweep man away.' " For once he knew he had Reynolds, but he didn't gloat as he might have, said simply, "Matthew Arnold."

Reynolds watched him through half-closed eyes and scratched his belly through the old sweatshirt he often wore at home. He still couldn't talk about Jim Abernathy without a stab of pain in his gut.

With thumb and index finger, Forester deftly pincered the ice cube from his drink and tossed it into the empty fireplace. "Don't like to dilute a good thing, eh?" He eyed Reynolds for another moment. "You had this in mind back in college?"

"No, not at first. I was satisfied with my enlon work in paraplegics."

"Yeah, I remember that. It was the first indication I had that I was rooming with a genius. That enlon really works, doesn't it?" He had a sly grin on his face. Britt had just come to the door and was waiting to say something.

"Yes, it really works," Reynolds said.

"Then," Hal said, "do you think I could have the operation? You know, hook it up direct to my dick?"

Reynolds laughed, knowing he had been set up. Britt gave a disgusted grunt and returned to the kitchen. She stood at the sink, staring out at the dreary fall day. He's such a boor, she thought. An overblown, arrogant, little-boy jerk. How could she ever have wanted him for herself, back there at that dance when she and Maia met him for the first time? Now she wondered how Maia had put up with him for so long. But he was probably the perfect gentleman with her, and Maia was so naive. She wondered how long it had taken Hal to get her into bed.

Blood suffused her face as she remembered the time, just a few months ago, when he had put his hand on the inside of her knee in an obvious invitation. She should have slapped his face like they did in her great-grandmother's time. Instead she had just said, "Hal!" and firmly lifted his hand away.

She knew Mercury had no real insight into the depths of her hatred for Hal Forester. He would not understand it. But he should have. In the four years he had roomed with Hal, Merc should have seen through him. Instead, he idolized him. Called him his hero. Merc contrasted his lean, kyphotic, limping body with that perfect physique of Hal's. He had no perception of his own very strong appeal to women. Every woman who met him forgot about his minor physical flaws once she got trapped by those eyes and the way he had of making her feel so important. And once she felt the power of his mind. But he did not know this.

In the living room, Forester and Reynolds were still talking about the transplants. Forester said, "How do you know what's going on in those brains you've transplanted?"

"We don't for sure. But we've got clues. The EEGs for one thing. We can tell if the brain's alive, of course, and we can tell from the type of waves what's going on. All very rough, not an exact science even yet." He glanced at Forester, said softly, "And . . . I seem to get messages."

"Messages?"

"This isn't for the newspapers, Hal. They'd think I was nuts, or something, but I do get fragments of thought once in a while."

"Thoughts?"

Reynolds got up, crossed the room, and stood looking out the window. Forester waited patiently. Finally Reynolds said, "I'm not sure. But once in a while, when I'm sitting beside one of the transplants, I do seem to know what they're thinking."

"Aren't they unconscious?"

"No, that's the point. They're not. They're unresponsive, but their brains are active. Or at least we think so. We won't know for sure until the first one talks to us."

"You've known for years you catch thoughts from other people. You've told me so. And demonstrated it!"

"Yes."

"Then," Forester said, "what's the problem?"

"Part of my job—before the transplant—is to get to know these people well: their jobs . . . their families . . . their hobbies . . . their likes and dislikes. We talk for hours. I let them ramble . . . spill out all their hopes and aspirations for the future. It does them a world of good—especially talking about the future—and helps us in our research. I keep detailed notes. The psychologists test them. After surgery we'll do the same tests, ask the same questions, see if they've lost anything."

"And maybe you're just thinking the way they *might* be thinking?"

"Yeah. But it seems more than that. So real, you know."

"Someday soon you'll find out."

"Maybe." Reynolds returned to his chair and plumped down in it. He was being pushed to a conclusion he was reluctant to make. "If they can remember back to those first few weeks, they might be able to corroborate what I seem to get from them."

"Why do you doubt now an ability you've always had?"

"I've never really been sure that I could actually catch whole thoughts when there weren't *other* clues to help me. Now I don't know. Maybe I can."

Forester studied him for a moment. " 'Modest doubt is called the beacon of the wise.' Shakespeare." He laughed, saw Reynolds' amused look, and added, "Really is this time. Hector."

Forester fixed himself another drink and stood looking out the window at the sun lighting the browning lawn. Britt crossed the room with a yellow plastic watering can to the row of plants on the window sill. Hal watched her for a moment, then moved to her side and draped a huge arm around her shoulders. She didn't shrug him off, but she did stiffen a bit.

"That's quite a guy, Britt, sitting over there so nonchalant in his chair. Quite a guy. You know that?"

She slipped from under his arm and walked back toward the kitchen. "I know," she said, and disappeared through the door.

He finished off the drink and started to make himself another one. "Yessir, he's quite a guy," he said, almost to himself, and walked a little unsteadily to his chair and sat down. And, he thought, that Britt is quite a girl. He wished Reynolds wasn't such a good friend. He'd like to make a real play for her again. He could break her down. He knew she was fighting a desire to be with him.

When Forester left, Reynolds walked

with him out to the courtyard. A wind had come up and there was a chill in the air. Forester shook Reynolds' hand, held it for a moment, and said, "Take care of that little girl in there."

He strode into the darkness, tall, strong, invulnerable. Reynolds went back into the house, built a fire in the fireplace, and turned the thermostat down to sixty. They pulled their chairs up close and he tried without success to concentrate on some recent technical journals while Britt curled up with a novel.

"Why are you and Hal at such odds?" he asked.

"At odds?"

"You know what I mean. He tries to be nice and you cut him off. Don't answer him or walk out of the room. Always just a bit of tension between you."

"I didn't think it was that bad." She curled the ends of her hair with her fingers as she often did when under strain. So he'd noticed. She should have known he would.

"I can almost feel the heat when you talk to each other."

"I've told you before that he repels me."

"I can't imagine why."

"Our chemistry just doesn't mix."

Or does it mix too well? he wondered, and said aloud, "He's always the perfect gentleman with you."

"Even when he puts his arm around

me?"

"Brotherly love," he said.

A barnyard epithet was on her tongue, but she held it back with effort. "I don't like it." She wondered if she should tell him outright about the passes Hal had made, about the innuendos and sly remarks he kept coming at her with. No, he has enough to worry about. Let this deepening hatred be her secret.

He was to remember that conversation later, when it made all the difference in the world to him how Britt reacted to Hal Forester.

16

Reynolds used one of the tickets to the Bears game on Sunday, but he didn't get a chance to talk to Hal. Pleading a head cold and fever, Britt stated flatly and vehemently that she wasn't going to sit in a cold football stadium and catch her death. Actually, the cold snap had ended and it was a warm misty day, the clouds overhead scudding across the city from the lake, the heavy smell of fog, soot and auto exhaust permeating their tight little apartment. But she didn't want to go, that was plain, and he didn't push her.

He never saw Hal Forester again. At least not the old Hal Forester he knew so well. But as the pressure eased at the lab, he began to follow football more closely and occasionally caught an Eagles game on television. He saw Hal on TV in his last game, a game which changed both their lives forever.

When he came home from the Bears game, Britt didn't even ask what the score was. Reynolds left her pouting in the living room and attacked a stack of research notes on his desk which needed annotating for the paper he was going to write when their first transplants were far enough along to evaluate. Already pressure was building to get into print. They well understood the fierce criticism which would arise from the scientific world if they delayed too long. But they were all too aware of the dangers of premature publication. The lay press, of course, was not at all inhibited and had seized the story with a vengeance. Steinke, so far, had kept the reporters off his back with short and devilishly cunning releases, but scarcely a day went by without some front page story about the work on brain transplants at Cook County Hospital.

Britt heard about Hal Forester from time to time in letters from Maia. Slowly the tone changed, from excited accounts of Hal's gridiron feats, to intricate, slightly ironic analyses of their long-distance romance, and finally to the terse announcement that they were no longer seeing each other. Reynolds wasn't surprised. If anything, he was surprised that Forester had stayed with her for so long. It wasn't in his character to build his life around any woman; he knew instinctively that a close relationship must either grow or wither. Growth implied moving towards marriage, or in this day and age at least to living together. Wither implied dissolution; this is the route he had chosen before and now chose for Maia.

She came to see Britt a few weeks after the breakup. As before, they met her at the airport, and she seemed to be none the worse for the insult to her ego. In fact, she seemed more radiant than ever. She wore a new fur coat—a "going-away present," she confided—and in it looked more like Britt than ever before. Hal had shown her the world outside the library and outside Charlottesville. She had never been a recluse, not at all, but now there was a subtle confidence in her walk, a casualness that heightened her attractiveness. Yes, he had been good for her.

On the drive home, she didn't even talk about Forester. Instead she pumped Reynolds for news of his work. He laughed gently and told her briefly what was happening. When they reached home, he escaped to his study, but he could hear the two sisters in eager conversation in the living room. Never an eavesdropper, he could hardly help hearing the postmortem on Hal Forester.

"I never did understand how you could keep seeing him," Britt said.

"Really? You never said anything."

"It wasn't any of my business."

Maia laughed. "No, I suppose not. But he was good for me. While it lasted. I've never known anyone like him . . ."

"He's not so unusual!" Britt interjected.

Maia went on as if she hadn't heard, "So big and gentle at the same time."

"Big Ben," Britt said drily.

Maia laughed again, the chuckle starting deep in her throat, bubbling up to the surface. "Yes, you could say that, I guess."

"I don't see how you can take this so coolly," Britt said, her voice rising at the end, almost shrill.

Maia glanced at her sharply. "What else am I expected to do?"

"You've gone out with this guy for a year, given him every spare minute, presumably given him lots more than that, and then when he thinks the parson's getting too hot on his trail, he just dumps you. And you sit back and say he was just a big gentle bear."

"Britt, he didn't just dump me. We talked things over and decided between us that we'd gone as far as we could without getting married. And he didn't want to do that."

"You should have gotten lots more than a fur coat out of that jerk."

Maia's eyes widened in anger, then narrowed as she said, "He's not a jerk. And what more should I have gotten? Half his property? I don't want half his property, even if it is legal now . . . it wasn't his money that attracted me to him in the first place. I went with him because of *him*, and now that he's out of my life . . ." Her voice trailed off thinly, her eyes clouded. Then she sat up and said, "But that's ancient history already." Her eyes flashed merrily. "I never did like history. And there's lots more fish to fry."

Britt regarded her with disgust. "You don't seem all that upset." But she relaxed a little, the tenseness leaving the muscles around her eyes. She pushed her shoes off with her toes, tucked her bare feet up under her, skirt high around firmly rounded white thighs. She had studied that pose, practiced it, and now it came naturally even when there were no men around.

"Oh, I was, at first," Maia said. "It was a blow to my tender ego. But it didn't take long to realize that he wasn't actually giving *me* up. He was taking the easy way out of a situation which had to go one way or the other some day. We both knew we couldn't just keep drifting along . . ."

"Why on earth not?" Britt shot back. "Lots of people do. At least until someone else comes along."

Maia laughed. "The old wing-walkers' rule. Never let go of one handhold till you've got another. But that isn't what I wanted. Oh, I'm not saying that it was I who shut the door. It wasn't. He walked out on *me*. But it was partly my fault because I kept edging him toward the precipice. You know, make me an honest woman or get out."

Britt's icy stare softened just a bit. "That was the *eighteen*-nineties when they said that. You're a hundred years too late. But anyway, he got out."

"Mmm-hmm."

"I'm *glad*."

There was a prolonged silence as if there were more to be said. Reynolds sat in his study wondering a little about the missing pieces in that conversation. It didn't occur to him to try to intercept their thoughts, for that took intense concentration and he had enough to do. Later he wished he had.

He closed the door and worked on his notes instead. There were unmistakable signs that their first three transplants had taken. Two months before, one of the interns had burst into his office in Hektoen. "Dr. Reynolds, I know you'll want to hear this right away. On Marianna Crowley, in 3002, I'm sure I saw one eyelid twitch!"

Reynolds jumped to his feet. Marianna was the second transplant after Abernathy. He ran down the hall to alert Steinke, thinking that if the intern were right, it could mean only one thing: the nerve of Edinger-Westphal, buried deep in the third —oculomotor—nerve, had arrived at the tiny muscle which runs along the edge of the eyelid. Knowing that the same tiny filament also innervates the iris, they hurried over to see if shining a light into her pupil would cause it to contract. Nothing happened. The pupil remained widely dilated, unresponsive. Steinke glowered at the dejected intern, but Reynolds said, "We don't doubt your word. If you saw it, you saw it." The intern shot him a grateful glance.

And two days later there was a slight, almost imperceptible, contraction of the iris when Steinke shone his bright penlight into the pupil. Steinke stood back in awe, as if he hadn't really believed that it could happen. Gonzaga stood behind the head of the bed, his strong white teeth bared in a satisfied grin.

Their anatomy books told them that the cranial nerves would be the first to function, because all of them except the vagus were very short compared to the peripheral nerves. The vagus, which runs the entire length of the bowel and is by far the longest nerve in the body, would take many months to regenerate. In those early days they weren't sure how to test vagal function satisfactorily. The classic Hollander test for vagal function in the stomach involved the use of rather large doses of insulin and they were trying to avoid all drugs that weren't actually needed.

Then, one by one, the other cranial nerves showed signs of regeneration, not only in Marianna Crowley but two of the other early cases. It was a thrilling, supremely emotional experience for Reynolds each time he could perform a series of tests and then write in the chart, "Abducens shows slightly more function today. The oculomotor is fully functional. There may have been a slight glottal click today, not sure."

The thought kept recurring, "It's working, it's really working." After all the heartache of Abernathy, all the grinding hours in the laboratory, and all the soul-searching in the exhausted hours of the night, it was working.

Now, sitting in his living room later that night, after Britt had complained of a headache and had gone to bed, he experienced that same deep emotion as the thought came, "It's working."

Then Maia, sitting across from him sipping a Scotch and water, said, "Merc, can you tell me how you know your transplants are working?"

He looked up at her, no longer surprised that their minds had met so boldly again. He could tell by her expression that she really wanted to know, so he told her in as much detail as he thought she'd comprehend. She watched him as he talked, also aware of that odd meeting of their minds. She wondered, not at all idly, what would have happened between her and Mercury Reynolds if she hadn't been seeing Hal Forester when she met Reynolds in that restaurant in Charlottesville. Would Reynolds have chosen her rather than Britt? Would Britt have given him a choice?

Reynolds, watching her intently, saw that she easily absorbed the scientific information he fed her. Her mind was at least as sharp as Britt's, and more organized. She listened carefully until she began to lose the thread of the dissertation, then held an index finger up to stop him, and, in a characteristic gesture, ran it lightly down the bridge of her nose while she posed her question.

Reynolds thought how delightful that little habit was. Endearing, actually, and he loved to watch her fight for the right words. In fact, he loved to watch more than that about her. Her short ash-blonde hair bobbed slightly as she nodded in comprehension. Her wide pupils were a deep black within the rims of light blue irises. She lowered her long lashes and fumbled with the ring Hal had given her and which he had insisted she keep.

"Well," Reynolds said finally to break the awkwardness, "where to from here?"

"Back to Charlottesville, I suppose, for a while anyway. That's my life, you know. May not seem all that exciting to you, but I like it."

"You don't get bored?"

"Never. Or hardly ever. I know what you're thinking. You're in such an exciting field that you can't see anything very earth-shaking about cataloguing books. But that's just a small part of my work. I love looking over the new books that come in, exploring all those other areas of the world that I'll never see. I try to read all the best-sellers, fiction and non-fiction."

"You must be a speed-reader."

"Not really. Or at least not all the time. Sometimes I can just devour a book—a thriller or an adventure story. But the ones I like are those I can sit back and savor.

Purposely slowing down to a crawl. Writers of real talent shouldn't be skimmed. If they've spent an hour trying to get a paragraph just right, I should at least give it a minute or two."

He watched her as she talked. Her hands accompanied her voice, not like a hand-waving Italian, but more like a maestro conducting a symphony. Graceful movements of her hands, or even just the faintest flicker of a finger, illustrated her words.

"Why don't you move to Chicago?" he asked.

"I've thought about that. Then I could be with Britt more." She looked closely at him, her mood suddenly altered. "Have you noticed how nervous she seems?"

"Mmm, no, I don't think I have."

"Well, she is. She's always been high-strung—a thoroughbred racehorse—on a perpetual high. But she's . . . oh, I don't know . . . *jumpy*, more than she used to be."

"She's frustrated, maybe. Clerking at Wieboldt's!"

"Oh, it's much more than that. I wish I knew what it was. I know she feels the strain you've been under. Maybe now that things at the lab are getting more routine, you'll relax, and then she'll relax."

She lay back in the chair, mood changing again, a quizzical smile softening her features. "So," she said, "what about *you* now? Where do you go from here?"

"A damn good question. One that no

one else has asked yet." Intuitively she already understood that his association with the brain transplant team would end when Gonzaga and Steinke learned his part of the operation. It wasn't all that complicated. By the end of the year—or sooner—they would know as much as he did. He would have worked himself out of a job.

"Will you stay on here?" Maia asked.

"I don't know. For a while at least. It'll take months to get the data together for the preliminary report, once the first year of experimental work is over. I can see it coming; endless sessions, trying to evaluate what we've done. We'll probably declare a moratorium on new cases until we get a good long look at our results."

"That could happen before the year's up."

Again the penetrating insight. "It could."

"You have one advantage."

He searched her face.

"The people you're operating on," she continued, "they're already dead unless you do something quick."

He got up and threw another log on the fire. Showers of sparks shot up the chimney. He turned and stood with his hands behind his back, warming them with palms outward and fingers splayed. She had another question which he could feel working its way to the surface. It was the same question Kettering had asked, and one Reynolds was afraid to ask himself because he didn't know the answer. Now she was going to ask it. Damn her.

"Merc," she started, her voice as irresolute as he'd ever heard it. "Supposing, just supposing, that something goes wrong, and the brain you've transplanted never quite succeeds in 'establishing those vital connections' you were telling me about a minute ago. And supposing the EEG shows that the brain is alive inside that cranium..."

"...and the body is alive outside the brain, but they haven't ever joined in the formation of a new individual?"

"Yes." It was almost a whisper. "What would you do?"

He spun toward the fire, feeling her eyes on the back of his head. He hated even to think of such a monstrous disaster. The nightmare he'd had months before flashed through his mind, the train telescoping into a tight little box, he in it and unable to communicate with anyone, shut up there forever.

"I don't know," he answered finally. "I just don't know."

"God," she said.

The fire sizzled and a blue tongue of flame shot up the chimney as a pocket of resin caught fire and then exploded. Maybe, Reynolds thought, that's what would eventually happen to that man's brain. He would wait patiently during the weeks he knew had to pass before he received any stimuli from the outside world. He would have no way to reckon time, but eventually it would dawn on him that he should be feeling something. He would have no way of knowing of the frantic activity around his bed while the doctors, his trusted advocates, tried to figure out what had gone wrong so they could correct it. The psychological tension would build slowly but surely. Darkness and soundlessness and lack of tactile and olfactory sensations would slowly deprive him of reason. He would feel abandoned, detached from life, isolated from all awareness.

And then his brain would explode in a shower of sparks, not physically but psychologically. The door would close on rational thought. Hallucinations would surge riotously through his mind, with no way to stop them, until his frontal lobes and limbic system would merge in one huge paroxysm of claustrophobic fear.

Reynolds hadn't heard her get up, but he felt her hand on his shoulder and he shivered.

"Don't let it happen," Maia said, "just don't let it ever happen."

17

It became clear that they were turning out brain transplant cases faster than the ICU ward could absorb them. These patients needed constant supervision and monitoring. Each was still monitored by the computer in the lab at Hektoen, at least periodically, to save Steinke and Reynolds the effort of running over to the ward each time something needed checking out. But they had also set up a duplicate computer in Gonzaga's office for the use of the ward personnel who spent twelve to sixteen hours a day there.

The transplants were complicated nursing problems, each needing a Stryker frame or a circle bed. Steinke, working with administration through Miss Rogers, had anticipated this and had greatly expanded the nursing service to accommodate the biweekly case. Long before the first transplant, the best RNs and LPNs had been recruited from all over the state, men and women of proven talent and dedication. But by the end of three months five patients were on respirators and total body care. After eight months, that number had doubled and looked to remain at that level or increase slightly. These cases were, of course, in addition to the normal flow of neurosurgical patients.

The first cases were now beginning to need less care, for the cranial nerves had regenerated. They were able to see, hear, smell, and taste. The skull caps containing the sensors were removed, and the matted hair washed, cut or combed out. The patients looked human again, lifting the spirits of everyone.

But the rest of their bodies remained senseless and paralyzed, requiring the same care as quadriplegics. Weaning off the respirator became possible in the fourth month, when the nerves to pharynx, epiglottis and larynx resumed control and the upper thoracic nerves began to function. But it was almost another month before the respirator could be safely removed from the room.

The sensor vest was slipped off once a

day for the first three weeks to allow a complete bed bath. Steinke or Gonzaga supervised the replacement. Once the computer readouts showed good, early growth, three to five millimeters a day, the vest was left off all day except for replacement once on each eight-hour shift, supervised by the resident on call. The four enlon strands along the anterior surface of the spinal cord remained in place, the depolarizers stimulating continuous growth and the micro-silicon chips monitoring it.

The interns and residents soon learned to use the console in Gonzaga's office and merely phoned Steinke or Gonzaga with the information. They would sometimes be told to change the settings which the computer had indicated. This process was aided by instructions taped to the front of the console:

> To increase transmission: type I. The computer will ask for the number of pulses. WARNING: AVOID A CHANGE OF MORE THAN 10.
> To decrease transmission: type D. The computer will ask for the number of pulses. WARNING: AVOID A CHANGE OF MORE THAN 10.
> To change the ON/OFF state of depolarizer: type S
> WARNING: EXCESSIVE CHANGES MAY CAUSE LOCAL INSTABILITY. Although this is not serious, IT SHOULD BE AVOIDED.

BRAIN CHILD

But all of this, the medical monitoring and the nursing care, took time and personnel. They cut back to one case a month, were immediately glad that they had, and wondered why they hadn't done so before. The relief from the constant grinding pressure was immense; no longer did they go from one case to a frantic appraisal of the next candidate. As Reynolds looked back, he marvelled that they didn't make more errors in both technique and value judgement during those early months. Those that were detected were minor and easily corrected. All except for Jim Abernathy—he still haunted them all because they couldn't pinpoint any one error. Their final conclusion, an unsatisfying one, was that Gerard Houston's body—especially his heart—was just too weak after two weeks of vegetative life, despite their supportive measures.

They did lose three patients, number 7, 8, and 14. In each case the death was during the "late" postoperative phase, weeks or months after surgery. Case #7 had a heart attack three weeks after surgery and expired almost immediately. Case #8 died in the tenth week from a massive blood stream infection starting in a diseased gall bladder. Case #14, the saddest case of all, died when the tube in the trachea eroded through the wall and caused a hemorrhage which couldn't be controlled quickly enough to save her.

Repeated crises were an inescapable part of their work. They passed from one to another scarcely realizing when they were dealing with crucial decisions. Not so with Andrea Hughes. Within three weeks after her surgery, she was in deep trouble.

It started routinely enough, in January, 1994, a year after Jim Abernathy. She was Case #20, the third to be done after they switched from bi-weekly to monthly operations. She was a beautiful young girl—young woman actually, for she was twenty-six. But she looked eighteen or nineteen, frail, with long blonde hair and big hazel eyes. She had polycystic kidneys, almost functionless for five years, carried along on weekly dialysis treatments. In many ways she was similar to the second transplant, the first successful one, ten months before.

Before going in to see her, Reynolds studied her chart. She had been diagnosed early, at the age of eight. For four years she was treated medically without dialysis, her blood urea nitrogen (BUN) slowly rising to a level of 40-50 and her creatinine to 2-4. She had been able to lead a fairly normal life, for her body adjusted to the slow increase in uremic poisons.

By the time she was fourteen, just beginning high school, dialysis had to be started. At first she went in about once a month, felt well for the next two weeks, then slowly became more and more lethargic, finally had to be dialyzed. During the past three years, the kidneys slowly lost most of their function and now needed help about once a week.

The immunology team had worked her up thoroughly, had finally given up on her ever finding a donor kidney that would stand any chance of successful transplantation.

Reynolds' first interview with her was on the dialysis ward. She lay in bed, propped up so she could read while the three-hour procedure cleansed her blood of the wastes built up during the previous week. There were a dozen other patients in the room, so Reynolds' first question was whether she could talk freely.

"Sure, why not? These people are all like family." She looked around the room and rattled off the names of everyone there. They really were her family, after years of meeting so often. She smiled sweetly, and his heart went out to her. He checked himself. No identification, he told himself sternly. This is just another case for evaluation. Compassion, yes. Understanding, yes. Personal involvement, emphatically no.

"You'll understand," he started, "that this is just a preliminary talk . . ."

Her far-away eyes glinted with an intense fire. "Preliminary, hell. I've had it with this body. What's it ever given me but trouble? I can't take a vacation without wondering if I'll get sick before I get home. I can't go canoeing in Canada because I might break a leg and they couldn't get me out in time. I can't go to a foreign country without so much advance planning that it's hardly worth it. It's worse than being a diabetic. They can at least take their insulin with them. Or get a pancreas transplant and never have to worry again."

Reynolds nodded in agreement with all she said. "Alright, then, we'll skip the preliminaries. You've got things pretty well thought out. Is there anything that bothers you about the idea of a brain transplant?"

She laughed bitterly. "Everything about it bothers me. Will it work? Will I be *me* when it's all over, even if it does work? Can I get used to seeing someone else in the mirror when I wash my face? What will my friends think? Will they be able to accept me as Andrea Hughes even though I look like Sally Smith? Do I get a choice of what I look like. God, *yes*, there's a lot that bothers me."

"But you still want to go through with it, even with all these doubts?"

Tears came to her eyes. She wasn't as tough as she first pretended. "Yes." It was a whisper, yet decisive.

"Tell me about yourself."

She wiped the tears from her eyes with the back of her hand and blew her nose. "What do you want to know?"

"Oh, where you work, your boyfriends, your hobbies, what you like to do in your spare time. That kind of stuff."

"I don't work regularly. That's one of my biggest problems. Nobody'll hire me for any long-lasting jobs so I take waitress jobs until I'm sick too often for even that kind of a job. I'm a pariah. Nobody wants me. And boyfriends? Sure I've had boyfriends. But like in high school. Who'd want to get serious with a girl who might not live the year out? So I date a guy just long enough for him to find out that I'm not long for this world. I've had a couple of kooks propose marriage, but they were sado-masochists and just wanted to spend their lives getting their kicks out of my grief."

The scope of her vocabulary intrigued him. "You've obviously been to college."

"MA in sociology."

"You couldn't find work with a master's degree?"

"Hell, no."

"How would you feel if there was permanent brain damage?"

Her eyes widened. "Is that possible?"

"We don't guarantee a thing."

"What about those cases you've done?"

"Too early."

"Yet some of them are talking."

"Not enough to really tell."

"You aren't levelling with me."

He could feel the eyes of a dozen patients on the back of his head. She was right. But how to put it? Finally he said, "Miss Hughes, there's something you should know. I don't know quite how to say it. Until you came along, we haven't had anyone of your, shall I say, mental caliber..."

"You just been doing gorks?"

"That's putting it too strong, but they have been pretty well down the road by the time they got to us."

"So when you don't start with much, there's no way to tell what's left." She stopped, watched him closely as she asked, "But not one's come up totally *non compos mentis*?"

"Not yet."

She played with the tape holding the butterfly in her vein. "It really rips me open to think of what I could be doing if I didn't have to come in here every week for almost the whole day."

"Don't try to decide right now..."

"I've already decided, can't you get that through your head?" She sank back in the pillows and closed her eyes.

"Shall I come back later?"

She rolled her head slowly from side to side, a tear squeezing from under her closed lids. "No, I'll be alright. Sometimes the whole mess just gets to me and I have to sort it out."

It was less than a minute later when she pulled herself into a sitting position again. "Thanks, I'm OK now. Where were we? Oh, yes, I was just going to ask you what choice I have of... of... God, how do you say it without sounding like a ghoul? Do I have some say in what I look like?"

"No..."

"Then you could put me in some fifty

year old hag?"

He laughed but stopped when he saw she didn't think it was funny. He mused that his mother probably wouldn't have thought it very funny either. "It works this way. If you're selected . . ."

"You mean I might be turned down?"

Her habit of interrupting was annoying. "Yes, you might. I don't have the final say."

"Who does?"

"Dr. Steinke."

"That creep? I've seen him a few times when they were looking for a kidney for me."

"He's a brilliant and very compassionate man," he said, understanding her reaction.

"If you say so. But go on . . ."

"If you're accepted for the program . . ."

"What am I, some animal with a number?"

She was beginning to get to him, but he held himself in check and continued, ". . . you'll be admitted to the hospital and given a thorough exam—physical, mental, chemical, and X ray. Dr. Jon Kettering will tell us when you're ready. He's been in our program from the very start, a year and a half now. We'll already be keeping our eyes open for a candidate for your brain. Once Kettering gives us the go sign, you can go home unless there's a likely recipient already in the hospital. You'll have to be available every minute of every day, because sometimes we have to move in quickly."

She eyed him like a child watching an ice-cream cone melt in the sun. Her lower lip quivered but she was unaware of it. He had given her the facts straight across the counter. He had tried to remain unemotional, for the atmosphere was always so supercharged on the patient's side. Sometimes he longed to sit down with his arms around the patient, soothe him or her with platitudes. But that would not have worked. His job was to be as coolly scientific as he could, while showing signs of real concern for the needs of the patient.

"What do your parents think of all this?" he asked, to break up the tension a little.

"Wasn't that on my chart? My mother had polycystic kidneys too and lived just a few years after I was born. My father was in high steel, got blown off a girder seven hundred feet off the ground. Three years ago. No sibs. That's the main reason they couldn't find me a kidney. So this is my baby, all the way."

Rather than fluster her, talking about her father seemed to calm her. She went on for several minutes describing how great her dad had been to her, raising her without a woman in the house, remembering birthdays, sending her to the University of Illinois at Champaign-Urbana. "He never treated me as if I were handicapped. Made me clean up my room, carry out the garbage, pushed me to get into all the normal activities, you know? Then, when he could see I was starting to droop, he'd ease off a little, and pretty soon it was time for another dialysis. Unless I was really out on my feet—and we didn't usually let it go that long—he'd put me on a bus and I'd go down to the hospital by myself. At first I thought he was just trying to bury the thing, because of mother, you know, but I see now that he was trying to make me treat this whole mess with as much disdain as I could. Not let it interrupt my life any more than it had to. Not feel sorry for myself."

"It worked," he said.

"It worked." The quivering of her mouth was gone and she was sitting straight up in bed. "I hardly ever get bitter about it any more."

"Time's up," a technician said. She disconnected the unit, flushed the butterfly with heparin, capped the Luerlok, taped it securely to Andrea's arm.

Andrea got out of bed, stood defiantly before him. He struggled up out of his low chair and was surprised to find her eyes on a level with him.

"You're as tall as I am," he said.

She laughed and then the smile faded just a bit but hovered at the corners of her mouth. "Will I be? In my reincarnation?"

18

He tried not to wake Britt as he rolled out of bed and started dressing, but she reached up to the headboard light and turned it on. "What's the matter, Merc?" she asked as she covered her eyes with the back of her hand.

"Can't sleep. Keep thinking of that little gal we did ten days ago. Something's wrong and I can't figure what."

"You going down to the hospital?"

"I don't know."

"What could you do?"

"That's the frustrating thing. Probably nothing."

She was awake now and sat up. "I'll

make some coffee."

They sat in the cold glare of the kitchen lights, Reynolds wide awake, staring into his cup, Britt groggy but anxious. A heavy winter rain slashed at the windows. The lights flickered, dimmed, blacked out. He reached behind him and rummaged for a candle in the drawer and finally found one. He lit it, dripped some wax on the oilcloth and set the candle into it. The uneven light threw shadows upwards on their faces, accenting the dark circles under Britt's eyes and sharpening the planes on Reynolds' cheeks and jaws. They sipped their coffee in silence, listening to the thunder rumbling in the outside darkness.

The lights came back on and Britt stirred uneasily. "There's more to this case than you're telling me. You've never acted like this before." Her blue eyes watched him warily.

He nodded.

"Want to tell me about it?" she asked.

Should he? Would she understand? Yes, to both.

"It isn't just this case," he said. "It's been all of them, but this is the most intense."

"What *are* you *talk*ing about?" She felt a strange dread, a premonition of disaster, as if any moment the owl might call. She stared in Reynolds' blank eyes, listened to that hollow voice, watched the tic-like jerkiness of his fingers. She sat tensely, back stiff, both hands flat on the table, coffee forgotten.

"In every case, except one old codger, Case #7, that we probably shouldn't have done, I've had the feeling I knew what was going on in their minds."

She drew in a deep breath. "You mean before the transplant?"

He shook his head rapidly. "No, afterwards." He slumped on his spine, half-closed his eyes, and watched for her reaction. "When I stand close to them, and put my hand on their foreheads, I think I'm getting messages from those transplanted brains."

"Merc!" Her hands went to her face in an unconscious gesture of denial.

"I know. It sounds unreal. At first I didn't believe it myself."

"But now . . .?"

"The first ones we did are starting to talk. They're telling me what went on in their heads." He sat up slowly, eyes wide. "Britt, I *was* getting their thoughts."

A flash of lightning lit up the room and a crash of thunder jolted the entire house. It was in just such a thunder storm that Reynolds had been born and in which his father had died.

He closed his eyes. He could almost hear his heart beating. Sweat oozed out into the palms of his hand.

"Have you told anyone else?" Britt

asked in a whisper.

"Just Hal, a long time ago before I was even sure. But nobody at the hospital." He stood up. "I think I'll go in. She needs me."

Britt didn't ask what he meant by that. He was glad because he didn't know himself.

He nodded a greeting to the uniformed guard half asleep in the foyer, ran up the stairs to the third floor and walked rapidly down the corridor to Ward 30. His footsteps echoed eerily in the hush of the deserted hallway. He fished his keyring from his pocket and let himself into Gonzaga's office and switched on the computer console. He ordered up the information from the past three readings of the sensor skullcap and vest. There had been no change at all. That was the scary part.

He turned off the console, left the room and locked the door behind him. For just a moment he stood quietly, tapping the key in the palm of his hand. Then he shoved the keys into his pocket and strode toward Andrea's room.

She didn't look like Andrea Hughes, of course, for she was in another girl's body. It always took an actual effort of the will for Reynolds to re-adjust to a patient's new appearance. As the recipient of Andrea's brain, Steinke had found a pretty, blonde young girl of eighteen with a potentially perfect body and a pre-senile brain. Two years before, she had been hit by a variant of Alzheimer's disease, twenty years earlier than its average age of onset.

Although the cause of the premature brain degeneration was unknown, the doctors were convinced it *was* a disease of the brain and not of the peripheral nerves or spinal cord. They were certain that the muscles would return to normal once they were innervated by a normal brain. Inarticulate, and bedridden, Jenny Freeman had no memory of her past, no interest in her present, and no concern for her future. She was a vegetable.

Her parents had been quick to sign a permit to allow Andrea's brain to be implanted in Jenny's braincase. They just didn't ever want to see her after the operation. The doctors agreed that that was normal and much to be preferred. It would have been an impossible situation if they had wanted their daughter back.

The surgery had gone exceptionally well, the early postoperative course smoothly. It was now almost two weeks since the transplant.

The respirator triggered electronically every three seconds and Andrea's chest expanded slowly and contracted with a rush. The heart monitor above the bed showed a normal sinus rhythm and a steady rate of 110. She lay on her side, the upper leg held away from the lower by a thick pillow. Another pillow supported her back. The water mattress swayed gently with each respiration. Her color was good. Her long blonde hair was gone, of course, but the fluffy golden two weeks' growth was beginning to peak out from under the tightly-fitting skullcap sensor. The vest sensor moved rhythmically with her breathing and was in perfect position, its edges following the skin markings all around. She looked liked she was in a deep sleep.

He lifted an eyelid and shone his penlight into it. No reaction from the pupil. He didn't really expect any yet. But the fingers of his hand tingled with an increased warmth almost like an infinitesimal shock. He lifted his hand quickly. He resisted the urge to call the nurse and checked her temperature again and then the connections to all the electrical apparati: the bed itself, the heart monitor, the respirator, the black box into which the enlon cable went. He could find nothing wrong. He touched Andrea again and there it was, a peculiar sensation running through his fingers and spreading out all over his body. He lifted his hand and it disappeared.

He pulled up a chair and sat down, then lay his hand on her forehead. This time the sensation was different, still slightly electrical, but more pleasant. He closed his eyes and concentrated. He could feel the rhythmic movement of the respirator, synchronized his own respirations to it. The hum of the machinery was in itself hypnotic and he let himself slide down into the dark folds of velvety softness, farther, farther, still farther.

There was no blinding light, no burning bush, no rain of fire, no thundering voice from the sky, none of the signs the gods use to warn mortals that they are about to speak. But speech there was, in an inordinately simple manner. It was as if he were thinking his own thoughts. As if he were reading to himself, lips moving soundlessly as his eyes moved over the page. It seemed, too, as if someone were playing with the volume control, for the words rose and fell, sometimes almost inaudible and sometimes loud and clear. It was his own language, his own words, his own brain transcribing in its own images. But Andrea was directing those images, rambling, fading, catching hold, rambling again.

For twenty minutes he caught words and phrases separated by long pauses. He had the feeling that she may have been running on more coherently than he could tell, sending out those messages into the ether in a steady stream, some of which he caught and some he missed. He didn't know then, and he never found out.

What he did hear was chilling.

"There's a bright

BRAIN CHILD

        golden

                haze on . . .

Oooh . . .
There's

    a

        hand . . .

            touching . . .

    He's here . . .
        touching
         electrically . . .
            touching . . .

The corn is as high . . .

    Oh no!
    The girder

        daddy

            the girder
            watch
              out . . .

Alone

    no
      no
        not alone . . . he's here

A little brown maverick is . . .

Help me . . .

cold

hot

spinning . . . dark spinning
horrible dark

Alone . . . forever . . ."

He took his hand from her brow and watched the EKG monitor for signs of change. There were none. The respirations were totally controlled so there was no help there. Perhaps an EEG would help, but he didn't know how to interpret the waves, and couldn't have hooked up the machine at any rate. Besides, there was no doubt at all in his mind that he was really receiving Andrea's thoughts, just as they crossed that supposedly impenetrable barrier.

Had he helped her by being there? Had she really known he was there? And if she had, how? There could be no skin nerves yet to carry the information to her brain that a hand was touching her. Yet he had definitely gotten the words, "He's here, touching." He didn't know what was happening then, but much later he did.

He stood up. His shirt clung to his back, soaked through with perspiration. His pulse was racing. He counted it. One hundred and ten. The same as hers. Coincidence? He felt drained, limp. She was in trouble. He could feel it. But was it just the disconnected ramblings that they should expect in a transplanted brain, the same schizoid junk which would jam the mind of any human deprived of outside stimuli, such as a prisoner in a dark, soundless cell? No, there was terror in her "voice," a scream still controlled by the power of her mind but close to the breaking point, a panicky cry for help that none of the other transplant patients had made.

Suddenly, a shocking thought occurred to him. Did Andrea somehow sense that the transplant was failing? Was there some mechanism at work, telling her that the union of her nerves was not going to succeed? Could she sense, like a patient with terminal disease, that she was going to die? He knew of many scientific studies which showed that most people know when they are dying, even though they have never been told that they have a fatal illness. From his non-medical reading he knew that literature is full of stories which, though dramatized for fictional purposes, make it clear that man has always known he can sense his own impending death.

In the morning, groggy from lack of sleep, he dragged out of bed and began dressing. Britt awoke and mumbled from the bed, "Y'don't mind if I stay in bed?"

"No. No need for you to get up. Your

class doesn't meet today?"

"No, but I'm meeting Maia downtown for lunch."

"She really likes her new job, doesn't she?"

"Well, she's only been up here a month."

"Does she know you're taking a computer course?" He clipped his tie on his collar and opened the door.

"Know? She's the one who talked me into it, remember? Hey, you forgot something."

He chuckled and returned to bed. She grabbed his ears and kissed him. "Get a nap today so you'll stay awake tonight," she said.

He tweaked her nipples lightly through the thin cotton nightgown. "I'll do that."

He decided to walk to help wake himself up. The streets were still dark at 7:30 and the wind howled around his ears. He slitted his eyes and stretched out his legs. He knew that his rolling walk was ludicrous compared to the Hal Foresters of the world. Hal Forester. He hadn't heard from him or seen him for weeks. Since he had dropped Maia, actually. He was glad Maia had moved to Chicago. It had been good for both sisters. At least for Britt. Maia had talked her into quitting her "stupid job" at Wieboldts' where she was insulted by everyone from bag-women to Caddy-drivers. The Reynoldses certainly didn't need the money now that he had gotten such an incredible raise. He remembered now that Maia had encouraged Britt to take that crash course in computer science so she'd know what Reynolds was talking about.

All in all, it looked like things were working again. Britt was much calmer. Forester had disturbed her. Clerking at Wieboldts' had been demeaning. Having no family nearby had been depressing, especially with Reynolds under such continuous strain for the last year and a half. So now it was all coming together for her.

And falling apart for Andrea Hughes.

He stood at her bedside watching Helen Rogers checking out a new nurse on the monitor. He watched in silence for a moment, then moved unobtrusively to the head of the bed and lay his hand on Andrea's forehead. Nothing. He didn't know if he was disappointed or heartened. Had Andrea settled down? Perhaps he was wrought, and there was nothing wrong with Andrea at all.

"Seems to be doing OK, Dr. Reynolds," Miss Rogers said. The new nurse stared at him with frank admiration and a little awe.

"I'm not so sure. I was here last night and had the awful feeling that there *is* something wrong."

"Wrong?" She stood with her hand on the monitor and tapped it gently. "Everything looks OK here, surely? And your computer readouts?"

"The monitors are OK. The computer readouts are static. But no, nothing seems really badly wrong." He sensed he was stumbling, lamely trying to explain things which were at the moment unexplainable. Miss Rogers shot a sudden glance at the other nurse, then looked back at him. His face flushed and he backed out and moved down the ward to see some of the other patients. He couldn't tell Helen Rogers that he was sure something was wrong because Andrea Hughes had told him so. For one thing, Andrea hadn't actually told him anything so definite. But he couldn't rid himself of the feeling that her mind shouldn't be swinging quite so wildly after only two weeks.

The next two evenings he went back to the hospital to sit with Andrea for an hour or so. He had not been wrong. Each night was a replay of that first night. He touched her forehead, felt a strange warmth, and then by concentrating he could hear her thoughts echoing in his brain. He tried breaking into them with thoughts of his own, soothing words which he hoped would help relieve her fears. But it didn't work in reverse. He remembered that his father Pan had been able to send messages to certain people who were receptive to him: his foster-mother Sylvia Reynolds, Phoebe certainly, and old Jed Schroeder. But Pan was different from Mercury. Pan could send beautiful dreams and wild flights of fancy. Mercury was the wing-footed messenger of the gods.

Then was Andrea Hughes sending a message, not *to* him, but *through* him?

It could be. And to whom?

Who else?

Victor Steinke.

19

He decided to pick his own time and place, knowing he didn't have forever. Victor Steinke was the most pragmatic man he'd ever known and would not even listen to a plea for re-operation unless the hard facts showed him that was the way to go. Reynolds remembered Miss Rogers' words, "Don't cross him unless you're really sure you're right. And he's rarely wrong."

So far there was very little about Andrea's case which would make a neurosurgeon seriously consider doing a nine-hour operation all over again. There were, however, a few minor aberrations which showed up on the graph, when compared to other patients they had done. Her pulse was a little faster. Her blood pressure remained higher, with occasional spikes to systolics of 180 or more. Even more disturbing—to Reynolds at least, who knew something was wrong—were the computer readouts. In all their previous cases, cranial nerve regeneration had begun on about the fifth day, the latest at eight days. Spinal cord regeneration was less predictable, but the latest was eleven days. It was now fourteen days since Andrea's surgery. The skullcap sensors showed that only two cranial nerves, the sixth and seventh, both pure motor, had started to grow. The spinal cord sensors showed no growth there at all.

Perhaps there was enough to challenge Steinke.

So Reynolds did, on rounds the next morning.

"Irrelevant at this stage," Steinke said. "In nerve regrowth we have seen all patterns. So far, third nerve has been first one. So far, spinal cord starts to grow in eleven days. There will be exception. This is it."

The abducens and facial growth continued slowly—half a millimeter a day. But the optic nerve—the nerve that sees—didn't begin growing. Nor did the olfactory, nor the auditory, nor any of the others, nor the spinal cord. And still Steinke persisted in his optimism.

Kettering was getting worried. Gonzaga remained loyal to Steinke. Helen

Rogers, true to her word, began to shoot dark looks at Reynolds whenever he pushed Steinke a little too hard.

Then one night almost three weeks after Andrea's surgery, Reynolds had the same nightmare he'd had before: the train car telescoping into a tight little box. But it was different in one important aspect. There was another person in there with him. The cheeks and eyes were covered by long blonde hair, the rest of the face bathed in bloody sweat. He looked closer and saw that there was no body attached to the head. It hung there in space like Macbeth's head on Macduff's claymore as the room shrank around them. The air was compressed till it was as dense as water. His ears ached and his sinuses throbbed. He swallowed and yawned but could not equalize the pressure fast enough. The pain became unbearable. The bloodied head hung inches from his face. Andrea Hughes. He screamed and woke up.

Now there was no doubt in his mind at all that Andrea Hughes's brain was still completely dissociated from the body into which she had been placed. It lay there neatly sewn to the spinal cord and nerve endings of the eighteen-year-old. The arteries had healed and pumped oxygenated blood into Andrea's brain. That was certain. Her brain was not dead. It was very much alive. He could hear it.

But nobody else could.

He could hardly restrain himself from calling Steinke and rushing down to the hospital to set in motion the train of events which would take Andrea to the operating room again. He sat on the edge of the bed, hands clenched, cold sweat drenching his body. The smell of fear permeated the room, emanating from his own apocrine glands.

His scream awakened Britt and she sat behind him on the bed, legs tucked under her, hands rubbing the muscles of his shoulders and back. She knew what was wrong.

"Go back to sleep, Britt," he said. "There's nothing you can do. Nothing *I* can do. I'll be alright."

Slowly her hands ran down the middle of his back, then fell away. She slid down into bed, her breathing rapid, tears in her eyes. He lay down, too, hands behind his head in the dark, practicing little speeches for Steinke until his mind was awhirl with nonsense phrases. There was nothing he could say which made any sense unless he could convince Steinke that he was really getting messages from Andrea. That big fat face of Steinke's rose before him like a moon over the ocean, laughing, deriding, finally fading away as he fell into a fitful sleep. The last thing he remembered seeing before he dropped off was a disembodied hand scratching on a tattoo on a disembodied arm.

He walked to the hospital the next morning, despite the freezing rain that slashed against him in the wind tunnel that was Harrison Street. The face he had seen in the bathroom mirror was drawn and grey, the lines etched deeply like those of a fifty-year-old man. He had cut himself twice and drops of dried blood clung to his neck and the corner of his nose. When he absently picked them off the bleeding started again.

Until that morning, Andrea had communicated with him only during the late evening when he was alone with her and her brain function was at its nocturnal peak. Now, as he walked into her room, he could feel the emanations even though there was a nurse in the room and the usual morning hubbub penetrated from the ward. At first it was just a low hum, like high tension wires, with a few unintelligible words breaking through. But when he put his hand on her forehead and closed his eyes as if thinking, her thoughts bombarded his brain as if she were talking through a bull-horn.

"Doctor . . .

> Dr. Reynolds . . .

>> I'm going, going . . .

Going to die . . .

> die . . .

BRAIN CHILD

      not gently . . .

      not softly . . .

    Do not go gentle . . .

Loudly . . .

  no . . . no . . .

   thunder rumbling

      on a frozen lake

Screaming at me . . .

      Dr. Reynolds . . .

Don't let me die . . .

   lightning flashes

      thunder

He's falling . . .
   don't let him fall

   he's my daddy

   catch him . . .

No, not him . . .

   me . . .

   I'm falling . . . falling . . .

    going . . . going . . ."

He took his hand off her forehead, gripped the edge of the bed to steady himself. He looked around helplessly, knowing no one had heard what he had. But not wondering at all why she quoted Dylan Thomas; she would not go gentle into that dark night. But go she would, unless something was done quickly.

"Get the EEG machine over here," he ordered.

"The EEG?" said a voice behind him. He turned his head and there stood Helen Rogers, her face almost catatonic. One hand gripped her uniform at the neck, the other out to the side, fingers shaking as if she held a thermometer. "You know you have to clear that with Dr. Steinke," she said.

"Find him then," he pleaded.

Gonzaga came in, took Reynolds' arm in his strong fingers. "What's the matter?"

"She's dying. I can hear her screaming. She can't stand it any more."

Gonzaga looked at Helen Rogers, then at the other nurse who stood frozen at the bedside, the IV tubing clutched tightly in her hand. "Did you hear anything?" Gonzaga asked. Both nurses shook their heads. He let go of Reynolds' arm, put his hand on Reynolds' shoulder. "Maybe I didn't hear you right, Merc."

"You heard me."

Reynolds was in full control again and knew he was looking the fool. "Get Dr.

Steinke, will you please? It's very important!"

The IV nurse fled from the room.

He felt a little dizzy and rested his arms on the high headboard of Andrea's bed. A deepening fatigue engulfed him and he lay his head on his arms. A peculiar odor drifted up from his hand, the one which had lain on Andrea's forehead. Not a smell he had ever detected from his own body, but one he had smelled somewhere before.

Slowly a scene formed before his eyes: a dark room, shades drawn, drapes closed, a bed tipped crazily on its side, the covers and mattress slashed by a knife. On the floor of that room lay a young woman, barely alive, her breathing like harsh snores. Blood from both her wrists lay in puddles on the floor and scattered in scarlet splotches on carpet and furniture. Besides the blood-smell, a sweetish smell of human sweat permeated the airless room. The psychiatrist with Reynolds had wrinkled his nose and said, "Typical of the far-advanced schizophrenic. You smell it once, you never forget it."

Andrea's brain was splitting in half, was at least in the first stages of a deepening paranoia, losing contact with itself as it had already lost contact with the rest of the world. Reynolds started to place his hand on her forehead again, but before he could do so, Steinke shouldered into the room, head thrust forward on his thick neck like an enraged bull, mustaches drooping, little pig eyes darting from the girl on the bed to Reynolds, saliva spilling out of the corner of his mouth into his grey beard. Reynolds recoiled.

Steinke stopped in the middle of the room, straightened up and wiped his mouth with the back of his hand. "Tell me already, what is this foolishness?"

Helen Rogers, following him into the room, started to say something, but Steinke waved her into silence with an imperious hand. "He will tell," he said and scratched furiously at his tattoo.

Tell him what? Reynolds asked himself. And answered: all. And so, in a flat monotone devoid of histrionics, he told Steinke of Andrea's early ramblings, of her later rational pleas for help, and finally of the terror-filled cries he had just heard.

Steinke listened to it all, taking it in as if it could really be true. Reynolds even deluded himself for a while that he was going to buy it.

When he finished there was a silence in the room that was broken only by the gentle pulsing of the respirator, the hollow hum of the machines. Steinke stood stolidly, arms folded on his chest, predatory eyes watching Reynolds like a cheetah stalking a gazelle, daring him to break and run. Helen Rogers stood sideways to Reynolds, eyes darting from him to Steinke. Gonzaga leaned against the wall, dark eyes bemused, wondering if Reynolds had finally gone bonkers.

Steinke broke the impasse. "You want we should do the operation all over again, is that it, Dr. Reynolds?" There was no sarcasm in his voice, just a hard unbelieving tone.

Perversely, his strident words revived for Reynolds the aching poignancy of his original interview with Andrea Hughes, recalled the Attic statement that she could no longer bear to live the rest of her life in a body which had given her nothing but trouble. It was time for him to take a stand.

"Yes, sir. If she dies I'll never be able to prove that I've been hearing her voice, receiving signals the rest of you can't hear. But I do. I've always been able to . . ."

"You can tell what I'm thinking right now?" Steinke said, his eyes mocking.

Reynolds allowed a small smile to play on his lips. "That would be too easy, Dr. Steinke. Everyone in this room knows."

Steinke didn't like that. And Reynolds didn't really blame him. He had been a little too cute. He went on, knowing he was licked, and knowing deep down inside him that if he didn't win this one he was through at Hektoen. Maybe he was, anyway. And knowing that Andrea was through as well.

"At least," Reynolds said in as level a tone as he could, "let's get the EEG on her, Dr. Steinke. See what the brain waves are doing."

He was surprised when Steinke turned and stared at Gonzaga, tacitly inviting him to intervene. Gonzaga leaned forward, hands resting on the siderails, brown eyes flashing. He was enjoying this emotional confrontation, a much more common phenomenon in his Islands than in the States. It was obvious however that he disliked taking sides. His answer was a masterpiece of shrewd compromise. "It might show us something," were his words for Reynolds, but his tone—for Steinke—indicated that he expected the EEG to dispel any doubts about Andrea's progress.

Steinke motioned toward the door with his head. Gonzaga and Miss Rogers hurried out. Reynolds left, too, uncomfortable now alone in the room with Steinke. He went down to Gonzaga's office and sat in the chair under the pickled brain and the pretty bikini. He wondered if Britt would be sad or glad if he had to leave Hektoen. Then he remembered the many times Maia and he had caught each other's thoughts in midair, knew she would understand this whole phenomenon—would believe him if he said he was receiving messages from a distracted brain.

He heard a clattering in the hallway and looked up to see the cumbersome EEG machine being trundled into the ward by the technician. It would take a half hour, maybe more, to set up the machine, attach the eight electrodes on Andrea's skull, and then get a satisfactory read-out.

He swiveled in the desk chair and searched the bookshelf over his head for a text on the non-surgical, non-infectious diseases of the Central Nervous System. With moist fingertips he thumbed the index and read the section on premature senility. Not being a doctor of medicine himself, he had never really challenged the choice of Jenny as the recipient for Andrea's brain. Surely Steinke and Gonzaga—perhaps even Kettering—would know if there was a contra-indication to using such a patient.

He read quickly through all the dementias, skimming page after page for some clue that nerve regeneration could be expected to be faulty. He alternated between hope that he would find something (and could run screaming into Andrea's room with the bitter knowledge), and hope that he wouldn't find anything (for he didn't want to be hit in the face with even a hint that his cohorts had been guilty of such an omission).

Just as he concluded that there was in fact no reason not to use the body of such a patient, a student nurse rounded the corner and stood breathlessly in the doorway. "You're to come right away, please, Dr. Reynolds. Dr. Steinke wants you."

20

Reynolds started off on the run for Andrea's room, the fat little student puffing at his side, her eyes wide and mouth agape. He ignored her. The EEG machine stood in the center of the room, as incontestable as a lie detector, the focus of everyone's attention. Steinke's back was toward the door, hands clasped behind him, Germanic. Reynolds had never hated him so much. Gonzaga was on his left, his profile inscrutable. Kettering, summoned by Steinke and informed of Reynolds' odd behavior, fixed Reynolds with a baleful stare, then swung his gaze back to the EEG paper rolling out of the machine onto the floor. Helen Rogers had pushed in between the bed and the far wall, facing the door, wringing her hands in her usual neurotic way.

It was in her eyes that Reynolds caught a glimmer of fear, and knew that he had won.

Although no one in that room was considered an expert at reading EEG tracings, not even Steinke, everyone could recognize normal tracings and knew a great deal about abnormal ones. Reynolds could see at first glance what had triggered the exaggerated responses in the people standing around Andrea's bed.

They should have seen the rhythmic, low voltage, oscillating alpha waves, ten cycles per second, of a brain at rest but not asleep. Or perhaps the slower, higher voltage waves of a brain asleep. Instead they could all see the basic pattern of beta waves, running at over twenty per second, interspersed from time to time by erratic discharges of ominous delta waves running at only one or two per second, indicative of brain damage or tumor. Occasionally the delta waves themselves were broken by slightly faster and very high voltage waves in high peaks indicating imminent coma.

Gonzaga was the first to break the tension. His voice was tremulous, so uncharacteristic of him that Reynolds had to look twice to see if it were really he speaking. He averted his eyes from Reynolds. "This doesn't mean," he said to no on in particular, "that the surgery's at fault. Maybe she's just being pushed past the breaking point . . ."

Steinke's bullet head jerked from side to side. "In no patients done to now have we seen this. Even in those with the slowest recovery. Something is wrong, terribly wrong."

Without moving his feet, he twisted his body in a slow arc so that he could see Reynolds. Wary now, not knowing just what demons possessed Reynolds, Steinke faced absolute proof that Reynolds knew something he didn't. Begrudging every word, he said, "You would be so kind as to alert the OR?"

Reynolds nodded and ran from the room. In the corridor, even as his feet carried him toward the phone, he had to fight down an urge to return to Andrea. His instincts of self-preservation prevented him. He just couldn't bear to make a further spectacle of himself in front of Steinke and Helen Rogers. Perhaps there would be a moment later on when he could be alone with her.

The next few hours were burned forever into his brain. He sat at his console in the Hektoen Institute while Gonzaga and Steinke worked feverishly to right whatever had gone wrong. Reynolds hadn't had a chance to get back to Andrea, and hoped she didn't feel abandoned. Fear of desertion might be all she needed to crack that schizoid brain right down the middle. He hunched despairingly in front of the monitors, deeply frustrated. For the first time he wondered how John Reynolds had reacted to the inevitable roadblocks in his Grand Experiment. Better than Mercury Reynolds, he conceded. Cooler, no doubt, and perhaps more self-confident. For good reason: John Reynolds was in total control of events.

He watched them turn the bone flap, the dissection easier than the first time because the bony union was not yet solid. Steinke ran his fingers under the temporal lobes and felt for the arteries. His voice came to Reynolds clearly through the microphone above his head. "Nothing wrong here, Dr. Gonzaga."

Painstakingly Steinke checked the positioning of the enlon strands to the unmylinated nerves and then to the spinal cord itself. He straightened, looked up at the TV monitoring camera. Reynolds had the peculiar feeling Steinke was an actor or an anchor man, gazing directly into his eyes. And his soul. "Nothing I find wrong with the placement, Dr. Reynolds," he said. "Do you want to check out yourself?"

"No," he said emphatically. And almost added that Steinke knew as much about it as he did.

"What do your monitors show, Dr.

Reynolds?"

"A very fast pulse, but you can see that. Nothing else . . ."

But suddenly there was something else. And he knew that no one across the street in that bright operating room could detect it. At first he wasn't sure of it himself, but then it became stronger.

He closed his eyes.

It was just the faintest whisper, a strangling monotone struggling across the abysmal void, unintelligible sounds gurgling from a Cretin's drooling mouth. Gone now all semblance of the girlish voice of Andrea Hughes which had said bitterly, "What will I look like in my reincarnation?" and which pleaded, "Don't let me die, Dr. Reynolds," and which had screamed, "I'm falling, falling, dying, dying, going going . . ."

And now dropped lower and lower into the depths, disappearing from Reynolds' ken. Gone.

He opened his eyes and saw the faint flicker of her pulse on the screen. Agonal beats, one a second, then every couple of seconds, then no more. As in a dream he heard the anesthesiologist singing out his doomsday song and watched the frenzy of resuscitation, knowing it was no good. But they had to do it, had to atone in the only way acceptable, had to massage the heart and shoot drugs and count the seconds and minutes away as if there was one chance in hell of saving her.

He sat there watching the nonsensical activity of mortal men playing with the immortal soul, trying to recall an already disembodied spirit, not knowing yet that it was in vain.

But he knew.

For he had heard her die.

The hackneyed phrase kept repeating itself in his brain: a part of me died with her this day. It was true. He doubted that he could ever again sit at a bedside and counsel a patient to have his brain transplanted into another body. He didn't try then to sort out all the conflicting emotions which assailed him. One thing seemed clear: he was through at Hektoen. They might go on, probably should go on, but he could no longer be part of it.

He didn't even want to go back to the OR. What good would it do? Andrea was dead, and he didn't want to confront Steinke.

The mid-winter day was cold and lightly overcast. Snow was starting to fall through the pale yellow light of the sun hanging blurred in the mackerel sky. He stood on the sidewalk in front of Hektoen, looking down Wood Street toward the Dental Tower of the University of Illinois, heard the roar of traffic behind him on Harrison, felt the nudge of white-coated doctors hurrying past him through the brisk wind, smelled the putresecent odor of the stockyards, all his senses sharp and clear.

He thought of Andrea Hughes. No more would she see or hear or feel or smell the world about her. That's what death is, he thought. You don't have to be buried to die. Just lie senseless in your grave of bone, unable to see or hear or feel or smell the world about you. Andrea had been as good as dead for almost a month. Her adopted body had lived on, unable to either use or kill the parasite within it. Until finally the parasite destroyed itself and its host as well.

A hand touched his arm, gripped firmly through the thick wool of his coat, shook him gently.

"Merc," Maia said. When he didn't respond, she said it again.

He turned to her then, saw her fear-filled eyes, and for the first time in days, smiled. He didn't even wonder then what she was doing there, didn't feel surprise that she had appeared just when he needed her most.

"I thought you were in a trance," she said, and tried to smile, too.

He wanted to say he had fallen from Mt. Olympus, his winged feet turned to clay, walking now like any mortal, no longer the messenger of Zeus sent to challenge the right of Calypso to hold Ulysses prisoner. He was afraid she wouldn't understand, would think he had really lost contact with reality. Later, of course, he realized he had been wrong.

But now he only said, "We lost a patient."

He could feel the fingers of her hand tightening on his arm, consoling him more than any words could have. He longed to take her in his arms, or rather let her take him in hers, cradle him against her breast, brush his hair, let him cry a little. She sensed this and took him by the hand and said, "Come on, I'll buy you a cup of coffee."

Almost immediately she dropped his hand and he saw why. Victor Steinke was bearing down on them from across the street, still in his scrub clothes, the loose fabric flapping in the cold breeze. Maia did not know Steinke, of course, but it was obvious from his attitude that he was coming toward them. Reynolds braced himself.

Steinke placed himself before them like a Greek at Thermopylae. Reynolds did not feel like Attila. Mechanically he started to introduce Maia but Steinke was not listening and interrupted, "You saw the monitors?"

Reynolds didn't tell him he knew she was dead before the monitors showed it. He merely nodded his head.

"We did all we could," Steinke said.

Was he apologizing? Was this his way of telling Reynolds he was sorry? Reynolds waited. Steinke waited. Maia watched them both, eyelids half closed as if her eyes could give her thoughts away. Maybe they could have.

"The anastamoses were perfect, Merc, perfect."

Reynolds found his voice. "Then what went wrong?"

"We do not know." He brushed his mustache downwards as though stroking a cat. His pig eyes squinted into the snow. "It was only the fourth we have lost."

Reynolds wanted to scream that that wasn't the point. The point was that they hadn't listened to him. Had ignored his pleas and warnings. Rage rose and boiled and then subsided into a terrible ennui. What could he say? Steinke was the ultimate pragmatist, born into a kill-or-be-killed world, raised in the holocaust of Hitler's Aryan supremacy. At that moment Reynolds felt almost as sorry for Steinke as he did for Andrea Hughes.

Steinke hugged his fat chest with both arms, the cold beginning to penetrate the light cotton scrub suit. The sun was gone and the snow was getting heavier. "Come see me this afternoon, we talk."

Reynolds nodded curtly, knowing he would have to, even if it were just to tell Steinke he was leaving. Together he and Maia sidestepped past him.

They found a booth in the far corner of the coffee shop across from the main County Hospital. When the waitress had brought their coffee, Maia leaned forward across the table and took both his hands in hers. "You don't have to tell me," she said. He no longer wondered how she knew what he wanted to do.

"I'd like to," he answered, and pushed back into the corner of the booth so he could look out the window onto the street.

She sipped her coffee and waited.

"I want to tell you something I've never told anyone else in the whole world. Not even Britt."

"Not even Britt? Merc, she's your *wife*."

"That's precisely why I couldn't tell her. Not yet, anyway. Maybe someday."

"Then why are you telling me?"

"You'll understand."

Her eyes mirrored her compassion and spoke her thanks.

"I've got to start a little obliquely so you'll have the whole picture. Bear with me."

She nodded. "I will."

He set his coffee cup down, untasted, and looked out the window at the swirling snow. He told her about John Reynolds and his Grand Experiment which had produced the interspecific being, the blond young giant Pan. How Pan and Phoebe fell in love and had a baby boy they named Mercury Reynolds. How that boy grew into manhood knowing he was a child of the gods, knowing he was not only different from other mortals but had a mission to perform. Had had thrust upon him the onus of responsibility to expiate the sins of the first Dr. Reynolds.

When he finished he sat back, tipped his head against the wall and looked through hooded eyes across the restaurant into the blizzard now raging outside.

"Go on, Merc," Maia said. "You haven't told me this for nothing. Something triggered it. The girl, presumably."

So he told her, beginning with the clairaudient "readings" of the very first transplants, right up to the final terrifying moments of Andrea's death.

As he finished his longish monologue he saw that she had indeed comprehended what he was trying to say. He sat forward in his seat, elbows on the table, hands clasped in front of him. He was aware of an incredible lightening of his spirit, a peacefulness spreading throughout his body. He expressed it in the conventional way, "I feel a hundred pounds lighter, just talking about it."

She reached out and placed her hand on his. "And I thank you for it. Makes a lot of things clear that I couldn't understand before."

"Or more confused."

"No, clear." She traced a pattern in spilled coffee and went on. "You've always frightened me just a little, ever since we first met in that restaurant in Charlottesville. I didn't know why then. And now that I know why, I'm not frightened."

Her eyes held his, turned his topsy-turvy world right side up again.

21

It was several moments before either felt like talking. They sipped their coffee, watched the other patrons—mostly Cook County Hospital interns, residents and nurses—and slid down off the emotional high they had both been on. Reynolds was drained, enervated. Maia sensed this and gave him time.

Finally he said, "Haven't even asked you what you're doing down here."

She almost said, "You needed me, didn't you?" There had been a strange foreboding when she awakened that morning. Instead, she said, "It's my day off. I was on my way to your house, actually, to have lunch with Britt after her computer class. But I was early and decided to drop in at your lab for that tour you've been promising me for two years."

Her smile was infectious and his spirits lifted.

"You never have," she added.

"I know. Won't you be late?"

"No. You don't have to."

"I'd like to."

So he gave her a Cook's tour of Hektoen. It was all very unsatisfactory. He was tired and kept thinking of Andrea Hughes. Maia was still overwhelmed by Reynolds' story. But she responded with the expected "oohs" and "ahs" and "I sees."

On the way down in the elevator she said with a note of apology in her voice, "It really is terribly exciting here, Merc. Unbelievable what you've done. And here's me, little Maia Reardon from Charlottesville, riding in the elevator with the man who's responsible for all of it."

He thought maybe she was making fun, but the look in her eyes told him that she was as serious as she could be. She was really impressed and in her ingenuous way had expressed it.

They followed the tunnels to the front of the main hospital and caught a bus there. Hanging from straps in the packed bus, they watched the snow swirling into dirty slush in the streets, remarking to each other that winter is not Chicago's best season.

His mind shifted inevitably to the horror of Andrea's last moments. In retrospect now, he wondered if there had ever been a chance to save her. Her brain had exploded in a shower of sparks and then just sank away like a torpedoed ship. He knew he himself would never be able to stand the claustrophobia of being reduced from a 155 pound man with muscles and bones and fingers and toes to a three pound mass of jello.

He had almost forgotten Maia when the bus jerked to a stop and threw him against her. She gripped his arm and he felt a delicious warmth. She smiled and let loose. He returned her smile and knew suddenly that Maia must wonder why he had told her his story when he had never even told Britt. He knew why: he was afraid he'd lose Britt if she reacted negatively — and he was quite sure she would. With Maia he had been able to be frank — even intimate — because if she were turned off by his tale, he would lose only a friend, not a wife. And, he mused, he had been considerably more certain of a positive reaction from Maia.

Britt was at that moment opening the door to their small apartment, fumbling with the lock because she could hear the phone ringing. Finally she dropped her books on the floor and used two hands to manipulate the key and doorknob. She rushed across the room and picked up the phone.

"Dr. Reynolds' residence," she said.

"Oh, it is, is it?" Hal Forester's deep voice rumbled across the line.

"Hal," she said in exasperation. "I've told you not to keep calling me."

"Britt, darling . . ."

"And don't call me that any more. I don't want to see you. I don't want to talk to you. I don't want to have anything to do with you."

"I thought, maybe, once more, for old times sake . . ."

She slammed down the phone. She expected Maia any minute and didn't want to be upset when she got there. But she couldn't help her reaction to Hal Forester, as irrational as it was. She shouldn't nourish this hate the way she did. It had gotten a hold on her and she couldn't shake it. Not that there wasn't good reason.

She tried to drive him from her mind as she retrieved her books from the hallway. The computer course was extremely enjoyable. It gave her something worthwhile to do, and when she finished it, she would know programming thoroughly and would at least have an idea about developing those programs. And she would know the language and could understand what people—including her own husband—were talking about.

She plumped down on the sofa and swung her feet up. Her face burned again as she recalled that phone call from Hal Forester. Why did he persist? Weren't there other women around whom he could sweet-talk? With hatred raging up inside her again she remembered the day he had come to her apartment, a few months before she met Mercury Reynolds. She had been seeing Hal for almost a year. It had been a ball, right up until then. Then, on that awful day, he barged in, eyes alight, smile inviting her to make love to him. Instead he left in one hell of a hurry. As soon as she told him she was pregnant.

"My God," he said, eyes sparking in fear instead of love, "aren't you on the pill? Or did you forget? Maybe on purpose?"

"You egotistical *beast*," she said. "Is your mind so warped with football and Shakespeare that you think I'd try something like that?" Her laughter was shrill, out of control, and Forester had the strange feeling that that was exactly what she'd done.

He tried to calm her down by sitting beside her and putting his arm around her shoulders. Roughly she hit his arm away. "No, you've soft-soaped me for the last time. All I want from you now is the money to get an abortion."

That hurt him worse than the blow on his arm. He was not a gut-level, right-to-lifer, nor a religious fanatic, but abortion to him was murder. In this case it would be murder of his own child.

"You wouldn't!"

"Oh, yes I would. You don't think I'm going to have the baby, do you?" Her eyes were unnaturally bright and Forester had the feeling she was losing control.

"You could have the baby and then put it up for adoption."

"Are you crazy? Where would I hide for six months?"

"You'd have to hide?" He almost added, "In this day and age?" But that was unreasonable. Social mores may have changed over the past twenty to thirty years, but there were millions of girls, perhaps still a majority, who would be mortified, shamed, to have a baby out of wedlock. Many others wouldn't mind for themselves, but knew that their parents would be horrified.

"Yes, I'd have to hide! Charlottesville isn't New York, you know . . . and my parents aren't New Yorkers . . . it'd kill them . . . and I wouldn't want Maia to know." She started to cry and he moved toward her again. "Get away from me!" She ran into the bedroom and slammed the door.

He had left then. As she thought of that scene now she remembered that at least two things were missing from it. He had never suggested marriage. And he had never said he loved her. Everything could have been different if he'd said either or both. They'd had a glorious year. She had been proud of him. He had seemed proud of her. But that all changed when he left her to work things out for herself, alone again.

And now, as she sat in her living room waiting for Maia to come, her rage built up again. She recalled that a month later, when she was in New York having that damn abortion, Forester, god-damn him, had gone right after Maia. That son of a bitch had gone after Maia, for God's sake, that little snip, with no more personality that a sea-urchin. Less. At least an urchin could sting you and wake you up.

No, that wasn't fair to Maia. She'd been awfully nice this past year. She shouldn't share Forester's guilt. She was a good kid in her way, if naive—but Forester had probably fixed that real quick. And now he'd left *her*.

She thought maybe she'd cool off a little after the abortion. She hadn't. She hated him even more. What Forester's actions—and reactions—had begun, years of morbid concentration had now welded into an unreasoning hate. There was no longer jealousy, nor fear, nor the slightest bit of love left. Just pure hate, digging and gnawing at the roots of her soul, till it drove out reason.

She had hid the depths of her hate from Mercury. She had not allowed it to poison their marriage. Or at least she didn't think it had. But she could hardly stand it when Forester came to visit them, especially when he touched her. She knew that her attitude kept him from coming to visit Merc, and wondered if Merc would figure it out before she had to tell him.

The door opened and Mercury and Maia came in. She looked up and smiled. "Well, where did you find *him*?"

"Lounging at the street corner. Trying to pick up a sexy blonde. Instead he got me!"

He sat beside Britt on the sofa, hands between his knees, and told her in some detail about what had happened at the hospital. He knew Maia was wondering if he was going to tell Britt what he had told her. He didn't. But he would have to soon, he knew that.

Britt sat rigidly on the sofa, feet tucked up under her, curling the ends of her hair with her fingers.

"You're really going to give up the project then?" she asked. "After all this?"

He nodded. "My mind's made up." He played with the coffee cup Britt had brought him, tried to find the right words, wished he smoked a pipe so he could fiddle with it before going on. Instead, he sat back in his chair, closed his eyes, then half opened them and watched her. She waited patiently, finally asked, "Where would you go?"

Until that moment he hadn't really given it much thought, but suddenly he knew. He glanced at Maia sitting half-turned away from them by the fireplace. Had she said something to start his mind working? No, at least not out loud.

"The girl we used," he said, "Jenny, the recipient for Andrea Hughes' brain. Except for her age, she was an almost classic case of a common form of pre-senile dementia. No one knows the cause. But they're working on it. Maybe I could get into that research."

Britt's eyes widened in fright. "Is it contagious?"

"No, or at least we don't think so. Wouldn't have used her as a recipient if it was."

Maia turned partway around and asked, "Where are they doing most of the work?"

"Temple University. In Philadelphia."

His leave-taking was an anti-climax, not nearly as exciting as his arrival. He wrapped it all up by working with Steinke and Gonzaga in the laboratory and in the OR, making sure that they knew all he could teach them about the theory and practice of using the enlon implants. When he finally convinced them that he was actually leaving, both became avid students. He worked with them on two implants, despite the earlier promise to himself that he wouldn't. Steinke eliminated the dissociated monitor, able now to handle the whole procedure directly in the OR. It worked well, perhaps more smoothly overall than when Reynolds had been part of the team. The monitor system had been indispensable at first. Now it was an anachronism.

Steinke was almost maudlin as Reynolds sat across from him in his room on the last afternoon. "Mercury," he said, slowly scratching his faded blue tattoo, "another like you we will never have here in the Hektoen."

"Bull," Reynolds said, trying to make light of the deep emotions he also felt at this parting.

"No, it is true. OK, we do now, sure, without you. But it is all because of you that we do what we do. We go on. Jim Abernathy we forget, and Randolph Johnson, and Anne Moylan . . . even we forget Andrea Hughes . . ."

"Never . . ."

"We must. No, you're right. Not forget. Just not let *them* make us forget all the others who go out of here with new lives because of what one man—Mercury Reynolds—has done for them. And for science . . ."

Reynolds stood up, crossed the room with his hand outstretched. Steinke stood up also, came around the desk and took the hand in both of his. Their eyes met in mutual understanding.

"I'll never forget you and the Hektoen," Reynolds said. "Our paths will cross again some day."

They parted then, not knowing just how true those words were. Reynolds returned to his office, cleared out his desk, looked out the window once more, and left. No fanfare. No teary farewells. He had the feeling that someone at least should have sung, "Till we meet again."

PART THREE

22

Reynolds had no problem getting onto the research staff at Temple. They welcomed him with open arms, for his name was known to every one there.

The head of the project in which he was interested was a chunky, fortyish man by the name of Chester Snapper. He lived up to his name. He didn't walk, he bustled. He didn't sit down, he dropped into a chair. His round, florid head was completely free of hair and in frustrated moments he sat in front of the blank wall by his desk and banged his forehead against it. His nickname was Red, though no one knew if he had ever had hair at all.

He wanted to know why Reynolds had left the brain transplant project.

"Several reasons," Reynolds answered. He hesitated. Should he tell him about Andrea Hughes and the girl with presenile dementia who had been her recipient body? Snapper would be greatly interested. Later. "Mainly because I had contributed all I could and thought it was time to move on."

Snapper accepted that and said no more about it. He had talked to Victor Steinke and knew that Reynolds had left freely and under no cloud. If Reynolds did not want to confide in him yet, so be it. They went out into the labs, and Snapper said with a flourish of his hand toward the complex, "This is where you'll work—first for us, then with us, and eventually, no doubt"—his smile was sardonic—"over us."

Flamboyantly he described his work and then slowly began to lead Reynolds into the specific research he wanted Reynolds to do. "For many years all we knew about presenile dementia was that it was always fatal. Now we're on to something. Some day soon, someone—maybe you—will put it all together."

He took a deep breath, let it out in a rush. "Our research is along two lines. One, our neurologists are doing in-depth studies of living patients, cataloguing every detail" —he pinched his thumb and index finger together—"every symptom, no matter how trivial, every physical sign, no matter how minor. All this information is fed into our computer for storage and later analysis."

He plumped his round body onto the edge of a desk. "The second line of investigation is in this lab—the meticulous postmortem dissection of the bodies of the victims, especially the central nervous system: brain, cranial nerves, spinal cord, peripheral nerves." He giggled. "You may have to sleep in the bathtub. You'll smell like a freshman medical student from the formaldehyde."

Reynolds and Britt found an apartment in downtown Philadephia, in a row house, an easy drive from the university. They moved in their collection of motley furniture and almost immediately felt at home. There was even a working fireplace in the living room, which Reynolds thought would be handy for Hal Forester to throw his ice cubes into whenever he came for a visit. If he ever did. Hal was still with the Philadelphia Eagles, and had an apartment somewhere in town, though Reynolds was no longer sure he had the right address. They had drifted apart since Forester had kicked Maia out.

Maia had stayed in Chicago, disappointed that the Reynoldses had moved, wishing she could stay close to Britt whom she felt still needed her close by, more now than ever. And she missed Mercury, too. He had become very important in her life. But she couldn't just follow them around the country every time they moved. She had her own life to lead, and it should not depend on either Mercury or Britt Reynolds.

The work Reynolds did now was pure, primary research. He felt that he had come home, back into the lab where he belonged, away from the strange world of crowded wards and breaking hearts, isolated from the staring eyes and pleading voices of little girls like Andrea Hughes.

He was not ignorant of the fact that the specimens he worked on came from once-living people. But he did not have to watch them—or hear them—die. The specimens had already been cultured by the bacteriologists and virologists, studied by electron-photo-micrography by the cellular biologists, and then came to him for what turned out to be incredibly complex and demanding work.

And Snapper was right: he went home each night smelling of formaldehyde, despite all attempts to wash the stuff off.

For several months, from his arrival in March, up until mid-October, he worked twelve to fourteen hours a day: eight to ten hours in the lab, then several more hours at night reading and studying. Then he began to notice that he couldn't concentrate at night for as long as he once did, had trouble motivating himself to get out of bed in the morning. He tired more easily, needed more sleep at night and frequently took naps during the daytime, something he had seldom done before unless he had been up all night.

One night Britt eyed him anxiously and spoke to him about it. He tried to laugh it off by saying, "You don't realize that I'm not the young buck you married."

She didn't share his optimism, didn't think it at all funny. "You can't even climb a flight of stairs anymore without stopping to catch your breath at the top. You used to *run* up stairs and never even breathe hard."

He pulled up his pant legs and held his pale limbs up for her to see. "See, no ankle edema."

"Don't joke. I didn't say you had heart disease. Just that you're not yourself."

"Maybe I need a vacation. Haven't really had one since the Caymans."

Her eyes lit up. "Let's go back."

"You know I can't take that much time now."

"Well, let's go *some*where. Please, Merc?"

So they did. They packed up the car and drove south into the warm late summer. Each day he felt his strength improving and by the time they had visited his mother at Standing Oaks, he was back to his normal self. Britt was overjoyed. He wondered if his illness had been psychosomatic.

"See," he said, "that was all I needed."

But within a week after returning, all his old symptoms were back. He began, finally, to worry.

He asked a lab tech to do a blood count. When it came back normal, he felt better for a couple of days. Surely, he thought, there can't be anything seriously wrong if the red cells are unaffected. He was sure he didn't have heart disease. He knew just enough about medicine to be a danger to himself.

He continued to plug along, driving himself with the exhilaration of the work. I can't stop now, he told himself, not when things are going so well.

One morning he couldn't even get out of bed without feeling dizzy. He sat on the edge of the bed and slowly collapsed on the floor. Britt heard the thump and the next thing he knew he was in an ambulance on the way to the university hospital.

A few days later, after he'd submitted to a battery of tests, Dr. Thomas, his internist, came in and sat down in the chair beside the bed. He looked like he was on his way to a wake. His big lumpy body sagged and the flesh on his plump middle-aged face seemed to lack the strength to hold his nose in place. He ran a pudgy hand through thinning hair and had trouble meeting Reynolds' eyes. He kept looking out the window, at the TV, at the picture on the opposite wall. As Thomas began to talk, Reynolds looked at the picture also and later could still remember every detail—a green promontory jutting out into an azure lake—a small outboard-powered rowboat trolling planers—breakers frothing against the rocky shoreline—Lake Superior troutmen cruising for coasters.

"We think we've located your trouble," Thomas said finally.

He had something to say. Reynolds gave him room and remained silent.

"They tell me you work with formaldehyde," he said.

Reynolds nodded. "Have for years. More, lately."

"It's affecting your blood."

"The count was normal."

"At first, yes. Not now."

"The arterial oxygen tension was OK." He was getting uneasy.

"That's true."

"So?"

"Have you ever heard of chronic formaldehyde poisoning?"

"It's rare as hen's teeth."

"Not quite that rare. Very uncommon, yes. And less common than the acute variety. But we see it once in a while."

"So all I have to do is quit the lab?"

"Not as easy as that."

"What are you trying to say?"

It's not easy to tell a man he's dying, and Dr. Thomas was not very good at it. But he got through to Reynolds finally. The blood-forming organs—the bone marrow, lymph nodes, liver, spleen—were on the verge of total collapse. The body cells suffered from "histotoxic hypoxia," an inability to use oxygen even though the oxygen circulating in the blood stream was normal. It was like the poisoning from narcotics, alcohol, acetone, and certain anesthetics. It was just like cyanide poisoning, only slower. Just as deadly.

When he had gone—with a gentle wave of his hand and a "We'll do what we can"—Reynolds lay back on the bed and stared at the ceiling. It was one of those textured ceilings with swirls made by big brushes. He counted the rows and found where the brush made one more swirl in one row than in the others. But he couldn't find the transition. He puzzled on that awhile.

Then he looked again at the painting across the room. And decided that those fishermen had something after all. The steady drone of the outboard. The gentle tug of the lines in the water. Waves slapping rhythmically at the boat. Then a stronger tug, the line slipping off the planer and running off the reel with a tinny scream. "Fish on!" someone would cry, and for the next five or ten minutes they had nothing on their minds except to bring in that brown, or salmon, or rainbow, or whatever they'd caught.

Nothing on their minds but a fish to

bring to net. Forgotten for the moment was their mortality, their inevitable confrontation with the messenger from the gods bearing in his hands the golden scroll on which was written, "It's time to go now."

But, he thought, when you're Mercury, the messenger of the gods, who came to *you* with the golden scroll? Who was messenger to the messenger? Dr. Thomas?

He closed his eyes and, for the first time in years, wept.

23

There was anguish in Britt's beautiful blue eyes when he told her what Dr. Thomas had said. She sat in the chair close to his bed, listening with disbelief, then sobbed violently and lay her head on the bed near his hand. He smoothed back the blonde hair from her forehead while she mumbled incoherently. Her words were those of women down through the ages, but they were still true: he was too young to die, too valuable to science. Self-pity crept in, inseparable as always from concern for the dying: what would she do without her husband and her lover, how could she go on living? She went on and on, scarcely knowing what she was saying, and then lay still except for an occasional sob which racked her body.

Finally she raised her head and looked at him. "How long?"

"Six months. A year."

"God," she said, and closed her eyes. Then opened them. Stared at him. He knew what she was thinking.

He shook his head violently. "I couldn't," he said. And meant it then. The thought of his brain in someone else's body nauseated him. He had seen too much. Had known Andrea Hughes too well.

He thought he had been famous when healthy; he was even more so when ill. As with his move to Cook County, his transfer to Temple had been widely publicized. Now his illness was news. The Philadelphia Inquirer's one million Sunday-supplement readers re-read the entire story of the "magic thread of life." Letters and cards poured in by the thousands. One was from Mariana Crowley, the very first brain transplant to show signs of nerve regrowth, now fully recovered and living with a sister in Atlanta. She said, "Think about it." He knew what she meant.

The techniques of late twentieth century medicine were marshalled to save the life—or prolong useful life—of the great Dr. Mercury Reynolds. For ten days they transfused him daily with packed red blood cells. They gave him bone marrow transplants to try to instigate some blood-producing capability of his own. They discussed taking out his spleen, finally decided against it. They stuffed him with medicines which were unproven but might possibly help. They never gave up. They did not ask him about a brain transplant.

After a couple of weeks he did feel strong enough to leave the hospital. He went back to work at the lab, but not in the formalin-stinking dissection room. Snapper gave him a job in the computer section of the dementia project, which did not utilize his great talent for original research but kept him close to the work. They could still tap the deep flow of his genius even though the artesian wells were no longer bubbling. He stuck at it for almost a year, periodically returning to the hospital for transfusions, medications and bone marrow transplants.

Britt clung to him, more and more despondent. She thrived on his love and he couldn't give her enough. She lived on his adulation and he had retreated too far into himself to show it. He knew he was dying; she knew he was dying. The knowledge hung between them, formless but palpable, never out of their thoughts for a moment. She was drinking more than she should, more than she ever had. She seemed to be deteriorating almost as rapidly as he. He noticed it, of course, and tried to reshape his own attitudes. She saw him making the attempt and this cut even deeper into her feelings of guilt and inadequacy.

Maia came frequently, her visits helpful but leaving Britt even more morose when she left. Sometimes Maia longed to be the great man's comforter. She hid it well and was sure Britt never knew. She was just as sure that Reynolds did know. How could he not know? It showed in her eyes and sped across the ether to him. They never talked about it. He couldn't and she didn't want to.

During the summer, his hospitalizations became more frequent and more prolonged. The deterioration he knew would come, had come. In September he left the hospital after almost two weeks of treatment and knew he would never go back to work. Dr. Thomas had said, "Perhaps you'd better take it easy now, Merc."

"Thanks, Randy," he had answered. "I'll do that."

But there was something he had to do before making up his mind whether he would rather die than have a brain transplant.

He called his mother at Standing Oaks and told her he was coming home. They had been in touch frequently by phone and she had come up for a day or two every month. He had told her not to come at all for it would only disrupt her schedule at the university. But she had come anyway and he was glad. Now he asked her if she could get a few days off and drive with him and Britt into the foothills of the Appalachians. Would she take them to Jed Schroeder's shack and then onto the mountain where she had lived with Pan?

"Yes, of course, I will," she answered. "But Britt? You want to bring Britt?"

"Yes. I want her to know. I should have told her long ago."

"No, you were right not to."

"Maybe. But now I want to."

Yes, he wanted to. Indeed, he had to. Britt must know all about him before . . . before what? Before he died? Before he had a brain transplant? She must be fully aware of what went through his mind in order to help him decide what to do. They must decide together. It was not to be a unilateral venture. They were in this marriage together, for better or worse . . . in sickness and in health . . . until Death do us part . . .

On the way to Standing Oaks, Britt asked, "Why are we doing this, Merc? Shouldn't you be saving your strength?"

He resisted the urge to say, "Save it for what?" and merely said, "It's something I've got to do. You'll see why when we get there. There's a lot I've got to think about—and there's a lot you've got to know so you can help me."

"Alright," she said, staring straight ahead with almost sightless eyes, trying to concentrate on her driving. Didn't she have enough to worry about without putting more on her plate?

They stayed overnight at Standing Oaks. Reynolds sat in the big living room where John and Sylvia Reynolds had conceived the Grand Experiment almost half a century before. The old country estate in its forest of oaks had not changed much over the years. To Reynolds it was haunted. It was here his father had been born and his grandmother Penelope had died.

Phoebe took Britt into her bedroom that evening and told her the story. They came out together after half an hour, Phoebe red-eyed and Britt staring. Reynolds watched them come. Britt's shoulders slumped and her hair hung limply about her ashen face. She stood for a moment in front of Reynolds, speechless, half-demented. Clearly Reynolds heard her mind repeating over and over, "He's an *ape*-man. I'm married to an *ape*-man." He shook his head from side to side and started to get up. She put out her hand to stop him and then let Phoebe lead her to her room.

Reynolds sank back in his chair, eyes closed, tears dripping silently down his cheeks. He should have spared her this. He should have known she wasn't strong enough—like Maia—to handle it. But if she were to participate in his decision, she should know what he had hidden from her all these years. He still had confidence that she would make it alright. His own illness had drawn from him whatever sensitivity he had had to Britt's feelings. And he had never had much.

It was early fall in Appalachia when they drove slowly through the little village where Pan had gotten off the pigtruck so many years before. On the far side of town they stopped long enough for Phoebe to point out the restaurant where Pan had bought a roll and coffee and had been told he could get work out at Jed Schroeder's coulee up in the hills. "It was just a little place then, with a big 'EAT' sign on the roof."

As they turned onto the little country road, well-gravelled and graded now, no longer a green tunnel through the forest, she continued, "Jed was black, you know, but he took your father in and treated him as one of his own. Pan never told him the whole story about his parentage. Jed thought he was bewitched or something when he went into his rages. But Pan went up into the mountains, determined to rid himself of his devils, and lived there for two years in a lean-to he constructed."

"Two years," Reynolds mused. "What a waste."

"No," Phoebe said. "Not a waste. He had to. Nothing's a waste when you have to do it."

They turned left into the hills, following the meandering sandy track as it climbed slowly to Jed's old shack. The timbers were grey, curling away as the nails rusted and fell out, the roof falling in and the veranda collapsing. Phoebe said, "You lived here with me for two years, too, you know. Used to play in the pine needles at the foot of those giant white pines that still sort of guard the place."

He got out and walked around. Just to put his feet on ground where his father had walked gave him a strange sense of peace. Phoebe watched him, a sadness touching her eyes. She could still see the vibrant, handsome, blond giant striding across that packed red clay. Reynolds tried the pump handle. After a few foamy rust-colored spurts, a stream of pure sweet water gushed forth.

Britt remained in the car, quiet, dry-eyed, still almost out of contact. Phoebe and Reynolds sat on the crumbling porch and looked out over the valley at the fiery hardwoods on the small mountains in the near distance.

With a gentle wave of her hand toward the mountain, Phoebe said, "Pan came out of there after two years, Merc. Thought he'd worked out his problems and could live with people again. He couldn't. So he went back into the bush, this time without fire and without shelter and almost without clothes. He lived there like an animal for three more years. Jed Schroeder knew where he was, of course, and sort of kept an eye on him. But Pan stayed away."

She wiped a hand across her eyes and swept back the greying hair from her temples. "That was when Jennifer and I went into the mountains on spring break from college. Pan saw us, watched us, finally cut off his beard and trimmed his hair and put on some old deerskin clothes he'd made years before. He sent me a message the night before he came down to our camp, even before we knew he was out there."

"A message?"

"In the flames of the campfire. I saw him as plainly as I see you now, and knew he was coming. He came, the next morning, and I loved him from the start. He came every day then, and when Jennifer went back to school, I stayed with him."

There was a light in her eyes and Reynolds knew she had been in heaven that year with Pan, knew she had had enough love during that year to last her a lifetime. With a great ache deep in his guts he longed to have known his father.

"Let's go up on the mountain," he said, and took her hand and lifted her from the porch.

She drove them along the valley floor, across the little stream which had its start in a cold spring high in the hills, and parked at the foot of a huge pine.

"This is where Jennifer and I camped. And where Pan came to us. It's hard for you to grasp now, I'm sure, Merc, but he was younger then than you are now. He played the pipes he'd made from hollow reeds and hypnotized us. Or at least, me."

They were an odd trio to be climbing a mountain. Phoebe, a robust but greying middle-aged woman; Reynolds, a dying, emaciated young man; Britt, a silent shadow between them. He had lost almost twenty pounds of muscle and looked it. The skin on his neck and arms hung in loose folds. But they made it up the trail almost grown over with brush. They climbed to the rock-facing where Pan and Phoebe had lived, stopping often, for Reynolds was very short of breath and tired quickly. Nothing remained to indicate that anyone had ever been there, much less lived there for six years.

Skirting the rock face, they groped slowly upward another five hundred feet and stood staring at a mammoth dead pine. At its base was an oblong pile of rocks. In a voice tremulous with suppressed emotion, Phoebe said, "You can tell by the branching that this was a white pine, the way it's gnarled near the top, and doesn't branch regularly like others around here. It was alive then."

She wasn't looking at the tree, and Reynolds knew she didn't give a damn whether it was a white pine or a purple one. She was gazing in reverent awe at the rock pile and just trying to maintain control.

Finally a few tears slid down her face and he lay his arm across her shoulders. She struggled for words, finally whispered, "That's where he's buried."

"Pan—my father—is buried there?" he asked, his mind now swirling with love and awe and frustration . . . and an ethereal joy that he had finally come to the end of a long quest.

"Jed Schroeder did that," Phoebe said, "when he came up here alone and found him. Before Pan fell from the tree, he left you up there, a tiny infant, just born, wrapped in his leather shirt. Jed, withered leg and all, climbed up and brought you down. Then he covered Pan with rocks and carried you down to me at the camp."

Reynolds sat at the base of the white pine and leaned back against its smooth, weathered, barkless bole. It would come crashing down one of these days, in a storm. The same kind of storm which had taken his father's life. And would have taken his own, but for Jed Schroeder.

"It's all written out for you to read, Merc, his creation, his life, and his death. And your birth."

He wasn't sure he wanted to know any more. But she fumbled in her shoulder bag and brought out a yellowed manuscript, handed it to him, and started down the mountain. "Come down to the car when you've finished."

He read the fragile pages and handed

them one by one to Britt. She read them with increasing consternation and long before the end moved across the clearing and lay down in the soft grass, unable to continue. By the time Reynolds had finished, two hours later, the sun was beginning to drop behind the mountain across the valley. Phoebe was sitting in the car in the passenger's seat. Reynolds helped Britt into the back seat, started up the engine and drove out of the mountains to the highway.

There was no question now what he had to do. In his twenty-four years, his father had experienced a lifetime of love and hate, pain and laughter, frustration and joy. Though conceived in evil, he had been born in innocence. Though living a life of guiltlessness, he had died in horror, unfulfilled.

He wished that Hal Forester were there to bring everything into proper perspective with some quote from the great literature of the world. Then he remembered one himself, and with a grim smile, quoted out loud, "Better pass boldly into that other world, in the full glory of some passion, than fade and wither dismally with age."

His mother was looking at him strangely but with understanding, then took his hand when he added, "Or dismally with disease."

James Joyce was right. If he, Mercury Reynolds, were to dismiss his genius and die dismally now, with only a whisper and without a bold fight, both his life and his father's would have been in vain. There was too much to live for—too much yet to be done. He saw that clearly now.

24

Phoebe, Britt, and Reynolds returned to Philadelphia straight from Appalachia. En route, Phoebe called her department head from a phone booth in a gas station and told him she was taking an indefinite leave of absence. No, she didn't care if it did cost her her job. She'd get in touch with him when she was ready to come back to see if the job was still open.

Reynolds went right to the hospital, worn out, scarcely able to put one foot in front of another. They transfused him again, filled him full of blood and bone marrow and medicines. Phoebe stayed with Britt and brought her to the hospital each day to visit with Reynolds. Britt seemed to be coming slowly to grips with her new knowledge.

His strength returned and with it a bit of hope. When he told Dr. Thomas of his decision to go through with the operation, Thomas nodded his head and said, "I thought you might. If anyone knows what he's doing, I suppose it's you. I can't even counsel you one way or another."

"But you don't like it, do you?"

He shrugged and smiled. "If I'd been in practice thirty years ago, I'd probably have been leery of heart transplants."

Reynolds said, "If I can get Dr. Steinke on the phone, would you talk to him?"

"Sure."

Reynolds dialled direct to one of Steinke's command post phones, hoping he was there. He was. Reynolds tried to sound light-hearted, but failed miserably. "I think I've got a candidate for you, Dr. Steinke," he said.

"Oh?"

"Me."

There was a long silence at the other end, and then an explosive, "Mein Gott!"

Reynolds handed the phone to Thomas, who introduced himself and gave Steinke a brief but thorough summary of the case history. So clinical were they that several times Reynolds had to remind himself that it was he they were talking about. When they were through, Thomas handed the phone back to Reynolds. "He wants to talk to you."

Reynolds gripped the phone with a sweaty hand. "You see how it is, Victor." He had never called him Victor before.

"Yes, I see. Sick I knew you were. Whole world did. But this bad already?"

"This bad."

He grunted. "When you make history, you make history." His voice was guttural, as Reynolds remembered it when he was caught up in an unfamiliar emotion. Reynolds could almost see him scratching his tattoo and fingering the stethoscope in his lab coat pocket.

Reynolds forced himself to ask the question. "Do you have a candidate in mind, Victor?"

"No, not right now. How that goes you know already." He forced a little laugh. "But come ahead, we find someone."

Reynolds remembered his preoperative conversation with Andrea Hughes. She had wanted to know if she had any choice in what she looked like. It was no longer a rhetorical question for him either.

Britt found a room just a few blocks south of their old place on Harrison, on Polk Street near the rounded dome of the Greek Orthodox church. Phoebe arrived two days later after a hurried trip to Charlottesville to arrange a long leave of absence. Reynolds insisted—with some opposition from Britt—that Phoebe move in with her. He did not want her to be alone.

Britt had not fully recovered from the traumatic trip to Virginia. She smiled seldom, laughed never. She sat alone now in the falling dusk, staring out the window at some children playing in the street. She had lost weight and looked gaunt. Dark grey patches under her blank eyes never went away now, even when she took a sleeping pill to drive the torment from her mind. Her shining blonde hair had a dull look. Her mind churned slowly over the events of the last disastrous year. How did they expect her to be the same stable, reliable old Britt that she was before all this happened? She should be the anchor to which Mercury could moor. He needed her now and would need her more after surgery. She did not feel like anyone's anchor.

Reynolds had talked with her again and again about his interspecific heritage. He tried to convince her that his background was no different from hers or anyone else's on earth. Yes, some of his genes had come from Hermes of the *Pan* clan, but they had been corrected—relocated, inverted, or whatever. But he had failed to still the gnawing doubt in her heart. Yes, Merc, I understand. Yes, Merc, you don't have to say it again. Yes, in my *mind*, I see it. But when he stopped, she always said to herself, but no, Merc, in my *heart* I can't.

She looked down again at the children on the street. God, what if she and Merc had had kids! What the god-damn hell would *they* have looked like?

A great wave of anguish flowed through her and she fell sobbing on the floor.

Maia came to see him in the evening of the second day after his admission. She stood in the doorway for a moment watching him. He lay with his eyes closed but didn't seem to be asleep. She hadn't seen him for almost three months and was appalled at the change in him. She blocked out the morbid thoughts that crowded her mind and said softly, "Mercury."

He opened his eyes and turned his head toward her. At first he mistook her for Britt. How beautiful she looks, he thought, her pupils wide in the dim light, her golden hair backlighted . . . then he saw that her hair was not long like Britt's, but short like Maia's.

"Hello, Maia. Come in. I thought you were Britt."

She smiled. "Sorry to disappoint you."

"I'm not disappointed. Sit down over here." He sat up on the edge of the bed as she crossed the room to the chair by the window. She bent to kiss his cheek and then sat down.

"Welcome home," she said, crossing her knees and folding her hands in her lap.

A wan smile tugged at his lips and didn't quite make it. "Thanks. Strange homecoming."

There was an awkward pause. What do you say to your sister-in-law when you're about to have your brain transplanted? Do you ask for her advice when you've already made up your mind? What does she say to you? Will she tell you what she really thinks?

She will, and she did. "You're doing the right thing," she said simply.

"I think so. I hope so."

"I don't doubt your judgement for a moment."

"Britt does."

"She'll accept it. Eventually."

"Someone should be with her at all times."

Her eyes shifted uneasily. "You don't think . . .?"

"I don't know what to think any more."

"Merc . . . we can't baby-sit her . . . she'd never allow it . . . you know how independent she is . . ."

"Was. She's changed so I hardly know her."

"We'll try. Phoebe and I, we'll try."

"I'll feel better knowing that."

"Does she know . . .?"

"About my father? Yes, she knows everything. That's a big part of the problem. Mother told her, when we were down there last week. She went with us up on the mountain."

"You have no idea," she asked, "when you'll have the surgery?"

"It could be any time. In a week. In a month. If they don't find someone in a few days, I'll go home—wherever that is—probably to Britt's room. Maybe Mother could come to you . . .?"

"Of course." She stood up. "You've got my number?"

He nodded. Smiled. "Thanks for coming."

She wanted to smother him in her arms. Instead she quickly pecked him on the cheek and left. He turned to watch her go, then lay back on the bed and stared at the ceiling.

They ran him through the familiar gamut of tests. His old friend and sometimes conscience, Dr. Jon Kettering, had finished his residency and moved to Florida, his place taken by a serious young man by the name of Dr. Johnny Speers, whom Reynolds had known casually as a junior resident. The name didn't ingratiate him with Victor Steinke. But Steinke told Reynolds that Speers was a good man, a man to be trusted, Speers was short, athletic, dark-haired, with a baby-face that would always look young. He was well aware of his responsibility to the man who was the inventor of enlon, but he was not overwhelmed by it.

Gonzaga, too, had finished his residency but had stayed on with Steinke. Reynolds was glad for that. He trusted Gonzaga's judgment and his skill with the scalpel. His arrogance had tempered a bit in the past year, but there was still the slight hint of superiority in his eyes that is the hallmark of the neurosurgeon. Reynolds liked that.

Together Speers and Gonzaga readied Reynolds for the transplant. They found little wrong except his total inability to manufacture red blood cells. Another paradox.

Gonzaga soon formed the habit of dropping in to see Reynolds after his work for the day was done. He was in one of the private rooms along the main hallway, two doors down from Miss Rogers' office. The room was bare except for the nightstand with the inevitable Gideon Bible and a few of Reynolds' personal things. Gonzaga had even found a 27 inch TV set which he hung from a nail on the wall opposite the bed.

On Monday night, four days after Reynolds' entry into the hospital, Gonzaga appeared in the doorway with a broad smile on his handsome brown face. "I've decided you need a few new bones, not a whole new body."

"One of the things you guys haven't come up with yet."

"Maybe that should be *your* next job."

Reynolds liked that, too. The way Gonzaga kept talking about how things were going to be when he recovered.

They watched the Monday night football game, along with a few million other men—and not a few women. Reynolds was doubly pleased because the Dallas Cowboys and the Philadelphia Eagles were playing. He knew it would be his last chance for six months or more to see a game. To see Hal Forester was a bonus.

Dallas dominated play in the first half and the teams went into the locker rooms with the Cowboys ahead 28-19.

"Not too much of a lead," Gonzaga said.

"Not in pro ball." Reynolds pushed himself up in bed and said, "I guess if you had any likely prospects you'd have said something already."

"Yes," Gonzaga answered. "Thought we had one earlier today but she pooped out on us."

Reynolds almost missed the pronoun, then spun on Gonzaga, ready to blast him. But there was a glint in Gonzaga's eyes as he said, "We haven't come to that yet, Merc." He chuckled, low in his throat at first and ending in a high giggle. He was coming around, alright.

Reynolds lay back on the bed. "That'd be worse than a black man in a white man's body."

"Yeah, I can't imagine now how we ever

even considered that." He swung his eyes to the TV for a moment, then glanced quickly at Reynolds. "You worried about what you're going to look like?"

"Wouldn't anyone?"

"There are more important things."

"I'm worried about what Britt will think more than anything."

"She'll stick."

Reynolds wondered. But it was too late to worry. "You're not stuck to anyone yet?" he asked with a teasing smile.

Gonzaga laughed and shook his head. "Still playing the field."

They sat in friendly silence while the bands marched and the cheerleaders flipped their saucy skirts in endlessly complicated routines. Reynolds felt a wave of self-pity sweeping over him, a nostalgia for simpler college days, an altered form of "Why me, God?" He fought down the black mood and concentrated on the game.

The third quarter was scoreless until only a minute remained. Then the Eagles drove to the thirty yard line and were held there for three tough downs. They lined up on the twenty-eight, and their kicker sent the ball squarely between the uprights.

"Just one TD behind," Reynolds said. "They can do it."

"Just give your old roomie the ball and let him run?"

Reynolds smiled. "Quote some Shakespeare in the huddle and watch his eyes light up."

"Half those guys never heard of Shakespeare."

The fourth quarter was played in a drizzle. The field began to soften. With only a few minutes to play, the Eagles got the ball on the Cowboys' forty yard line, only six points behind. Two plays off-tackle put them on the thirty-one, third and one.

"They've got to have the TD," Gonzaga said. "And the extra point."

"They'll go for the first down."

"Not if Bart Starr was coaching they wouldn't."

"It's too slippery to chance it on third and short."

But they did. The tight end came in with the play. They lined up in I-formation, quarterback over the ball, Hal Forester behind him, the other back a step behind Hal. The isolated camera picked up Forester and showed his moves in a corner of the screen. On the snap Reynolds watched Hal. Suddenly his heart beat faster, and he wanted to shout, "Watch it, Hal, watch it. Don't go for it."

But Forester had already swung wide to the right of the line and was streaking for the corner. He had double coverage as always. The quarterback faked a hand-off and dropped back into the pocket. Downfield, with an incredible move, Hal ducked to the inside, left one man there with egg on his face, and now with the ball in the air he cut to the outside and gained a precious half-step on the other defender.

Reynolds closed his eyes, then opened them to watch in fear, for across the thousand miles from Philadelphia to Chicago had come a premonitory warning. Hal leaped for the ball, snared it with those amazing hands, and at the same time was hit from the side by the free safety. A nice clean tackle. But Hal was off balance from his acrobatic leap off the soggy turf. He came down with all the force of the tackle plus the combined weight of both men. On his head. His helmet flew off. He lay still, the ball still clutched to his chest, a few yards over the goal. The crowd went wild.

Gonzaga bounced to his feet shouting, *"Bueno, bueno."*

The camera panned the crowd, then zoomed in on Hal Forester. His tackler got up slowly, turned away in dejection, then looked back at Hal. Something in the odd way he lay there caught the Cowboy's eye. He leaned forward and spoke. Reynolds couldn't hear, of course, but he knew what was being said. "Forester, hey, guy, you can get up now."

But he didn't get up. And Reynolds knew he wouldn't. Forester lay still, screened by trainers and coaches and no doubt a doctor. The station broke for a commercial but Reynolds' mind still pictured that crumpled body lying twisted and still.

Slowly, almost imperceptibly, a whole new pattern of thought began to form in his head. There were no calliopes nor ferris wheels but there was a distinct sense—or quality—of grotesque carnival, a Mardi Gras. Oblivious now to the TV and Gonzaga, he concentrated on this strange phenomenon. Mardi Gras. Fat Tuesday. Carnival? Clowns? What did it mean?

Slow comprehension. Not carnival. Not clowns. Mardi Gras all right. But masks and wigs and costumes and harlequins and impersonators and . . . and . . . and what? Masquerade?

And why Mardi Gras?

Because tonight was Monday and therefore tomorrow was Tuesday and the day he would assume his disguise. His domino. Yes, his new face.

It was all too clear.

25

He crossed the room and switched off the TV, then turned to Gonzaga and said, "How would you like to take a trip to Philly?"

Gonzaga stared in amazement. "To Philly? What the hell for?"

"To bring back Hal Forester."

"Are you serious?" Consternation twisted his face but he perceived from Reynolds' look that he was deadly serious. Reynolds needed Hal Forester now more than he had ever needed anyone. And there was no time to lose.

Reynolds knew the Chief of Neurosurgery at Temple, Dr. Harvey Summerfield. While working on pre-senile dementia, Reynolds had sat in on dozens of conferences with him, had talked with him on many occasions about his own work at Cook County. Summerfield had been anxious to get a transplant team organized and thought Reynolds would be the perfect man to head it up. It had hurt a little to disappoint him, but Reynolds couldn't bring himself to agree. If he ever went back into brain transplant work—and that was very unlikely—it would be at Cook County.

So he gave Gonzaga the name and asked him to get in touch with Summerfield as soon as he arrived in Philadelphia. He would already have been alerted. Gonzaga gave him that raised-eyebrow look but his memory of Andrea Hughes was too fresh to allow him to doubt Reynolds' prescience.

"We'll have to clear this with Steinke," he said.

"I know. I'll handle it. You just get moving."

He moved. Reynolds called Britt, asked her to come down to the hospital. God bless her, he thought, she didn't even ask for details, just said, "OK, be right there."

While he waited for her, the phone rang. Steinke.

"Now what gives with you, Mercury?"

Reynolds laughed, euphoric. He felt better than he had for months. That his joy was totally based on self-indulgence at the expense of the life of his closest friend did not sink home just then. That came later. With a vengeance.

"I've asked Fred Gonzaga," he said, "to go to Philly and bring back Hal Forester for me."

"So I am informed. And who is this Hal Forester?"

Reynolds told him.

"Simple like this it is not," Steinke said.

"God-damn it, Victor, I know the routine as well as you. I'm going to use Hal Forester's body for the rest of my natural life, or know the reason why. If you don't agree, I'll fly to Philadelphia, show the crew there how to implant the enlon electrodes, and have Gonzaga do the surgery there. I'm sure there wouldn't be any problem getting temporary privileges for him. His name carries a lot of clout now, you know. Thanks to you."

Steinke blustered for a moment more and then said, "I get back to you, Merc. Do nothing drastic."

Steinke knew that Reynolds would never carry out such a fool scheme. He was just bluffing. You don't just walk into a hospital and show *anyone*, even Dr. Harvey Summerfield, how to do a brain transplant in a few hours. It would be like a medical student doing his first appendectomy by reading Christopher's Textbook of Surgery. Or worse. He hung up the phone, then picked it up again and asked the hospital operator to get him Dr. Harvey Summerfield at Temple University.

Across the street, on Ward 30, Britt came into Reynolds' room with Phoebe just as he put down the phone. "Merc," Britt asked, "what's happening?"

He told them. Phoebe sat motionless, her eyes shifting from Britt to Reynolds. Britt won't be able to handle this, Phoebe thought, she'll split right down the middle like Andrea Hughes did. Britt stared at Reynolds, her pupils little islands of aquamarine in pools of milk. Before he was through she was jerking her head rapidly from side to side. She got up and paced in the tiny room. "No," she said when he was done. "No, I couldn't stand it."

He was shaken. "Couldn't stand what?" he asked, knowing suddenly what she meant before she could answer.

She turned and glared at him, blue eyes still surrounded by white sclera. "You *know* how I feel about Hal Forester."

"Britt. It wouldn't be Hal any more. It would be me. Me, Mercury Reynolds. Sure, I'd look different, but you've been getting used to that." He tried to be nonchalant, even diffident. But it didn't work.

She lowered herself into a chair and cowered there, hands over her eyes, long blonde hair hanging limply around her face. Phoebe moved to her side and stood with her hand on Britt's shoulder.

"It'd be *too* much," Britt said, finally, lifting her eyes to meet his. "Merc, don't *do* this to me. I'm just getting used to . . . to what I heard in Virginia. Now you're asking . . ." She caught herself in mid-sentence and stared up at him. "How do you know . . . maybe Hal's not . . ."

"He is."

She stumbled out of the room whimpering, "I can't, I can't." Phoebe went with her, whispering to her words of comfort. Reynolds let them go and fell back heavily on the bed.

The machinery was set in motion. The logistics were almost insurmountable, transporting an unconscious man with a rapidly deteriorating sensorium almost a thousand miles. But they did it. Nine hours later Hal Forester lay in the neurosurgical intensive care unit of Cook County Hospital, on Ward 30, an EEG machine hooked up to his shaven scalp. As Reynolds had predicted, the waves were flat.

He had planned to remain cool, detached, scientific. It didn't work. As he lay there in bed, IV running, EKG monitor taped to his chest and back, nurses and house staff running to and fro, he remembered that fantastic leaping catch for the winning touchdown. Flooding his brain came vignettes of Forester lying on his cot in their dorm, quoting first from Kafka and then from newspaper articles describing his gridiron heroics. There were so many times in college when Reynolds had watched Hal Forester doing what he did best and envied him his strength and agility, his glue-fingers, his broken-field maneuverability. As surely as the gods had made Reynolds in the modern day image of Mercury, they had made Hal Forester in the likeness of Hercules. The gods that made him, as Dashiell Hammett said, had plenty of material, and gave it time to harden.

There were times, too, when Reynolds had longed for Hal's easy way with people, his friendly charisma, the feeling that what he did was right just because it was he doing it. Reynolds saw him now with Maia and with a dozen other girls hanging from his arm. From the dark recesses of the past he dredged up bits of conversation from their school days and from their meetings over the past few years. There was no way he could dissociate himself from the man Hal Forester. Forester was his friend. He loved him.

Now if everything worked out, Reynolds would have that body to do his bidding. The perfect brain in the perfect body. But at what price? He dared not think on it too much, yet what else was there to do?

He remembered the old saw about "not being able to afford a yacht if you have to ask the price," and knew that it applied to him and to Hal Forester. The price of the yacht was his life and Forester's death. They both had paid the price without asking what it was. Reynolds could afford it. He never had had a chance to ask Hal if he could. He thought the answer would have been, "No."

But now Forester had paid the ultimate price. He had bought the yacht, not knowing the price was so high.

26

Victor Steinke stood in the doorway of OR E, pudgy arms folded across his chest, green scrub-suit creasing the rolls of fat on his back and shoulders. Like a pilot ready to take off, Steinke's little pig-eyes swept methodically around the room, making check marks on an invisible list in his head.

Hal Forester's superb body lay naked under a white cotton blanket. His head lay twisted to the right, a thin clear plastic tube issuing from his nostril to the respirator. His eyes were closed. His grand sweep of reddish-brown hair had been shaved off, leaving his dull white scalp obscenely naked. There were no bruises.

Dr. Harry Jankowicz, the anesthesiologist, sat calmly in the hub of furious activity. Around him buzzed nurses, interns, residents, technicians. He was fifty-five, tall, lean, with a beginning pot, slope-shouldered from years of swimming, blonde hair close-cropped and eyes light brown. Reynolds had chosen him. Jankowicz was pleased—even honored—but not surprised. He knew he was the best on the staff. He tipped his head back a bit to bring the dials of the respirator into focus.

"Hell of a waste, Victor," he said, nodding in Forester's direction. "He was sure to be a Hall of Famer."

Steinke grunted. He knew of six million people who had been wasted with less profit. But no, that was not the way to think. He would feel different if Hal Forester was his son. "Thankful we must be that he serves some purpose."

"There's that."

Steinke's gaze continued to drift over the OR. Scrub nurse gowning. Myra Lockridge. Reynolds had asked for her. Good choice. Circulating nurse moving smoothly about her myriad tasks. Jamie Jefferson. Her great-great-grandfather probably took that name when he was freed. She's the most important person in this room, Steinke mused. She can make or break any operation. He wondered if she knew that he was aware of her role in the conduct of Mercury Reynolds' brain transplant.

He heard a bustle behind him. An orderly wheeled Reynolds by on a cart, started to turn into the narrow hallway between OR E and the scrub rooms. Steinke laid his hand on the cart and the orderly stopped.

As Reynolds turned his head to look at Steinke, he caught a glimpse of Hal Forester through the jumble of machines and people. His eyes darted up to Steinke, then back to Forester.

"I can't quite take it in," Reynolds said. "It's . . ." He stopped, unable to continue.

Steinke said, "Don't force, Merc. I know what you think." And he did. Reynolds could look ten feet across the room at his own body. In just a few hours he would be inside that body, not controlling it yet but prepared to do so when the signals started coming through. Steinke grunted. He had made an unintentional parallel. In reverse. Reynolds brain would now be calling the signals for Forester's body.

Even after—how many cases now?—thirty-seven?—he remained awed at what he was doing. The first ones were living near-normal lives now, getting used to their new faces and toes and everything else in between. There were now seven deaths. Eight if you included that poor little girl who jumped off the breakwater near Navy Pier. Twenty percent died. No, eighty percent lived. Almost all of them had had some form of complication: the usual ones

Birney Dibble M.D.

following any surgery, easily handled; and those unique to brain transplants, usually some form of nerve dysfunction, like a cranial nerve not completing its growth. The physiotherapists were busy. But there still had been no host-rejections of the transplanted brain.

Reynolds put out his hand and Steinke took it. "See you later, Victor." He smiled. "In a few months."

"I see you inside in a minute, Merc. You don't see me, but I see you."

"Thanks, Victor. Don't let my soul get away."

"The lid we put down fast, just let devils out."

"Not all of them. Be a dull life."

As the orderly pushed Reynolds away, Steinke thought what an irony this was. The prime candidate for a Nobel Prize in medicine was about to have the operation that earned him that prize. But there were many historical precedents. The surgeon who did the first total removal of a lung for cancer underwent the same operation years later. The pathologist who did the first post-mortem on a Lassa-fever victim died of the same disease. The list was endless.

Dr. Mercury Reynolds, the scientist who had discovered the "magic thread of life," now would add himself to the list. In the most significant manner possible, he would test that invention.

In the waiting room, five floors below, Maia and Phoebe sat in straightback chairs. Britt had come with them from the ward, fidgeted for fifteen or twenty minutes, then left abruptly with a farewell wave of her hand and, "You can find me at home. If I'm not back when they bring him down, call me."

Maia shook her head slowly and said, "She's going bananas, Phoebe."

Phoebe thoughtfully rested her elbow on her crossed knees and her chin in her hand. "I don't understand it. I thought she'd be stronger."

"What happened in Virginia?" Maia asked.

"She found out about Mercury's background. How much do *you* know?"

"He told me a long time ago—after he lost a patient he thinks he might have saved if he'd been more aggressive."

Phoebe nodded. "Mmm-hmm. Andrea Hughes. I remember that. He left County right after." She looked intently at Maia. "Interesting that he told you and not Britt."

"He used me as a sounding board."

"It doesn't seem to bother you."

Maia smiled. "Why should it?"

"For the same reason it bothers Britt."

"We're different people."

Phoebe stood up and moved gracefully to the small window that looked out on Wood Street. She shuddered involuntarily as she looked at the facade of the Hektoen Institute across the street. She played the same game that Reynolds had—*if* he hadn't come to Hektoen, *if* he hadn't gotten interested in pre-senile dementia, *if* Hal hadn't been injured, if, if, if . . . And the final if—if Britt hadn't married him, Maia might have, and there wouldn't be any problem with Britt now. She had often thought how much more suitable Maia would have been for Mercury. But you couldn't blame him. He was a man, and young, and had fallen, predictably, for the more glamorous of the two.

She roamed the tiny room for a moment, picked up a magazine and thumbed it, stood in the doorway and watched the activity on the ward, switched on the TV and immediately turned it off.

She returned to her chair. "Britt has more than an average dislike for Hal Forester."

Maia met her eyes, recognized the invitation. She could ignore it. Or she could tell Phoebe what she knew about Hal Forester and Britt Reardon. Would it help? Or would it be gossiping? Presumably Merc himself didn't know. Would it be fair to him if his mother knew and he didn't? She weighed the pros and cons and made her decision.

"Phoebe," she said, "I think it would help you to understand Britt—and help you to help her—if I told you what I know about

Hal and Britt."

A shadow crossed Phoebe's beautiful eyes but it was gone as quickly as it came. God bless her, Maia thought, she's the strongest person I've ever known. But look at the fire in which the steel of her character was forged.

"Britt and I met Hal Forester the same night—at an open-house dance at college. We were both at Mary Washington in Fredericksburg. Hal was already playing for the Eagles." She smiled wanly. "He never even knew I was there. Britt had that loose-limbed sway as she danced—provocative to say the least. They left together and I didn't see her for two days. That was the start of an affair that lasted for almost a year."

"I don't think Mercury has any idea of this."

"I'm sure he doesn't. Anyway, Britt and I had lunch together one day—she'd graduated already and had come up to Mary Washington to see me. She told me that she and Hal were washed up and she was going to New York to take a modelling job. I bought it."

"I'm beginning to get the picture."

"I'm sure you are. She hadn't been gone two weeks when I got a call from Hal. He was coming to Charlottesville and wanted to drive up to see me. Somehow it didn't seem right—but Britt had let him go —and he was such a gorgeous hunk of man! I let him come."

"And Britt?"

"She came back a few weeks later. She had had, of course, an abortion. But I didn't know it at the time. I figured her job had bombed and she was broke."

There was a film of tears over Phoebe's eyes. "Mercury must never know about this."

"No. There's no reason to tell him now. But I thought you should know so you'd understand the hell Britt is going through —*has* gone through the past twenty-four hours—knowing her husband will look like the man she's hated for all these years."

"There was no way to stop it."

"No. No way."

Like a rink full of swirling hockey-players suddenly frozen for the face-off, the crew in OR E and then OR F formed a silent unmoving tableau around the unconscious man in one room and the anesthetized man in the other. Then small movements and soft voices began, as the surgeons made the incisions, drilled bone, turned the flaps and explored with gently probing fingers the source of one man's genius and another's skills.

One by one, Steinke cut the cranial nerves away from the brain of Dr. Mercury Reynolds. The nerve for smell, for sight, for eye motion, for facial sensation, for facial movements, for hearing, for voicebox and intestines, for swallowing, and finally at the far end of the *medulla oblongata,* for tongue movements.

He gingerly bit away the bone around the *sella turcica* and gently extracted the pituitary gland without tearing its fragile attachment to the hypothalamus. He kept up a mumbling monologue, *sotto voce,* reciting to himself, as most surgeons do, each tiny step of the way.

Then for the thirty-eighth time, he made an incision over the lower neck, unroofed the spinal cord, and cut it in two.

Now the brain of Mercury Reynolds lay dissociated from his body except for blood supply and drainage. It was Dr. Hiri Czrza's turn.

Czrza stood poised, gowned and gloved, at Steinke's elbow. Steinke stood up slowly, muscles stiff from the awkward posture. Czrza sat down and without a word began the dissection. Steinke waddled into Hal Forester's room where Gonzaga was almost finished with his work.

"Any problems?" Steinke asked.

"A hairline fracture of the right frontal bone. Massive acute subdural and intracerebral hemorrhage. No problems for Merc."

"No problems for the footballer either."

"No."

Czrza's voice from the other room shattered the sedate silence. "Dr. Steinke, would you come here please?"

Steinke rushed into the other OR.

Britt moved in a daze from the Ward 30 waiting room, high heels clicking on the grey terrazzo, oblivious to the stares of the interns and nurses. Several recognized her and slowed down to speak, but she ignored them with a shake of her head or a wave of her hand. She didn't want to talk to anyone.

Outside in front of the hospital, she stood undecided for a moment, then set off rapidly east on Harrison. She didn't want to sit in that horrible little room on Polk Street. She had said she was "going home," but it wasn't home. Her home was . . . where? In an ugly old rowhouse in Philadelphia? A lonely apartment in Chicago? Her parents' home in Charlottesville? Yes, all of those places, if Mercury were there. None of those places now. Mercury Reynolds would never come back to any of those places. He was gone.

The very moment he had said he was going to have a brain transplant, he had left her. And when he told her he was going to use Hal Forester's body, he had killed whatever feeling she had had for Mercury Reynolds. He might as well be dead. No, he *was* dead. She would never be able to abstract the man he had been from the face and body of Hal Forester. She knew that face and body too well. She had loved every nuance on that handsome Roman face. She had run her fingers over every inch of that Herculean body.

Then she had just as surely come to hate that face and that body. Even "hate" was a sorry term for the feeling she had for Hal Forester. She *loathed* him. She *abhorred* him. He *disgusted* her. He *repelled* her. It would have been far better if he had been allowed to die.

She clenched her teeth and slitted her eyes. Perhaps he would die now, and take the ape-man with him.

"I have just started," Czrza said, "and I find a thick placque of arteriosclerosis in the right middle cerebral artery."

"The arteriogram was normal," Steinke said.

"Yes."

"You can cut it lower down?"

"Only by taking the artery to the retina separately."

Almost to himself, Steinke said, "And then blind that eye would probably be."

Czrza did not comment.

"The placque is calcified?" Steinke asked.

"Undoubtedly."

"An endarterectomy you cannot do?"

"Technically possible," Czrza answered. "Practically speaking, I do not think it wise."

"It is your decision."

Czrza thought for a moment. "No."

Steinke sighed deeply. "The left side is

OK?"

"Yes."

"Then do what you have to do."

Czrza clipped and cut all the arteries and veins in the cranium except the right carotid artery and right retinal artery. He then cleared the loose tissue which fixed the retinal artery to the stump of the already-cut optic nerves, asked for a clip, then another, and finally the scalpel.

"Now," he said breathlessly, "we must move fast."

His associate had done the blood vessel work in Forester's cranium. The brain cavity was empty.

Quickly Czrza placed Reynolds' brain in the cavity, pulled up the operating microscope and began to sew the arteries together. First the right carotid, which went quickly. Then the much more difficult retinal artery. He used sutures so fine that Steinke, standing only five feet away, could hardly see them.

Then for five more interminable minutes he checked each tiny stitch. Finally satisfied, he whispered, "Take off the bulldog."

He nodded his head in great satisfaction. Without moving his head, his eyes glanced up from the microscope and fixed on Steinke. "The eye has blood now, Victor. How long was it without?"

"Thirty-five minutes, Hiri."

"Too long. He will be blind in that eye."

"No one could have done it faster."

"No."

"And the other one he still has."

"Yes."

He returned to his microscope and finished the main anastamoses. From time to time he took a deep breath and let it out slowly, unable to forget the unavoidable failure.

Together now, Steinke and Gonzaga meticulously re-sutured all twenty-four cranial nerves, a two hour job. Then, just as carefully, they inserted the twenty-four enlon depolarizers into the nuclei of the nerves and anchored them with tiny drops of chemically inert glue. When all were in place, they gathered them together into a cable and affixed the bundle to the undersurface of the dura with tiny stitches. The cable was then led out through one of the burr holes used to open the skull and carefully taped to the skin of the scalp.

Gonzaga closed the wound while Steinke moved the microscope and sutured the spinal cord, forty-four tiny stitches one millimeter apart. Then he slipped down the four spinal enlon strands along the front of the cord and fixed them to the dura with stitches. Excluding James Abernathy, where the enlon implants were never used, Steinke had now completed thirty-seven straight cases. The most important part of the operation had now become the easiest part.

Birney Dibble M.D.

Jamie Jefferson, the circulating nurse, handed Gonzaga the sensor skullcap. With a sterile spatula he smeared the inside with sterile adhesive and lovingly molded the cap to Reynolds' head. He snugged up the velcro, then trimmed the ends of the twenty-four-strand enlon cable and temporarily taped the cable to the cap.

"Ready to move," he said.

Four pairs of hands slid under Reynolds' prone body: Jankowicz under his head, Gonzaga under his chest, the intern under his hips, Jamie Jefferson under his shins. From the other side two people rolled Reynolds face up onto the waiting arms and they carefully slid him onto the waiting gurney. The sensor vest was molded to his back and secured to his chest with velcro straps.

En route to the ward Reynolds was taken to X ray where a total head and body CT scan was done to accurately pinpoint the position of all twenty-four cranial nerve depolarizer nodules and all 124 spinal cord nodules. This information would then be fed into the computer for permanent points of reference.

Dr. Victor Steinke had successfully transplanted the brain of Dr. Mercury Reynolds, the inventor of enlon, into the body of Hal Forester, the Philadelphia Eagles' football star.

27

It was an odd feeling. Just to lie there knowing that all there was left of him was his brain. Head gone, eyes and nose and ears and everything gone. No chest, heart, or lungs. No abdomen, legs, arms or feet. All gone, his ashes spread with the night wind blowing out over Lake Michigan. But as consciousness returned, he fastened on one fact that neither fantasy nor delusion could dispell: he was still alive.

He couldn't see, didn't even know if his eyes were open. There was no sensation of light, nor of darkness. In order to perceive light or darkness, one must have eyes connected to a brain. This he did not have.

Might never have.

Meanwhile he was blind. Deaf. Dumb. The sensations which even now were bombarding his eyes and nose and ears and fingertips dissipated in the brain-stem and never penetrated to his brain. Conversely, no voluntary motor impulses stirred the synapses in the muscles, for no stimuli could leave the brain.

Oh, God, he thought, perhaps some day.

And so there he lay, or at least all that was left of him. A 1700-gram mass of protoplasm, connected to life by only a thousand tiny stitches, letting his past go in the cool glare of the operating light. At least they must have hooked up the arteries right, he thought, or his brain wouldn't be getting blood and he *wouldn't* be thinking. A wry smile formed in his brain and went nowhere.

He had no concept of time, not knowing whether hours or days went by. He slept, if that is the proper term for the loss of consciousness in a brain which has been transplanted from one human being to another. He floated in a black void. The thought came often that the world must have been like this when God was alone and had not yet created the earth and the stars and the heavenly bodies.

Perhaps there was an analogy after all. He, Mercury Reynolds, was without form, and void. Faceless, headless, formless.

Lungless, too, and gutless (in the anatomical sense), heartless (also anatomically). Formless. Just a brain, and presumably a soul. (Steinke had promised not to let it loose!) He could feel tight little rings of panic pull together around his thoughts like a purse-string. He blacked out, and when he regained consciousness, he thought, "I'm dead." But immediately a second thought intruded, "If I'm dead, where am I?" He was assailed again with the awful truth that he was indeed alive if he could think he might be dead. His mind subsided into a dreadful ennui, while Hal Forester's body lay limp and lifeless.

He wondered often in those first long days whether Forester was somewhere where he could see what had happened to his body. Would he laugh? Or cry?

Alfredo Gonzaga stood in the hallway outside Reynolds' room, watching Britt at the bedside. She had left her short beige coat on, and was hatless. Her long blonde hair was windblown; she tossed it back with irritation from time to time. She rested her hands on the bedrails. Her eyes were directed toward Reynolds, but in them was no sign of recognition, of love, of anything except, what? Gonzaga wondered. Derision? No. Hate? No, not quite, but yes, a little. Repulsion? Yes.

He started toward the door but she saw him and came around the bed and passed him by before he could mutter more than, "Good morning." He turned to watch her stride down the ward corridor and disappear into the main hallway. He wished she would talk to him—or Steinke or Phoebe Reynolds—or *someone*. But she never did. She came alone, stayed a few seconds or a minute at the most, then left. Today was the first time he'd seen so much in her face. Usually her face was blank. She would never make progress toward accepting Mercury Reynolds at this rate.

He shrugged and went into Reynolds' room. Britt Reynolds was not really his responsibility, but Mercury was. He was very satisfied with the progress his star patient had made in the three weeks since surgery. Soon now, in a week or two, the two branches of the auditory nerve should reach the inner ear and Reynolds would be able to hear and to sense movement of his head. This they knew from previous cases.

He checked the sensor skull cap and the sensor vest. Both were positioned perfectly. The computer readout this morning had shown normal regrowth of all the cranial nerves and the spinal cord. He moved around behind the respirator and checked the radio-receiver in the little black box. No problems.

Britt meanwhile walked slowly in the cool November sunshine toward her room on Polk Street. A plan was forming in her head. With the calculating precision of a robot, she had lost all human feelings for either Mercury Reynolds—whom she already thought of as dead—or for Hal Forester—whom she wanted dead.

She remembered vividly how Andrea Hughes had died. Mercury had told her in detail. Her death had not been pleasant but it had been quick and it had been painless. All she, Britt, had to do was get into the computer directing and recording Forester's progress, capture the information, and replace it with telemetry from a previous patient.

She could then do two things: transmit this misinformation, with that of a previous patient, from the computer in Reynolds' office to the one in Gonzaga's. And she would program, on a floppy disk, a new set of instructions which would transmit "null" information to Forester's body to stop growth at all lead points. Steinke and Gonzaga would act on this information as if it were Forester's. Or rather, they would *not* act on the readouts because they would see continued normal data. Meanwhile, the cranial nerves and spinal cord would cease to grow, and Forester would do what Andrea had done: his mind would become schizophrenic and he would die, literally without knowing what was happening.

She knew she could do it. She could walk into the laboratory—everyone there knew her—and make her floppy disk program. She could say, "May I borrow the computer for a few minutes?" No one would think a thing of it. She thanked God that she had taken the computer course to refresh the memories of her high school courses. But she must act before the auditory nerve completed its growth. She did not want Forester to be able to receive any outside stimuli, for that might prolong the dying or even wreck her plans.

He lay locked in a tight little bony box scarcely the volume of a quart jar, a coiled-up spring, ready to explode like a jack-in-the-box. The immensity of the concept overwhelmed him.

He didn't know if being a scientist helped or made things worse.

The scientist tried to be rational, even objective. The patient worried, no, anguished.

The scientist tried to anticipate those reactions which needed nerve connections and those which would respond to humoral substances circulating in the blood. The patient was apprehensive because there *were* no reactions, and the total absence of stimuli began to have its effect. He could no longer separate fact from fantasy, dreams from reality (whatever reality may be in such a state). He slipped in and out of consciousness without knowing what was real and what wasn't. As far as he could tell at the time, that horrible no-stimuli period may have gone on for months before sensation appeared.

Toward the end of the third week he woke from a sleep phase to the sound of his own name being repeated over and over again. A deep sense of peace surrounded him like a hand cradling a newborn puppy. A few moments passed before he realized that it was too early to be hearing voices through normal nerve pathways. For several minutes he waited for more words to come, but none did. Had he hallucinated? Dreamed? Yes, probably, he had heard all kinds of weird sounds, including voices, during the past weeks. But no, it was simpler than that. He was still Mercury Reynolds, despite the loss of his body. Someone "Out There" was thinking his name, or saying it, and he was "hearing" it. It was like Andrea Hughes in reverse. He was now the patient, listening to someone at his bedside.

An odd sensation occurred just before the words came through. He had the feeling of warmth on his forehead, a physical impossibility since his skin nerves were not working yet. Still, there it was, that comforting hand settling on his brow. He set his mind to the problem, glad for something concrete to work on. Eventually the explanation came. He knew that every animal gives off an aura comprised of heat and smell. The distance from which it can be detected depends on the strength of that signal, the environmental temperature, humidity, wind, and most importantly, the ability of other animals to register it on their sense organs. Dogs really can "smell" fear.

Someone was breaking into *his* aura. The blood circulating on his forehead was picking up the signals and sending them to his brain. He knew now how Andrea Hughes could say, "He's touching, touching . . ."

The incredible feeling of joy, almost ecstasy, stimulated his brain to heights of insight which it had seldom reached before. Suddenly, in a brilliant flash, he comprehended just how his brain worked when he "heard" unspoken words. It was so obvious that he wondered why it had never occurred to him before. A couple of decades before, a researcher had shown clearly that Broca-Wernicke's area of the left brain hemisphere—the main speech center—sends out wordwaves a fraction of a second before the word is spoken. And that brain wave is sent out even if the person only thinks the word without saying it.

He knew that most people could not sense these electrical impulses because they are very weak. But he could. This was part of his inheritance. Somewhere in the deoxyribonucleic acid on the double helix of his 47th chromosome was a receptor system for the unspoken word. It was not magic, nor supernatural. Not, therefore, inexplicable. He knew as surely as he lay there in his bony box that the explanation was not metaphysical, but based on sound genetics.

So, as he had done so many times before the operation, he sent himself into a state of total relaxation. By concentrating on blocking out all extraneous thoughts, he actually went through the motions of relaxing his muscles one by one. He drew a dark curtain down across his eyes to shut out all light perception. He knew that there were no muscles to relax, no light to shut out, but the mental exercise was an ingrained habit that had become a form of self-hypnosis.

It worked. He began to see words forming on the screen of his brain, a strange combination of voice and written word. It was more than a voice-print which shows sounds on a graph, needing interpretation by an expert. The words were as clear to him as if they were being typed in capital letters, yet at the same time he knew that it was a woman's *voice* creating those words. The words he heard were soothing ones, like those used by a mother to a sick child. Maia's words.

He did not wonder why he didn't sense Britt there at his bedside. He assumed that she was there but was unable to communicate with him as Maia did. But that was alright. In a very short time he would actually hear her voice. Then everything would be OK again. She would get used to the new Mercury Reynolds, perhaps even love him more without the humpback and the limp. He hadn't thought of it before but he wondered with grim humor if he would have Hal Forester's football skills.

One day, when he was in one of his more lucid states, able to concentrate on his mental gymnastics, he felt another sensation, strange yet familiar. It passed over and was gone. Then there it was again: the feeling of being on a merry-go-round, whirling faster and faster. Then dizziness, almost to the point of nausea, gripped him. If he could have screamed he would have. The horror of being unable to *say* anything or *do* anything gripped him like a steel hand. As quickly as it had come, the dizziness vanished. He had actually responded to some *external* stimulus. Abruptly he knew what it was. The nurses were turning his body to avoid bed sores, and the nerves from the semi-circular canals in Hal Forester's cochlea had relayed the information through *his own* nerves to his brain.

As distressing as the sensation was, it was a bench mark. He was *feeling* again! For the first time since his operation he was really convinced that the surgery was going to be a success. If the cochlear branch worked, the vestibular branch would work and he would soon be hearing again. God almighty! Just to hear something . . .

And if the eighth nerve worked, so would the second and he would see again . . . and . . . all the others would work and the spinal cord would grow out and he would feel with his fingers and wiggle his toes. God!

He wanted to get up and jump around and shout, "I'm going to be alright, I'm going to live!"

28

Britt clutched her coat at the neck to keep out the cold night wind. A light snow drifted aslant as she turned the corner on Harrison and walked boldly up to the doors of the Hektoen Institute. She tried two or three of Reynolds' keys before she found the right one and then let herself into the dimly lighted building. She hoped the locks hadn't been changed on Reynolds' former office door. There would have been no reason to do that.

She heard footsteps approaching as she pushed the elevator button. The night watchman hailed her. "Say, miss, may I see . . . oh, it's you, Mrs. Reynolds. Cold night, ain't it? How's the doc doin'?"

She entered the car and said as the doors slid shut, "Coming along."

The car stopped at the ninth floor and she strode rapidly down the corridor to Reynolds' old office, soft-soled boots whispering in the eerie silence and leaving muddy prints on the waxed tile. She unlocked the door with no difficulty and went directly to the cabinet holding the racked laser disk-packs.

She turned the tiny key in the cabinet. Neatly labeled were the seventy-four plastic containers holding the permanent computer records of the brain transplant cases, two for each patient. In a separate drawer were another dozen unused disks in identical containers. She knew that while Reynolds was still at the lab, cases #1, 7, 8, and 14 had died. Almost any other would do. She reached at random and picked Case #15. Albert Grovener. She didn't remember the name. She thought she would have, if there had been any trouble with his progress.

She opened the container. The laser disk-pack was eighteen inches in diameter and held on it one billion bytes of information, more than enough to record the information obtained from the patient in the first month after surgery.

She exchanged an unused disk from the drawer for the one of Albert Grovener and replaced the container in the rack. She held Grovener's container in her hand for a moment, then locked the cabinet.

Now would come the tricky part. She left the room, took the elevator to the basement tunnel and found the door locked. She felt just a moment of panic when none of her keys fit, but then she got control again, climbed the steep concrete stairs to the first floor and crossed the street to the main hospital. She slowed down as she approached Gonzaga's office in the hallway outside the ward. The silence was profound. She stopped, listening. No footsteps coming from the ward. Quickly she opened Gonzaga's office door, breathing a sigh of relief, thankful that Reynolds had needed keys to all the rooms involved in the project.

She went to the console and typed in the command needed to change the receiving code so that the information would be coming from the computer on Reynolds' old desk in the lab at Hektoen. Then she changed the transmission code so that the computer could ask for the substituted telemetry data of Albert Grovener.

Convinced that she had done it correctly, she made the journey once again across the street to Hektoen. The guard looked at her quizzically so she smiled sweetly and said, "I think this'll be my last trip. I hope so." He relaxed with his coffee and paperback.

Letting herself into the laboratory, she

went directly to the computer console and inserted the disk. Quickly she set the transmission and reception codes and ordered the computer to show her Day 22 of Grovener's hospital course. Then she pulled from her shoulder bag the floppy disk on which she had made the new program and inserted it into the computer. Rapidly she typed out the necessary commands to the computer to allow the new program to be sent to the machine in Gonzaga's office on Ward 30.

It was almost too easy. A high school student could have done it. Until someone noticed the exchange, Gonzaga and Steinke would get readouts every twenty minutes from Grovener's laser disk-pack. And Forester's body would be getting "null" orders which would switch off the depolarizers and stop all nerve growth.

She sat for a moment in contemplation, wondering if she had forgotten anything. No, everything was perfect. She felt nothing except satisfaction of a job well done. No second thoughts. No remorse. She was only doing what she had to do. There was no other course of action open to her.

For four or five days after Britt's treachery, the impetus from the depolarizers continued to work. Her timing couldn't have been more perfect. Reynolds entered a state of wondrous euphoria as his senses awakened, one by one. So long dormant, like a seed buried in dry earth ready to burst open with the rain, his eyes and ears and other senses were waiting. And when the signal came, not once but with a million tiny, lightning-like probes, his eyes were ready to see, ears ready to hear, muscles ready to move, skin ready to sweat and feel and blush.

He rightly interpreted the crescendo of sensations as signs that his nerves were growing out into Forester's sense organs. But so long had the senses lain unchallenged and so erratic were the first nerve growths reaching them, that they responded crazily at first, often with weird effects.

Blinding flashes of light penetrated through to his awareness. Scintillating flickers of color turned as if in a kaleidoscope. Pounding and ringing noises alternated with piercing screeches as if a train were trying to brake to a stop from high speed. His jaws ached as if all the teeth were rotten. Nauseous odors flooded his constricted world as if the whole earth were gangrenous and putrid. Then those awful smells disappeared and the cloying odors of August flowers bathed his brain. For one whole day—or what he interpreted as a day —his tongue felt swollen and seemed to protrude from his mouth like a man who had been hung. Prickly ash on his cheeks, thistles on his forehead, and finally a pincushion on his scalp told him that sensation was returning to his face.

His face! Whose face? Mercury Reynolds' face? No, Hal Forester's face. The face that belonged to the only man he had ever loved, except for his father whom he could love only in memory. Could he ever look in the mirror again, seeing there different eyes, a different nose, a mouth not his own? What was Britt thinking, as she stood by his bed? Whom did she see? Merc Reynolds or Hal Forester? Are the eyes truly the windows of the soul, so that she could look into his now dark eyes and see her husband there? Or would the memory of his blue eyes cause her to turn away in tears?

Victor Steinke stood at the foot of Reynolds' bed, flow sheet in hand, watching Gonzaga measuring the amount of sweat on Reynolds' shoulder. Starting at the tip of the shoulder he ran the probe downward on the upper arm with short controlled strokes, marking each point where sweating stopped. Then with a tape he measured the furthest point.

"Seven-point-four centimeters," he said and looked up hopefully at Steinke.

"Yesterday was the same. And day before."

"I thought so. I was hoping I had remembered wrong."

Steinke tossed the chart on the bed

and scratched furiously at his tattoo. "Something *is* wrong."

Gonzaga straightened up, then bent over again and rubbed away the marks from Reynolds' arm. "The computer says everything is OK."

Steinke grunted. "An old man I am becoming. In the old days we practiced medicine with our eyes and ears and"—he gave Gonzaga one of his rare smiles—"sometimes our noses already. Go back I would not. But was not all bad. We had to think. So, OK, we think now. What we ourselves measure here on Merc is no good. What the sensors measure is good. We believe who already?"

Gonzaga shrugged and turned to greet Maia. "Is something wrong?" she asked as she came in and stood at the bedside, blue eyes anxious, smile tentative.

"Miss Reardon," Steinke said with a slight bow. "No, we do not think anything is wrong. Confusing findings we have from the examination, but the computer says nothing is wrong."

Her eyes darted quickly from Steinke to the still form on the bed. The respirator pulsed with a controlled breath once every three seconds. The IV dripped steadily into Reynolds' arm. The cardiac monitor showed a smooth tracing. Clearly nothing could go wrong now.

"We will leave you with him," Gonzaga said as he and Steinke headed for the door.

"Don't worry."

She laid a hand on Reynolds' forehead. It was damp now and there was a flicker of the eyelids. Both good signs, Gonzaga had told her. Without nerves, skin doesn't sweat and eyelids don't move.

She didn't know if she was doing him any good by trying to reach him with her mind. But he was so perceptive. And their minds had always touched, even before the operation. She looked down at his face as she spoke to him. "Mercury, I'm here. You're doing great. *Every*thing is going great. Just hang in there, Merc."

She spoke soothingly for five minutes, all the old cliches, caressing his mind with platitudes, telling him he was loved, urging him to fight with whatever forces he had left. She tried to keep the rising fear out of her voice. She lifted her hand from his forehead and wiped the back of it across her eyes.

She would come again in the afternoon, then again at night. She would repeat her little performance each time, not wondering at her devotion, not yet understanding the depths of her love.

Still confident that all was well, it took Reynolds several days to realize that he was feeling nothing new. The improvement had really been very slow, so slow that even a day by day appraisal yielded little information, especially in his altered mental state, when minutes sometimes seemed like hours and days like weeks. But there came a time when he knew someting was wrong.

Dreadfully wrong. He wasn't deteriorating. He knew that. But he wasn't progressing. Nothing changed. Just as in those first horrible weeks when no stimuli came through to him, he began to feel a rising panic, the feeling of a purse-string contracting around his consciousness, a band of blackness tightening around the middle of his mind. He fought for control and made it worse. For the first time he felt a pounding in his brain, a tattoo of terror drumming incessantly in time with his heart. He learned now by personal experience the irrational yet paralyzing fear of claustrophobia. There was nothing he could do to counteract it. He must get out!

He couldn't get out.

There was no way he could lift himself —all 1700 grams of him—out of his prison of solid bone. He needed help. He thought often of Andrea Hughes and this drove him closer and closer to the brink of total break with reality. His train-car dream was no longer a dream. It was real.

Two days later, Maia, too, was having trouble controlling herself. Gonzaga and Steinke were no longer able to comfort her with their talk about the normal computer readings. Their actions, especially their eyes, gave them away. Britt wandered in once or twice a day, a complacent smile on her face, and stood for a moment at the bedside and then left. She seemed to show no emotion at all. Her eyes were vacant, her features a cold mask.

Maia and Phoebe, leaving the ward that morning, met her in the corridor outside the ward. Britt ignored them, but Maia stepped in front of her.

"How can you stay so calm," Maia said, her voice trembling with rage, "when your husband lies in there and Steinke . . .?"

"My husband is dead," she said and brushed past.

Maia turned to watch her go, mouth hanging agape. "What in hell did she mean by that?" she said to Phoebe. "What *could* she mean? If she really thought that, why does she keep coming to see him?"

Phoebe's eyes were misted over. "I think I know. She's already counted Mercury dead. And she thinks it's Hal Forester that's dying and is glad."

"My God!" Maia said, then added, "Let's go back on the ward."

They followed Britt to Reynolds' room. She stood for a moment on the other side of the bed, facing the door. No one else was in the room. She touched her fingers to her lips and then laid her fingers on Reynolds' mouth.

Maia gripped Phoebe's arm. "She's saying goodbye. She *knows* he's going to die."

Phoebe nodded, tears started to flow down her cheeks. Britt came out of the room, quickly pushed past them, hardly knowing they were there. Phoebe and Maia turned, and, hand in hand, walked out into the cold November day.

For so many times now that he couldn't count them, Reynolds played out the scene with Andrea Hughes. He touched her forehead, felt the tiny electric shocks, knew she was talking to him, listened for her voice, heard it trailing off. Then he sat once more at his console in Hektoen, watching the computer readout, watching Steinke and Gonzaga battling desperately to save her, heard her brain split in two, smelled again that awful stench of schizophrenic sweat. And heard her die.

Now he imagined that he could smell that sour-sweet odor of schizophrenia again. But this time it was his own. His thoughts drifted high above his head, pulling him up, up out of himself like a patient with a high fever—or in cardiac arrest—watching his body down on the bed, seeing Hal Forester's mouth twist into a wizened grimace, a gruesome caricature of his handsome smile. A patient's chart lay on the bed below him—his own—but the pages were blank except for one word on each. Goodbye. Flick, the page turned. Adieu. Flick, another page. Sayonara. Flick.

Auf Wiedersehen. Flick, flick, flick. He was leaving the world.

But he was still rational enough to think: it was all worth it. I did what I could. I did what I had to. If I die now it will still be worth it. I've paid my dues. I *tried*. He didn't think in the grand terms of expiating the sins of the first Dr. Reynolds, but he knew he had done just that. The slate was wiped clean, and he was ready to go, at peace with himself and with the world. He was going to die, and he was ready.

Then suddenly he felt the unmistakable break in his aura, the presence of another's thoughts intruding on his. The vision of the inert form on the bed disappeared and he was back inside his claustrophobic box of bone. He felt a peculiar disappointment. He had been ready to leave—it had been kind of nice out there, outside his tiny prison for the first time in weeks. He was ready to die, to give up the long fight. Now he was back in the thick of it again.

The voice was so clear that he wondered for a moment if he was actually hearing her speak, then knew he wasn't. The words were forming directly on the corrugated screen of his brain, not streaming through his neural pathways. They were jarring—ruthless-insistent—imperative—banging away in capital letters:

"HOLD ON, MERC . . .
FIGHT IT, MERC . . .

DON'T LET GO . . .
HANG ON . . .
DON'T PANIC . . .
STAY CALM . . .
YOU'RE ALRIGHT, MERC . . .
WE LOVE YOU . . .

Then the words became muffled, drawing away from him, or he from them, he couldn't tell which. A great peace settled over him. Then her voice was gone completely and he smelled that awful odor again. He seemed to shoot in and out of a plunging cataract, hearing the roar of water, then the hush of the piney woods at dusk, then back into the maelstrom. Her mind drove persistently against his, struggling to free him of the panic that gripped him, fighting to expand that collapsing railroad car.

But he knew she couldn't win. He was going . . . going . . .

29

Steinke was on the verge of reoperating on Reynolds to find out what was going wrong with the depolarizers and sensors. Step by step they checked out the external enlon lines, the sensor skull cap, the sensor vest, the black radiobox on the table back of the respirator. Everything checked out. They even checked the data coming into the computer in Gonzaga's office on the ward. It looked fine. But no one thought to check out the laser disk-pack in the computer in the lab at Hektoen. And no one thought to check the transmission codes. No one had yet thought of sabotage. No one ever thinks the unthinkable.

Steinke ordered an EEG and watched the paper roll out of the machine onto the floor. It was Andrea Hughes all over again: the frantic pulse of beta waves over-ridden every second or two by delta waves, and the crash of high voltage peaks indicative of imminent coma.

"Maybe," Steinke said, "we go in again." He looked up at Johnny Speers and Alfredo Gonzaga. Speers pulled at an earlobe. Gonzaga stared at the tracings. Both felt once more the heavy burden thrust on Steinke: he could listen to advice from his colleagues, he could consult his textbooks, he could pray to God or flip a coin, but in the end it was he, Victor Steinke, who had to make the decision. There was no one else to whom he could pass the buck.

"Let's do a CT scan first," Speers said.

"What the hell for?" Gonzaga asked.

Speers shrugged. "God, I don't know. Might show us something."

"Do it," Steinke said.

They moved Reynolds to X ray and repeated the CT scan, something they had never needed to do before on a patient this late in the post-operative course.

Now Steinke, Gonzaga and Speers met back at the bedside. Steinke stood in the middle of the room, hands behind his back, head lowered like a bull, bald head reflecting the ceiling lights. Gonzaga was draped over the end of the bed, oozing concern and doubt. Speers sat on the bedside chair, studying a printed readout from the CT scan. Helen Rogers, quiet for once, stood in the doorway with hands folded in front of her, eyes shifting slowly from doctor to doctor. Behind her, Maia stood stiffly, almost at attention, arms down at her sides, fists clenched. Phoebe had not come in yet. Britt had not been seen for almost twenty-four hours, since Phoebe and Maia had seen her touching her fingers to Reynolds' lips.

Speers spoke, almost to himself, musingly. "We start with the fact that we expect greater physical changes than the computer shows. We know that the computer cannot give us erroneous information if it *receives* correct information. I see this CT scan now, done just this morning. I superimpose the depolarizers' images . . ." He looked up in dismay. He spoke quickly, his thin reedy voice charged with emotion. "The images superimposed on the CT scan are slightly off from what would be expected from the initial displacement of the depolarization nodules."

Gonzaga came to life. "They're *what*?"

"Slightly off from . . ." Speers started.

"Yes, yes," Steinke interrupted, "but what do you . . .?" He stopped. Blood rushed to his face and his little eyes bugged. His head dropped even lower on his neck, the rolls of fat bulging over his collar.

"There can be only one explanation,"

Speers said, almost triumphantly. "If you have ruled out all possible explanations but one, then that one, no matter how improbable, is the correct solution."

Helen Rogers said softly, "Thank you, Mr. Holmes," then stepped out of the way as the three doctors charged past her and disappeared down the hall.

"What . . .?" Maia asked.

Miss Rogers crossed the corridor to Maia. "They think they know what's wrong. Someone has tampered with the computer over in Hektoen."

Maia gasped. "Britt?" she whispered, her voice almost inaudible. Would she go to such length? No, not even in her demented state. No, she couldn't, she wouldn't.

Leaving Steinke far behind, Gonzaga and Speers raced down the stairs and across the street to Hektoen. Impatiently they waited for the elevator, and rode it to the ninth floor laboratory. Breathing heavily, unconscious of the stares of the scientists in the huge room, they rushed to the computer on Reynolds' old desk. Gonzaga sat and typed commands into it. Why he asked for the transmission and reception codes, not even he was sure, but there it was: two different codes where they should have been the same.

"Why are they different?" he asked.

It was a rhetorical question.

He extracted the disk-pack from the computer and with unbelieving eyes read the name on the platter. "Albert Grovener," he said to Speers, then looked up at Steinke waddling across the room toward them. "Which case was Grovener?"

"Fifteen, sixteen, somewhere early in our work," Steinke said.

They started on the run for Reynolds' old office where the laser disks were still stored. Without a word Steinke opened the cabinet. He pulled out the first disk-pack of #15, looked at it, and handed it to Gonzaga.

"A blank," Gonzaga said, "Who in the hell . . ."

"About that we worry later. Come."

An hour later, Maia and Phoebe walked slowly out of the hospital, turned down Harrison and then Ashland to Polk Street. The manager of Britt's apartment let them into her room after a brief explanation of why they had come. He stood quietly at the door as Phoebe and Maia entered the brightly sun-lit room. In the roll-away bed lay Britt, fully clothed, an empty bottle of seconal on the small table. Her face was turned toward the table, on which she had placed a picture of Mercury Reynolds taken on his graduation from the University of Virginia, in black robe and mortar board, golden hood draped over his shoulders.

Phoebe put her arm around Maia's waist. Maia turned toward her, eyes brimming with tears. "She didn't have . . ." Phoebe put her finger on Maia's lips. "No, don't. Come away now."

She led Maia down the narrow hallway to the front door. She turned to the manager, who had followed them dumbly down the stairs. "Lock the room. We'll take care of things."

He nodded and bowed them out the door.

Two months passed. Then three. Maia had lost her job at the library and spent much of every day at Reynolds' bedside. Phoebe stayed a week, long enough to be sure that everything was going smoothly again. Britt was cremated in Chicago and her ashes sent to her parents in Charlottesville. Neither Maia nor Phoebe went south to attend the private memorial services. Phoebe understood why Maia didn't go, but Mrs. Reardon was shocked and mortified. All Maia could say was, "Mother, if you knew the whole story . . ." Someday perhaps she would tell her. Now it was better to let things lie, especially since no one had suggested pressing charges of attempted murder against Britt.

Feeling returned to Reynolds' face, although there were patches of numbness which only slowly filled in. His ears began to make some sense out of the cacophony of sound which bombarded them. He could not talk yet because his voice box was above the level of the tracheostomy tube leading to the electronic respirator beside his bed.

So with special anxiousness he awaited the endless looping growth of the laryngeal nerves from high in the brain stem, through the neck, deep into the chest, under the arch of the aorta, and back up into the neck to the voicebox. Only when this occurred would the vocal cords stay open by themselves. Only then would his voice return. And only then could they safely take out the tracheostomy tube. Every week or so Gonzaga or Steinke stretched out a white-coated arm to occlude the tube and say, "Try to talk now, Merc." He ached to obey and couldn't. The hand receded into the background and despair descended around him like dark grey folds.

Then one day, when Gonzaga touched his finger to the tube and told him to speak, he did. "Fred," he said, and took a deep breath through his mouth.

"Good boy," Gonzaga answered, and gripped Reynolds' forehead with his hand in the way he would have gripped Reynolds' hand if he could have felt it. The nurse at his side lay her hand on Reynolds' temple with a tenderness that would have made Florence Nightingale breathe a deep sigh of satisfaction.

In surprisingly few days he was able to speak complete sentences, though slowly and with a raspiness which made him difficult to understand. But his voice was back, and with it the ability to communicate. Such a little thing. Never again would he forget that it is the ability to talk to one another, more than any other faculty, that separates man from the lower animals.

And little by little his vision returned. Later they would find that the macula of the right eye was gone, victim of the thirty-five minute period when the retinal artery was clamped, but the rest of the retina was normal. Now all he saw was a blurring of shapes that seemed to materialize and then fade away. But gradually the shapes became bottles and tubes and human forms.

And faces.

The faces he saw most often at his beside were Maia and Phoebe. It bothered him that he never saw Britt. Every time he woke up, he looked around anxiously for her.

One day Maia was there when he awakened. He opened his mouth to ask where Britt was. She anticipated the question. She leaned against the bedrail, put her hand on his forehead, and said, "She's not here, Merc. She's gone."

30

Britt was gone. That didn't make sense. She was his wife. At first he didn't try to figure that out. He just lay there in a daze, not able—not wanting—to make sense of it. Gradually the implication of Maia's words registered. Britt hadn't just gone downtown shopping. She had left him—had abandoned him. Why? Because he was Pan's son? Because he was in Forester's body? Both?

Britt was *gone*. He closed his eyes when the full realization hit him. Tears of self-pity welled up and rolled down his cheeks. Just when he needed all the support he could get, his wife, his darling, had abandoned him. Left him to fight that age-old battle against death, alone. Couldn't she have stayed on just a little longer? Fought down whatever conflicting emotions surged within her until later when he could handle the insult?

He felt a hand wiping away the tears, gently holding a handkerchief against the corners of his eyes. Not able to rotate his eyes laterally—the sixth cranial nerve being the longest and last to regenerate—he turned his head laboriously to the side and looked straight into Maia's eyes. She held his gaze for a long time and confirmed without words what he already knew: Britt had been gone for a long time. She wouldn't be back.

"She couldn't handle the switch," Maia said simply.

"Tell me . . . 'bout it."

"Do you want to know now?"

"Yes."

"Can't it wait?"

"No."

She sat back against her chair and he held her with his eyes. "Never be . . . better time," he said.

She rubbed her finger along the bridge of her nose as she always did when she was trying to find the right words. He closed his eyes and waited.

"She came to see you every day for a month after the surgery. Always alone. Wouldn't let anyone come with her."

She started to add something but blotted it out so fast he couldn't catch it. If it were important, he'd hear about it some day.

"One day I came up with your mother. We were just leaving when Britt came in. We watched her from the hall. She was standing by your bed, hands on the rails, so engrossed that she didn't even know we were there. Her lips moved and I could almost catch the words, but not quite. You should have seen her eyes, Merc. Filled with deep agony. She was hurting. Hurting way down inside where we don't have to go very often."

He knew the look. He'd seen it at least once before, a long time ago. Britt had been talking lightly about what their children would look like. He'd said something like, "Well, he wouldn't be a big football player like Hal Forester." That had quieted her. She sat gazing into the fireplace, her eyes heavily lidded, the corners of her mouth drawn back slightly but not enough to show her teeth. Something he'd said made her ache, deep, deep down inside. Suddenly she had looked up at him and the hurt changed to fear, and almost as quickly to a longing that struck him as being inappropriate to what he'd said. He'd smiled, not knowing what else to say, and her face relaxed again, all the little lines smoothing out like a pond when the wind suddenly quits.

"Then," Maia went on, drawing him back to the present, "she stretched out her hand and brushed back the damp hair from your forehead. She leaned forward over the side-rails, couldn't quite reach you with her lips, so she kissed her fingers and touched them to your mouth. It was goodbye, Merc, so obviously a goodbye. We tried to leave without her seeing us, but she straightened up and came out of the room so quickly we couldn't. It didn't matter. She was so wrapped up in her grief—yes, that's what it was—that she scarcely saw us. Just glanced up at us, nodded her head in a kind of resignation, and pushed by."

"And . . . she never . . . came back," Reynolds said softly.

Maia sat slumped in the chair, hands clasped tightly in her lap, eyes open, looking in the general direction of the floor unfocused. There was something wrong, dreadfully wrong.

She closed her eyes, forced herself to speak. "She won't ever come back. She can't, Merc. She's dead."

He rolled his head away from her and stared at the ceiling. Before he could say anything she began to tell him what had happened. It all poured out of her in a frenzy of catharsis. He couldn't have stopped her if he'd wanted to: the solitary visits Britt had made to his bedside, the switching of the laser disk-packs, Steinke's dreadful quandary when he was baffled by

Reynolds' clinical status compared to the computer readouts (he remembered that nightmare with awful clarity), the CT scan and Speers' recognition of the switch, and the finding of Britt in her room. She said nothing of her part in controlling Reynolds' mind in those last few days before the deception was detected. But he knew.

He could feel the fight go out of him even as he said to her, "I guess, Maia, I've got . . . you to thank . . . for my being here."

She smiled. "Not really. Not just me. I had help. Steinke. Gonzaga. Speers."

"But it was you I heard—you who stuck by me and told me to hang on." His eyes brimmed with tears. "And you who's here now."

For a moment her cool hand rested on his brow, then she was gone. She left, but he knew she'd be back.

He slipped back at least a month in his recovery. So much of his progress was dependent on his own desire to get well. When he realized that Britt was not there, and never would be, he lost some of that desire. He remembered her, inevitably, as she had been in Charlottesvile, in the Caymans, in their Harrison Street apartment. He dwelt on the mental images he had of her lips and her eyes from inches away. The way she scrunched up her nose and pouted when she was trying to get her way with something. The way her fingers felt on his face, on his eyelids, on his mouth. He wallowed in self-pity, wondering how she could do this to him.

Only on the edge of his irrationality did he consider what he had done to *her*. He had done what he had to do. He *had* to tell her about Pan. He *had* to have a transplant. He *had* to use Forester's body. He had made those decisions as he came to them—and if in retrospect any one or two or three were wrong . . . well . . .

Phoebe came up from Standing Oaks to be with him. She sat by his bed, quietly most of the time, occasionally reminding him how far he had come, minimizing how far he had to go. She, with Maia, became the solid ground, the rock, on which he would build his new life. She constantly reaffirmed by speech and actions that he was her son Mercury. The agony she endured he never heard—and never would hear—from her. Just imagine, he told himself a thousand times, what it must be like for a mother to raise a child and then see it transmogrified suddenly into another being.

For a while he faulted Britt for not accepting him as his mother had. He said as much to Phoebe one day and she turned him around by pointing out in no uncertain terms that mother-love is different from wifely love. Not necessarily stronger, but different. Not necessarily withstanding tougher tests, but different ones.

So he began again to take an interest

in his recovery. He was still quadriplegic. He knew this was to be expected, for the peripheral nerves to arms and feet and muscles had such a long way to go. But beneath the rational scientist's optimism, there lingered the patient's nagging doubt that he would ever have full use of Hal Forester's body.

Meanwhile, someone was burning his thigh, then his feet and then his buttocks. Sometimes the firebrands struck him everywhere at once and he couldn't stand the pain and called out for relief. The morphine relieved the pain, but did so by releasing floods of endorphans, which made him temporarily schizophrenic, or at least schizoid. He didn't progress utterly to the point of delusions of grandeur where he wanted to put on the robes of Caesar or carry the cross of Christ. But he had the horrible feeling that he was no longer Mercury Reynolds.

At the same time he had the same horrible feeling of not being Hal Forester either. For a short period of time he was one person, then for awhile the other. And he couldn't get the two together, nor separate them either. It was like staring at a line drawing of boxes which change perspective as one gazes fixedly at them. He almost welcomed the return of pain as the morphine wore off, for then he could better fuse the two men he had become.

And all the time he knew that he

should be happy about the pain, and the itching which sometimes followed or preceded the pain. This was sure proof that the sensory nerve fibers were actually penetrating the suture line in the third ventricle and entering the nuclei of the pain-carrying fasciculi (the spino-thalamic and others). If the sensory nerves could grow upward, certainly the motor fibers could grow downward and eventually his brain would send nerves to the muscles of Hal's body.

He forced himself to stop thinking of "Hal's body." Hal Forester is dead, he kept telling himself, killed by a massive, uncontrollable hemorrhage at the base of his brain. His death was imminent from the moment blood began to pour into the anterior fossa, shutting off his life as surely as a hand squeezing his neck.

So Hal is dead, and I'm alive, Hal is dead and I'm alive, he repeated over and over again. I have a new body—it's mine—not someone else's. New lips with which to talk, new hands with which to work, new feet with which to walk, but with the same old brain with which to think! For the first time in months he actually felt like laughing when he asked himself, "Is that *good*?"

Down the length of his body the nerves grew, providing new pathways from brain to muscle for the tiny electrical end-impulses which give tone to muscle. When the tone returned, the muscle could move and then strengthen with use. One by one his bodily functions returned. Muscles began to twitch in his neck, then the shoulders, and out into the arms. The muscles between the ribs began to function; to strengthen them Gonzaga allowed him to breathe independently of the respirator for increasingly long periods.

When the phrenic nerve had made its long journey from the brain stem through the chest and out onto the diaphragm, hiccups began which lasted for almost two weeks. His entire body jerked like a puppet, arms and legs flailing, belly tightening, mouth filling with vomitus which he had to swallow and spit. That was when Gonzaga was first certain that he *could* swallow, and cautiously gave him water and tea and milk. When he handled those liquids well, Gonzaga ordered custards and jello and ice cream, and eventually mashed potatoes and meat loaf and pureed vegetables.

The marvel was that he could actually taste the food.

He tried to smile.

That worked, too, but it made Maia cry.

At the end of the fourth month two strong pairs of arms slid him off the ICU bed into a wheelchair. Maia pushed him into room 3015 on Ward 30. It was like coming home. She sat in a chair opposite him and took his hand in hers.

"We've come a long way, baby," she

said and flicked an imaginary cigarette.

He nodded, squeezed her hand. With his other hand he occluded the tracheostomy tube and said, "I'd like . . . a mirror."

Her hand tightened in his, but without a word she let it go and fished a small compact out of her purse. With only a moment of hesitation he reached out and took it from her. His fingers fumbled with the clasp. He didn't know if it was because of nervousness or lack of coordination. Before he got it open, he looked up at her. She smiled encouragement, her long lashes low, partly covering her blue eyes.

"You're doing great," she said.

The clasp came open and he raised the mirror to his face.

31

His mother went home to her teaching job before he was discharged from intensive care, but she came back to County every couple of weeks to sit with him. She listened in awe as he told her in great detail some of what he had experienced during those long months of confinement in the prison of his own mind. She waited patiently while he spoke, so hesitantly at first, two and three words at a time.

"Now," she said, "perhaps you know a little of what your father experienced, trapped in a brain that did strange things to him that he couldn't control."

"Mother," he said, "everybody experiences that."

Her eyes widened in sudden comprehension.

"So we do," she answered.

Maia reacted in a somewhat different way. Unlike his mother, she didn't try to hide from him the fact that he looked like Hal Forester. She felt his biceps and said, "Hey, man, you'll never catch a pass with those scrawny arms," and brought him a pair of dumbbells to work out with. Or, "I do like a man who has piercing black eyes," and pretended that she was melting away like a teenager at a rock festival. It was discomfiting at first but it helped him immensely in the long run to get used to his new physique and his new face.

When it was time to leave the hospital, there was no discussion at all. She picked him up in her car, drove him to a small apartment on Taylor which she had rented in order for him to be close to Cook County, and moved in with him.

She had transformed the little apartment into one an invalid could live in: no throw rugs, all the lamps with big switches, toilet with handrails alongside, high, hard chairs, wall-switches with little glow-lights, long handles on the water taps, walk-in shower instead of a tub. And in the common room she had installed an electric hospital bed which did everything but fly. In short, she had made everything easy for a man as uncoordinated as Reynolds expected to be for many months.

Their lives assumed a certain married complacency. Maia got him up early, served breakfast, then went off to the downtown library where she had gotten her old job back. He puttered around the apartment, exercising his legs and arms constantly, and when it was nice outside, took long walks around the block.

Actually the physical adjustments were relatively minor compared to his mental turmoil whenever he passed a friend on the street and received no sign of recognition. He couldn't go up to everyone and say, "Hey, look at me. I'm Mercury Reynolds. Take a good look so you'll know me next time." Sometimes he wondered if that is just what he should have done, but he couldn't.

He had endless hours to spend and decided to take the advice that the Turk gave to Candide: "Work keeps at bay three great evils: boredom, vice, and need." He wasn't too concerned about vice and need, but boredom would be a problem unless he had something to work at. His work was reading. He read everything, but concentrated on neurology and neurosurgery texts and periodicals. He made lists of articles for Maia to dig out of the university library and soon knew all there was to know about the degenerative diseases of the nervous system. He began writing the authors of the more lucid articles, asking questions, once in a while making suggestions for further research.

Replies started to come in, tentative at first despite his reputation, then in a flood. He began to correlate his own knowledge of presenile dementia with what he read. Slowly, slowly, a comprehension of the entire subject formed in his mind. Then one morning, he let his book drop in his lap and sat staring across the room. His mind twisted and turned and grappled with the concept that had just leaped into his mind. "Yes, yes," he cried, and leaped to his feet. "That's it. The key. It is, it is!" He pulled pen and paper onto the desk and sat down to put his thoughts down.

Why hadn't anyone thought of it before? He didn't know. But he did know that every idea which comes to the attention of men must come to one man first. The concept of the sun as the center of our solar system, the law of energy as the mass of an object times the square of the speed of light, the realization that blood actually circulates in the body: all these and thousands more, first thought of by one man and communicated to the rest of mankind.

He knew that he had received a divine spark which must be tested and proven, and tested again and again, in order to make it acceptable to the skeptic. But he held the flint and the tinder in his hand. All he needed was the laboratory in which to strike the flint and time in which to blow the spark into flame. He could hardly wait to get started.

His enthrallment had a beneficent side effect. He didn't miss Britt as much as he thought he would. That great psychological friend of all men—repression—was hard at work. It excluded from his consciousness—at least temporarily—the painful thoughts which would have made life unbearable. He wasn't ready then, in those early months, to handle past history and present trials together. The present was enough, for he was a driven man: driven to learn everything he possibly could about the disease he had been working on when he got sick.

Not too far in the back of his mind was the awful realization that Britt had abandoned him, and that she was dead, but he couldn't spare the emotional energy to delve too deeply into all the ramifications. He knew in general why she had disappeared, could even understand (if not condone) her attempt to kill him in such a gruesome way. For him, at that time, it was enough. He didn't allow himself to miss her. He tried not to judge her too harshly, for her mind had been possessed by the devil himself. To her he had not been the Mercury Reynolds she loved. He was another being, a creature she loathed in unreasoning, cold fury. And she, he mused, was not the Britt he had loved. He would not have recognized in her the beautiful blonde enchantress with whom he had fallen in love in that Charlottesville restaurant so long ago.

During those days he had time to consider what they had accomplished in the field of brain transplants. He was living testimony to what could be done by good men breeching the walls of skepticism. They had stormed those walls with ladders of faith, knocked them down with the battering-rams of courage, shaken off the arrows of prejudice with the chain mail of wisdom. The battle was not won, but the walls were down. The castle keep, where were hid the secrets of the universe, was no longer impregnable. If their triumph was not yet complete, it was in sight down the dimly lit corridors of time.

More important to him, right then, was his own personal triumph. In a very real way, he had vindicated the Reynolds name, had done what he had set out to do. He remembered thinking those same thoughts when he knew he was dying. He had been content to die then. Now he knew he still had work to do.

But one evening he came in from a particularly exhilarating walk. The air had been as clear as it ever gets in Chicago in February, pushing in from the northwest where there were few factories, shoving the smog and smell of steel mills and stockyards into northern Indiana. Maia looked up from her book, saw a flash of fire in his eyes that hadn't been there—except for very brief moments—for a year or more.

She laid her book aside and smiled. "You look like a college boy just back from a hot date."

"Feel like it."

She motioned to a chair like a corporation president to a junior executive. "Time to talk," she said. She slid forward in her overstuffed chair, clasped her hands together near the floor, arms between her knees pushing the long skirt tightly around her thighs.

He sighed. "OK," he said. "But relax, I'm ready."

Her eyes glowed with a peculiar sad amusement. She pushed herself back in the chair and crossed her ankles on the ottoman.

She didn't know where to start. He helped her by saying, "Once upon a time . . ."

"Good as any. Once upon a time there was a handsome football player named Hal Forester and a young model named Britt Reardon . . ."

Britt Reardon? He could feel his eyebrows lifting and his eyes staring. This wasn't what he expected at all. As soon as she saw his reaction she dropped the fairytale prose and began again in earnest.

"Britt was Hal's girl for a year before I started going out with him. When he stopped seeing her, he called me at school and we started dating." She smiled. "I was second choice."

He returned the smile. "I think you would have been my first choice if you hadn't been going with Hal when we met."

"I'm not so sure, but thanks for playing the gallant." There was a luminosity in her wide pupils that stirred him in a way he hadn't felt since long before his operation. "Anyway," she continued, "she told me one night that she was going to New York to get a modelling job and that she and Hal had split up. She didn't elaborate, and I didn't push her. It wasn't any of my business if she didn't want to tell me more. I figured she was tired of Charlottesville and needed a whole new change of environment."

"You figured wrong?"

"Right. I figured wrong. She went to New York because she was pregnant. She went to get an abortion."

She watched him carefully, not knowing what to expect. Four years ago he might have exploded. Now he just stared at her, words forming, disappearing before he could get them out. Finally he stood up and said, "I feel like a beer."

She tried to smile. "You don't look like one."

He chuckled sourly and got a couple from the 'fridg and handed her one. She took it and drank half of it chug-a-lug. She wasn't laughing. He wasn't either. He felt sort of sick inside.

"Thanks," she said. "I needed that."

Their emotions were so deep that all they could come up with were cliches. He sipped his beer, not tasting it. He had to know something else.

"Did Hal know?" he asked.

"Of course he knew." Her eyes blazed. "He wouldn't even consider marriage."

"He didn't consider it his fault."

"No." She sucked in her breath convulsively, but it was not a sob. She looked down at her hands.

"What is it, Maia?" he asked, and slid forward in his chair, ready to get up.

She looked up at him. There was a film of moisture in her eyes but her smile was genuinely happy. "I just had the weirdest feeling—for just a split second—that I was talking to Hal Forester."

He snorted gently, the corners of his eyes and mouth curling slightly in a wan smile. He got up, walked across the room to the small mirror, and looked at himself.

"I can see why," he said.

"But your eyes are different from his. That must come from inside. His were always just a little mocking, as if he knew a secret about you that he couldn't quite conceal."

"And mine?"

She sniffed, then blew her nose quietly. "Yours are from another world, as if you know things we mere mortals could never understand."

"Now you're teasing me."

She shook her head slowly, holding his eyes with hers. "No," she said.

"Well," he said, returning to his chair, "to get back to Hal. Not too many years ago your Dad would have been there with the shotgun."

"It was a good system."

"I'm not sure." He toyed with his can of beer. "You didn't know all this when we met in that restaurant?"

"God, no. You think I could have gone out with Hal Forester if I'd known? As far as I was concerned, Britt had gone to New York to find a better job, found she couldn't, came home after a month. Meanwhile Hal had started dating me. It was a good story. Believable. Everyone bought it."

He felt a peculiar sort of jealousy. Jealousy that Hal Forester had known Maia in such an intimate way, whereas he was just beginning to know her in a much different way. But the early stirrings of love were there, seeping into his consciousness. Imperceptibly the nurse-patient relationship was changing. He couldn't help wondering if the feeling Maia had for him was one of sympathy rather than love. Then he remembered what Lawrence Durrell said in *Justine:* "Love is so much truer when sympathy and not desire make the match." If this were true, Maia could already be in love with him. Perhaps without knowing it.

Perhaps knowing it.

She got up and knelt in front of him as

Britt had done so long ago the night they first made love. She laid her head on his knees and he leaned back in his chair and stroked the short blonde hair back from her brow. He didn't want things to move too fast. He wasn't sure he was ready. Even as she relaxed against him he thought of Britt and what she must have gone through in that month in New York.

"There's just one thing more I'd like to know," he said. "How long after she went to New York did you meet me in that restaurant with my mother?"

"Hal and I had just picked her up at the airport."

"My God."

"You caught her on the rebound."

"But Hal was so casual about it all."

"That's one reason Britt hated him so."

She didn't need to spell it out any better. "But why," he asked, "didn't she ever say anything? How could she just let me go on thinking . . .?"

"It was over with. Done. Caput. All it would have done would have soured your relationship with Hal. She knew how strong your affection was for him. I think she was right. It wouldn't have done any good, and could have done irreparable harm."

"And after the transplant?"

"She tried. Oh, how she tried. I told you. I could see the wheels turning. She desperately wanted to accept you as Mercury Reynolds. But she couldn't. For too many years she had harbored a hatred for the very man she saw lying in that bed. She couldn't see your mind, couldn't hear you talk, couldn't recover all the little things that made you Mercury Reynolds. She tried to kill Hal Forester, not Mercury Reynolds. Don't fault her too much, Merc. She tried so hard."

He lifted her to her feet, took her head between his hands and kissed her. There was no great passion, just a hint of love which could grow between them if they gave it time. And if he could resolve in his own mind the strange fact that Maia saw in him—at one and the same time—Mercury Reynolds' mind and Hal Forester's body.